INTRIGUED

"From the first time I saw your picture in your magazine and read your editorial, I wanted to get to know you."

Wishing it didn't make her feel as wonderful as it did, Shay also confessed, "I've been intrigued by you too."

"You have?"

"I've read every article about you, Braxton. Probably seen every time you were on television too."

Braxton couldn't believe this. "This is deep. So you've been reading about me, I've been reading about you, and we've been fascinated by each other. So now that we've had a little time together, what do you think?" He couldn't help moving closer. "Are you still intrigued?"

Shay was aware of his closeness. His scent was ever so intoxicating. Something maddeningly intense filled her. It had been a long time coming, but she was attracted to someone again. She was feeling those feelings that made a woman feel sensually alive and so attuned with her femininity. His kiss, she wondered how it would taste. His chest, her fingers ached to caress its hardness again. Her own body, she trembled for it to be touched by him. Overall, she wanted to be enraptured by romance. But why with this man? What was it about Braxton that ignited those sensations in her? A man she hardly knew. The one who was going to try his best to incarcerate her.

Other Books by Louré Bussy

A TASTE OF LOVE
LOVE SO TRUE
TWIST OF FATE
MOST OF ALL
NIGHTFALL

Published by BET/Arabesque Books

IMAGES OF ECSTASY

Louré Bussey

BET Publications, LLC
www.msbet.com
www.arabesquebooks.com

ARABESQUE BOOKS are published by

BET Publications, LLC
c/o BET BOOKS
One BET Plaza
1900 W Place NE
Washington, D.C. 20018-1211

First Printing: July, 2000
10 9 8 7 6 5 4 3 2 1

Printed in the United States of America

ACKNOWLEDGMENTS

To all my family and friends, especially "Baby"; thank you for your love and support.

To my editor, Karen Thomas, and publishers, Linda Gill and Kelly Richardson; thank you for making another dream come true for me.

To those who have been so kind in helping me share my work worldwide; thank you Brenda Woodbury, Nicki Hand, www.romantictales.com, Memphis Vaughn, www.timbooktu.com, Sharon, www.blacksocialcalendar.com and my producers.

One

"I love you."

"I don't love you back."

Shay Hilton looked up from her desk at the man who had betrayed her in a way that no woman could bear. Her response was heartfelt. It had been three years since she last stared into the eyes of her ex-love, and the shock of his barging in her office, spouting words she knew he didn't know the meaning of, impacted her like a spaceship landing in the room. He had never apologized for what he put her through. He never made the smallest attempt to make up for the inhumanity of it all. Then again, he couldn't. So why did he appear now? Why was he there? Up until that moment Shay had been having a wonderful day. Excited about the award she was receiving later, she couldn't concentrate on work. Instead she pushed her magazine's responsibilities aside to enjoy a newspaper article about that Braxton Steele.

Anytime Shay saw the district attorney of Englewood Cliffs featured in a press piece or television report, it commanded her attention. Except now Marquis Jackson stood directly in front of her after so many years and after what he did, she was astonished.

"You don't know how much I miss you," he admitted, his luminous dark eyes searching the face that he could never get out of his mind. The echo of *I don't love you back* was killing him, and he was desperate to detect something that proved it was a lie.

Certainly, the woman he thought about every day of his life had good reason to wish him a slow, tortuous death. During his flight from California to New Jersey, Marquis mentally prepared for a scene that he knew would be unpleasant. At the same time, he was counting on an old saying. It vowed that nothing could quench the fires of true love.

Was Shay's love for him really gone? Every drop of it? Marquis couldn't tell. He only knew that the warmth invading his blood, mixed with his raging heartbeat, screeched that the love of his life was finer than he remembered. Her caramel-kissed skin glowed like silken oil had been poured over it. The mocha crystals staring at him possessed a sparkle he'd never seen in them before. Adding to her sultry attributes, as she rose slowly from her chair, he couldn't miss that her body was more toned, more curvaceous and more succulent than he'd ever seen it. It was obvious to Marquis that life was treating Shay well. Or was someone making her look that way? If so, he had no qualms about getting rid of him.

"Not a day goes by that I don't think about you," he went on. His normally clear voice sounded gravelly, whispery and as if it came from somewhere deeper than his throat. "You're always right there in my heart. I was wrong. But I'm here today to make it right. My life hasn't been the same without you. I put on a good face for everyone, laughing on the outside, but inside it's a whole other story. I want you so bad."

Silent, Shay folded her arms while her gaze peeled his skin. How many times had she dreamed of this moment? The day when Marquis would face her, practically crawling, begging for a chance to reunite, and there she would stand, successful, looking good and so completely over him nothing he could say would matter to her anymore. Sure, she did feel a twinge of something—*mad*. Mad at him for forcing her to recall the greatest sword to slay her heart. It took her more than a year to get over what he'd done to her. One entire year of her thirty-four years wasted with crying, fear, confusion, insecurity, hopelessness and pure heartache.

Fortunately, time and many blessings had made all the difference in the world in mending her spirit from the heartbreak. Everything was going perfectly now. Her brother, Rakim, had always been the angel in her life, and somehow they had become closer. True friends, like her rocks, Christina Gracen and David Robertson, made the days all the more blissful. And her career had soared to such an outstanding height that Shay was being honored this evening at a black-tie ceremony for being one of the most dynamic female entrepreneurs of the year.

Her three year old *Love & Relationships* magazine was one of the fastest growing publications ever owned by a woman—a woman of color at that. What's more, after allowing for solely platonic relationships with the opposite sex, Shay had decided that perhaps Dr. David Robertson did deserve more than the friendship he accepted. Each time Shay was with him, his tender manner and the look in his eyes when he stared at her made it apparent that he desired much more. Tonight he was escorting her to the ceremony. Afterward, perhaps she would indulge in a little kissing with the sweet doctor. Marquis and all the misery he brought her were definitely in her past.

"Would you like my secretary to see you out?" Shay asked, unfolding her arms. "Or should I call security?"

Dabbing at the beads of perspiration that dotted the bare skin above his lip, Marquis moved closer to the sensual creature that aroused him with inexpressible desire. A subtle wind of strawberry wafted, making him inhale repeatedly until he could almost taste the fragrance on Shay's skin. Taste it the way he used to savor her unforgettable scent long ago, with long, erotic massages with his lips. If only he could indulge her that or merely touch her. If only he could have awakened in Shay what they once felt within each other's arms. Those feelings still had to be there. How could they perish when they were so strong? They were so alive in him.

"Not one step closer," she warned.

Her glower more than her words froze him.

"Shay, if you let me explain, then you can understand why I did what I did."

Shay pressed the buzzer on her intercom. "Anna, would you please get security up here? I want this man thrown out of my office."

"You got it, Shay. Will you be okay until they come?"

"I'll be fine. Thank you, sweetie."

Marquis was gripping the door handle when Shay looked up from the phone.

Hurt and disbelief masked his features. "It's all right. I know it's going to take some time to convince you that I'm the man for you. Actually, it's going to take some serious work. But as that old saying goes, Anything worth having is worth working for. I'll be patient. Get used to seeing me. We *are* going to be together."

Marquis closed the door. His heart was still thumping wildly; he couldn't move for thinking. It was only the sense that someone was watching him that tugged him out of the spell Shay had cast. He shot a glance near Shay's secretary's desk. Large, hazel eyes were rolling at him. Was the disgusted look because the woman was asked to call security on him? Was it because she had chased him earlier? Or had Shay told her what he'd done to her?

Eager to escape the leer, Marquis's slender frame hurried down the hall toward the elevators. His finger pressed the cold circle that displayed the down arrow. Of the three elevators in the posh reception area, the middle one arrived immediately. Empty, it reeked of fading cigar smoke.

Riding down to the lobby alone made it easy for Marquis to once again become absorbed in his mind. The thinking and visualizing wouldn't stop. He couldn't get over seeing Shay again. He couldn't get over how gorgeous she looked and how well she had done with her life. If he hadn't ruined everything they would be sharing her success together. Then again, they still could. Marquis had read the Englewood Cliff's paper. He hadn't missed the announcement about the ceremony tonight, honoring Shay and several other female entrepreneurs' achievements. Nothing would stop him from being there. Nothing would stop him from feeling her powerful affect on him, like he had felt in her office. Nothing, except death.

The elevator doors opened to the lambent glow of the building's lobby. Buttoning the top of his overcoat, preparing for the freezing February air, Marquis stepped onto a beige marble floor when an unwelcome sight appearing before him halted his tracks.

"What the hell are you doing here?" he growled. "Following me? Why don't you go back to wherever you came from? What do you want from me? My life?"

It's about time I found a hairstyle that I truly love, Shay thought. She was patting the short, layered locks that sculpted her oval-shaped face. Dressing up for the award's reception, she faced a cherrywood Victorian mirror and beheld her image against a backdrop of lavender-hued walls, curtains and beddings. Playing with the silky, loosely curled bangs that covered her brows, she loved the way they accentuated the big baby-doll eyes that her daddy had given her and those unusually long lashes, a legacy from her mother's family. For the first time she'd listened to her hairdresser's suggestion and had been persuaded to shed all those split ends that brushed her shoulders. She tried a cut that he'd envisioned specifically for her. Why had she been hanging on to that unhealthy hair anyway? For the sake of having long hair?

Marquis adored her hair long. She recalled that as her scrutiny toppled from her hair and makeup to her burgundy, velvet gown. But by the time her gaze reached the thigh-high slit, the scene in her office with Marquis had blurred away all that was in her view. She should have felt some perverse satisfaction that he desired her and she no longer desired him. Rather than that, Shay found herself merely wishing that she'd never met him at all.

Five years ago, she could barely pay her bills working as a journalist for a quarterly trade magazine called *Actor's Friend* when their paths crossed. The publication was targeted at those in film and theater, and at those pursuing careers in the industry. A new African-American actor had been gaining much praise for his small role in a BET feature film. Shay was assigned to interview him at a posh Manhattan eatery. His name was Marquis Jackson.

He impressed Shay as intelligent and funny that day. She had never laughed and listened so much. At the wind up of the interview, Shay felt inspired by a man who was determined to succeed with integrity in an industry where there were few positive roles for black males. His enthusiasm for his art was so fervent that Shay's fire was fueled for her own dream of creating a magazine about love and relationships.

Shay found Marquis interesting and even attractive. Although, his looks weren't the type she ordinarily gravitated to. His all too perfectly chiseled features and long, wavy hair gathered in a ponytail would have appeared almost feminine if she hadn't been charmed by the blatant masculinity in his manner and voice, as well as his exciting personality.

Telephone numbers were exchanged. Before long, they were enjoying lengthy conversations on the phone and dates that neither wanted to end. Somehow it seemed they had everything in common, from their unwavering passion to achieve their dreams, to their interest and hobbies, to their insatiable sexual chemistry. And as like grew to love, life became a dream that neither wanted to end.

Paper crushing under Shay's bottom as she plunked down on the vanity seat distracted her from cruising further down memory lane to the dramatic end to her relationship with Marquis. She raised herself up slightly, reaching underneath her lap to find a newspaper. Shay had brought it home from the office to continue reading the article about that fine Braxton Steele.

She wondered if he was capable of doing to a woman what Marquis had done to her. God knew she hoped not. Hoped not because there was just something about that man. Like a spell had befell her when she first saw him in the newspaper, and Shay was drawn to any press medium featuring the district attorney of Englewood Cliffs. Turning the pages until she reached his article, she knew this moment was no different.

Always struck by Braxton Steele's jaw-dropping sexiness, Shay also relished the fact that a brother from a working-class background like her own had grown up to become a lawyer who won nearly every case he prosecuted. As well, he provided thought-provoking statements that sometimes seemed spiritual whenever interviewed or quoted. Other times, he was so funny Shay found herself laughing out loud at the television or the paper interview. Still, as attractive and fascinating as Braxton Steele was to her, there was no way Shay could have anything to do with the man if they ever happened to meet in person. Rumor had it he was a ladies' man. Shay wasn't about to put up with a headache like that. At this point in her life, she was settling for no less than magic and the forever-more that magic was supposed to guarantee. If she ever bumped into the handsome district attorney, her motto with him would be, Look but don't touch.

The ringing penthouse doorbell nudged Shay away from the engrossing piece. The reminder that David, her very special escort, had arrived, prompted Shay to put the paper aside. As she rose to her feet, she reached for her Strawberry Victoria's Secret perfume. Spraying the areas that were pulse points, according to an aromatherapist she'd interviewed, she gave herself one final look in the mirror. She hoped David liked her dress. A prominent psychologist, David Robertson contributed a monthly col-umn to Shay's magazine, as well as other miscellaneous pieces in the publication. She admired all his knowledge in his field and loved his company so much, he'd become one of her closest friends.

Enjoying her fruitlike fragrance to the extent that she could have bitten herself, Shay swung her shapely hips toward the front door, scratching against the stiff lining of her gown. Opening the door, she decided that she loved David's scent too. He simply smelled soapy and clean.

"Smelling good and looking good," she greeted him, in-specting his black tuxedo, complete with his overcoat slung over his shoulder. She then raised her gaze to his broad

mouth. His showing-every-tooth-in-his-mouth smile always made her smile too. "What's that silly grin for?"

"For you." Lifting his glasses and shaking his head with
swearing conviction, he ran his eyes over her from head
to toe. "Pretty lady, you look so good I'd like to put you
on a plate and sop you up with a biscuit."

Shay laughed. "You're so silly." Knowing David hadn't
learned such a phrase from his wealthy upbringing but
from her made her laugh more as she guided him by the
hand into her gold-and-black-decorated living room.

Near the coat rack, he slid his coat off his shoulder and
noticed a few wet stains on it. "The snow is starting to
come down out there, just a little bit."

Shay went around the bar. "They expect a couple of
inches. Do you want to have a drink before we head out?"

"That would be nice of you." David made himself comfortable on the love seat. "You know what I like."

Loosening his tie a bit, he tried not to stare at what he
liked. God help him, he hoped tonight Shay would throw
away those barriers that laid across her heart and at least
let him kiss her—a real kiss, not those brotherly friendly
pecks. He hungered for the kind of kiss that he dreamed
about—the passionate ones he'd dreamed about with her.
Although, after hearing the story of Marquis's betrayal,
David understood her reluctance for intimacy. Despite it,
he clung to his wish for that wondrous day when Shay would
cease giving that fool power over her happiness.

"One glass of Cristal coming up," Shay promised,
searching the labels on the numerous bottles.

David soon watched her uncorking his favorite champagne. "Are you having some with me this time?" She
rarely drank. He smiled to himself, remembering how honest she became once when she did. Having too much
Cognac, Shay revealed that she had been celibate too long,

and her body was starving for good loving. David wouldn't have minded hearing her say that again. He wouldn't have minded taking care of her problem either. "Just one little drink won't hurt. It's a special occasion."

Impishly, Shay twisted her plump lips to one side. "I remember what you claimed I said when I had too much red wine."

"So you're saying you didn't say that? I was hearing things?"

Holding in a laugh, she began pouring the frothy liquid into two glasses. "Could be."

"So why don't you drink a lot tonight? I'll tape everything you say."

"So I can embarrass myself again."

David threw his head back, laughing. Laughing with him, Shay came toward him holding their drinks.

"Congratulations," he said, as she settled next to him. They were poised on the edge of the love seat, their glasses lightly tapping. "I hope tonight is the beginning of heaven on earth for you; may you get all that your heart desires; may all your career dreams come true. And all your dreams for love too." The last words were accompanied by a look so tender Shay was compelled to look away.

After sipping the tart-tasting drink, Shay licked her lips. "This is good." Still avoiding David's eyes, she set the glass back down on a coaster decorating the gold table. Marquis popped in her mind, but she didn't want to dampen the mood by mentioning his visit.

David's gaze never left her face as he swallowed several sips of the champagne. When the glass was nearly empty, he rested it. "Thanks for letting me be your date and share something so special with you. I know what this night means to you."

Nodding as she met his eyes, Shay's expression became

a mixture of joy and sadness. "It's funny. Back in those days when I was so poor that I had to ration a can of beans, I would imagine what it felt like to have my dreams come true, but I can tell you firsthand my imagination could never create how wonderful I feel tonight. I feel like magic is being sprinkled all over me, and inside me and around me. That's how good God can be. But enough of being all serious. We are going to have us some fun tonight."

"All right!" David bellowed. "Want some more to drink? The more you drink, the better it'll taste."

"Now, you know that's not true." Standing, she grasped his hand and started pulling him up from the love seat. "Mister, you better get up from there and take me to my party. You are not getting me drunk. I know what you're trying to do. You're not slick."

His loud, even laughter swirled through the air blending with hers.

"You go, girl!" Shay cheered, her voice drowned by booming applause as her friend, the owner of a special needs school, accepted her award for excellence in the ballroom of the President Chateau. Fighting the butterflies plaguing her as she braced herself for being called to the stage next, she hoped she didn't look too bad. On the way inside the building, snowflakes had messed with her do. Knowing David always made her feel better, she glanced at him beside her. That infectious grin of his flashed at her. Glimpsing her other side, one of Christina's kitten eyes gave her a wink. It had always been their private sign that meant everything would be all right.

But when Shay's name was called, she wasn't so sure about that. Walking up to the stage, she found that her new pumps were slippery and stomach flutters taunted her, even as the sensual curl of her lips entranced David and her sincerity touched the audience.

"I'd like to thank everyone for coming tonight to share this wonderful occasion with us honorees. And I'd like to thank those who made it possible for me to be here. But they told us we had to be brief, so I can't mention everyone. So first off, I give praise to my heavenly father. Without him, none of this would be possible. I give thanks to my wonderful brother, Rakim. And there are just too many loving things he's done for me to specify just one. I'd also like to thank Christina Gracen and Dr. David Robertson for their precious friendships. They keep my heart and soul together. Thank you all."

The master of ceremonies hugged Shay with his Santa-like body. Afterward, he handed her a gold, eagle-shaped trophy. Basking in a roar of hand-clapping, Shay gathered the bottommost portion of her gown, gracefully heading down the steps of the stage. With the awards part of the function over, guests began leaving their tables and socializing. A band started playing an instrumental version of R. Kelly's "I Believe I Can Fly." Waiters and waitresses circulated with cocktail trays.

Making her way through the packed room toward David and Christina, Shay only wished that Rakim had attended this ceremony like he had all the other important events in her life. She imagined how proud he would have looked. To her misfortune, his new career as an attorney had whisked him away on a business trip to Chicago. He was arriving back in New Jersey tonight, but his flight wasn't scheduled to land until an hour after the festivities were over. Christina mentioned that she was picking Rakim up at the airport. And that bothered Shay.

She wasn't blind to what had developed between her brother and her best friend. Truth was she had always believed that they would be perfect for each other. However, each of them knew why it wasn't the right time now for a romantic involvement. Shay wanted them to be together in the right way. Rakim had just separated from his wife of seven years—a wife who lived and breathed for her husband and desperately wanted her man back. It didn't matter that Janet's selfishness and superficiality had pushed him away. Shay wanted Rakim to get things straight with Janet before being with Christina. All in all, though, she knew it wasn't her business.

From a vast distance across the room, Shay spotted Christina and David mingling with some of the award recipients. She began winding through the pack, hurried to reach them. Imparting an "excuse me," and another "excuse me," she was halfway to her destination when a tuxedo appeared in front of her, the person wearing it purposely blocking her path. Snapping her attention up at the man's face, her frown hardly expressed the rage she felt at seeing Marquis again.

"What are you doing here!" The ballroom was so clamorous no one heard her loud, spiteful tone. "You have some nerve!"

"Shay, you have to listen to me."

"I don't have to do anything! You weren't invited here!" She rushed around him.

Marquis grasped both of her wrists, pulling her close, forcing Shay to face him. Probing her eyes gently, he thought of beautiful, brown diamonds. But these jewels were so alive with innate seduction, they promised unbearable pleasure all on their own. All too well Marquis knew they didn't merely promise. If there was anything in this life that he couldn't bear living without any longer, it was Shay as his lover, and eventually his wife.

"Eric told me the truth," he announced.

"I told you the truth! And you didn't believe me!" Shay jerked his hands off of her and attempted to move around him.

He sidestepped, thrusting his body in her path. "I know that now. I saw him not long ago. He almost died in a car accident and his father contacted me. Eric wanted to see me. So I visited the hospital. Because he thought he was about to die, he made a confession. He told me the truth." Recalling his idiocy lowered Marquis's head. "I'm so sorry about what I did to you. It was so wrong. And the baby . . ." The words choked in his throat and he looked up.

The sudden anguish on Shay's face was so startling Marquis reached out to her. His hand clasped around her wrist once again.

"Get your hands off!" she ordered, so wildly twisting her arm that her diamond bracelet dug into her skin. "You're hurting me! Let go!" She glimpsed several people noticing them.

Marquis moved both his hands to her waist. They clamped around her, enabling their bodies to nearly brush. "Can you feel it?"

"Yes! I feel like throwing up!" She pounded his chest and pushed it to free herself. "Now let go of me!"

"Yes, let her go!"

Hurling a glance over her shoulder, Shay was relieved to see David and Christina rushing toward them.

David grabbed Marquis by his ponytail. "Didn't I tell you to let her go!"

Fiery sensations prickling through Marquis's scalp impaired him from hearing a few spectators snickering at his assault. Automatically releasing Shay, he spun around with his fists drawn. "What the hell you putting your hands on me for?"

"Because you put your hands on Shay."

"Who the hell are you?"

The room became quieter. A small crowd started to surround the three.

"I'm Dr. David Robertson, and I'm with Shay this evening." David shoved his glasses higher on his broad nose. "And I don't appreciate you manhandling her. Now, who the hell are you?"

Marquis smirked. "The love of her life."

"The nightmare of my life!" Shay shouted.

"That's for sure," Christina added.

The circle of spectators grew larger. The room became even quieter.

David frowned. "This isn't . . . Is this the creep?"

"Creep!" Marquis shot back, narrowing his dark eyes. "Who are you calling a creep, you nerd?"

The name he'd been dubbed more than once during his childhood made David's mouth flop open. "I'll show you a nerd all right. This nerd will send you to your Maker."

"He's Marquis," Shay answered.

"A low-down dog," Christina mumbled, rolling her eyes at the man who'd nearly destroyed her best friend.

"Marquis!" David repeated. A clump of rage formed in his throat just saying that name. "You don't deserve to live, let alone touch her!"

David removed his jacket, ripped off his tie and handed his glasses to Christina. With the throng of onlookers including nearly everyone in the room now, the band stopped playing. Glaring at David, Marquis zealously rolled up his sleeves and raised his fists. Did this nerd think he was really that bad? He was going to kick his . . .

Observing the ruckus from across the room, Braxton Steele was as interested in watching a good fight as the rest of the attendees. Unlike them, however, he was an officer of the court. It was inappropriate for him to be an idle spectator.

Even so, with every fiber of his being, he could understand why the two men would battle over such a woman. No matter where he was in the ballroom or whom he was conversing with, Braxton couldn't keep his eyes away from her long. All night Shay Hilton had been getting under his skin. Although he wasn't surprised by the sexy magazine editor's affect on him.

A female colleague had given Braxton a present—a copy of *Love & Relationships* magazine and a subscription to it at the Bar Association's Christmas party two years ago. During the festivities the guys teased him about receiving such a *soft* magazine for a present. Caring less what they thought, he read some of the articles in full view of his buddies. Matter of fact, he found one particular page so intriguing that he went off by himself to appreciate it in seclusion. It was the editorial page. There was a photograph that his eyes were riveted to. Beneath the picture were the most profound words about love that he'd ever read.

In the privacy of his home later that day, Braxton read the magazine from front cover to back. During those moments of relaxation, he kept turning back to the editorial page. He couldn't get enough of looking at that fine editor Shay Hilton. Finding her sensuous and delicious, he could have taken a bite out of her. Neither could he stop reading over and over what she wrote. If her commentary truly flowed from her heart, he could conclude that she was smart, spiritual, optimistic, sexy, warm, funny, a dreamer and possibly his dream.

He was also impressed that she produced a quality publication full of provocative information. He had to meet her. The telephone number to her administrative offices was listed. Braxton picked up the receiver. Although just after dialing the first number, he hung up. Obeying his good sense, he realized how unlike him it was to call a woman based on her looks. He knew nothing about her. Not really. That evocative prose in her editorial could have been written by anyone, including a person she could have been pretending to be.

Still, Braxton didn't stop lusting. Like a schoolboy with a crush, he cherished each issue of *Love & Relationships*. Certainly, he was entertained by all of the content. However, it was the photo of Shay and her reflections that evoked the most passion from him.

The announcement in the paper about her receiving an award this evening, complete with the event's location, was definitely a sign to him that they should meet. When she stood at the podium there was such sultriness in the way she looked, and vitality in her voice. There was such aliveness about her that no camera or photo could capture it. Overall, there was just something about Shay Hilton that reached inside him and so God help him, it hadn't come out. All night he'd been threading through the swarm, trying to make his way over to her. Stopping him were people who knew him and knew of him. They pulled him aside for general conversation or to discuss legal matters.

But David's first punch to Marquis's jaw propelled Braxton into action, and he crossed the room to step through the crowd and between the two men. Centered amid the fury, his hand's flattened on each man's chest, Braxton didn't make eye contact with the guy who had removed his glasses or the guy with the ponytail, who looked somewhat familiar. He stared at the place from where he swore he heard his name being called. He stared into Shay Hilton's eyes.

* * *

Braxton Steele! What in the world is he doing here?

Shay was trying not to look at him. But how could she not when he was directly in front of her, breaking up a fight over her. Embarrassment quenched some of her anger. With her emotions heightened, there was awareness of him as if there were no one else in the room.

He had stepped right out of the press features and television reports, bringing his flesh-and-blood presence into the room with him, reminding Shay that she was made of flesh and blood, too. Flesh that had the ability to become warm when triggered by the right stimulus. Shay was losing the battle to keep her interest away from the well over six-feet broad-chest stimulus with eyes that whispered of intolerable pleasures and skin so Caribbean-tanned she ached to touch it.

"Shay, would you like to go home or stay?" David asked, maneuvering next to her, for he noticed where her eyes lingered a little too long. He looked over at the D.A., then with some abashment glimpsed everyone looking at him, Marquis and Shay. "Shay, would you like to go home or stay?" he repeated.

Shay refused to surrender to temptation any longer. She focused on David. "I—I just want to be alone for a while. Isn't there a lounge here?"

"There's one up there." Christina threw her head toward a red-carpeted stairwell.

Shay swept a glance at the gawking crowd. Hating Marquis even more for humiliating her like this, she looked back at David and Christina. All the while she was careful not to lend the slightest glance to Braxton. "I'm going upstairs."

"You sure you'll be all right alone?" David asked.

"I'll be fine. I just need to clear my head."

Shay headed to the staircase. Except before she could

mount it, Marquis blocked her passage. Swiftly, David made a move toward Marquis. Although, before he could take any action, Shay threw her hand up. The smack to Marquis's face silenced the room with quiet stiller than death.

Every eye in the room landed on Shay. Too aggravated now to be ashamed, she stared Marquis hard in the eyes. "It doesn't make a difference what you say. The simple fact is I hate you so much, I could kill you! *I could kill you!*"

Her black, velvet pumps then thumped into the carpet leading to the steps. Before long, Shay ascended the winding stairwell en route to the lounge. After digesting her parting words to the guy who he'd seen somewhere before, Braxton and the master of ceremonies persuaded everyone to resume enjoying the festivities. When it looked like everything had returned to normal, Braxton suddenly had an interest to check out what was up the stairs.

But everything wasn't normal. Another with rage in their heart watched from a secret place as Marquis was escorted out of the ballroom by security. Afterward their footsteps hurried up the fire exit passageway that led to the upstairs. Shay Hilton would be taken care of. She would be taken care of real good.

Shay had been standing by the window a few minutes, wondering why she allowed Marquis to ruin one of the happiest nights of her life, when she heard heavy footsteps thudding along the dense hallway carpeting. Getting closer to the lounge, they finally ceased right outside of it. Anger deepening her breaths and shrinking her eyes, Shay studied the door. If she saw Marquis's face one more time, she would kill him.

Two

"Is everything okay?"

Shay tried not to show her surprise or nervousness at seeing Braxton Steele standing in the partially open doorway. "I'm fine, thank you."

Braxton pushed the door a bit more, widening the entrance. "I'm Braxton Steele, the D.A." Extending his hand, his tall, broad-shouldered physique came toward her.

Drawn into eyes that were looking intensely into hers, Shay's dainty fingers, with pink-polished nails, reached out. "I'm—"

"Oh, I know who you are," he cut her off.

Shay managed a tiny smile while noticing that his warm, soothing hold of her hand lasted much longer than it should have. "I guess you would know who I am since you're here tonight. Did one of your friends receive an award?"

Foolish, he thought, to tell her he was there because he lusted after her picture. Therefore, Braxton thought of a partial truth. Since he was acquainted with the recipient who operated the special needs school, he offered, "I'm here because of Mary Greenwood."

Shay adored that lady, too. An older woman, she'd often given Shay professional and spiritual advice. "I know Mary. She's a sweetheart."

"Yes, she's something special all right." Tipping his

head slightly to the side, Braxton dipped his hands into his pockets. "You're pretty special too from what I've seen. That magazine of yours is excellent." He was losing himself in her eyes, hadn't found his way out of them since he'd entered the room. "The way you write about love is deep."

"Thank you," she said, feeling silly. Her heart was pacing a little faster with each second. It made her feel like a teenager who was being sweet-talked by the boy she'd had a crush on forever. Vowing not to fall for this sweet-talker's ladies' man charm, Shay slyly strolled away so that there was a considerable distance between them.

Braxton's gaze trailed her movements. "I guess you're a love expert." Sneakily, his eyes traced the curves of her body.

"I wouldn't consider myself a love expert."

"Oh, no?" Dimples poked into his smooth, tanned cheeks. "You sure worked something on those two brothers."

Shay would have been entranced into letting her smile join those two seductive indentations in his cheeks in a laugh, if she hadn't realized what he truly meant.

"Excuse me. Are you trying to say that I was sleeping with both of those men at the same time?"

Braxton stopped smiling.

That wasn't what he meant at all. He was merely trying to express that her unmistakable beauty, her personality and altogether being was so powerfully attractive to men that it practically enslaved them. He'd only wanted to compliment her. Not make her so mad that her sumptuously soft lips were now rounded in an enraged ball.

"I meant that you . . ." Searching for the right words, his eyes darted throughout the air.

"I know what you meant!" Her irked tone summoned

his attention back to her. "Well, I'll get you straight right now. If I wanted to sleep with two men at the same time, that would be my business! But for your information that is not my personal lifestyle preference. I'm a one-man woman!"

Delighted about her last bit of information, Braxton fought back a smile. "You misinterpreted what I was saying to you. You appear to be a very classy lady who just has some problems."

"Problems!" Shay made a squinting frown.

"I meant you have problems with men." He saw her eyebrows rising and regretted that his mouth often spoke before he thought. "I meant with those two guys."

"I don't have problems with both of them. Just one."

He recalled her parting threat to the pretty boy. "I know you do. You were very passionate about that."

"I'm passionate about a lot of things," she said, then realized the statement could have been misconstrued as flirting, especially to someone who wanted to be flirted with.

An inviting look in Braxton's eyes revealed that he perceived it as just that. "I have no problems with passion."

Shay succumbed to the allurement of the smoldering stare but quickly found something on her dress at her thigh to occupy her eyes. Looking down, she began smoothing a wrinkle. "Well, I won't be wasting any more passion of any kind on Marquis Jackson. He's out of my life."

"That's too bad for him." Braxton's hands dug deeper in his pockets as he strolled nearer to her. "You know, my mom used to tell my sister that the best way to get over a love is to get another one."

Shay looked up to see the distance between them diminishing. The pattering in her heart increased, but she hid her tension with a chuckle. "You sure your mama didn't tell *you that,* after you got on some poor girl's nerves?"

Dimples brightened his cheeks once again. "No, it was my sister. But back to you, is the other guy in your life?"

Shay half frowned, half smiled, his nerve annoying and amusing her at the same time. "Excuse me."

The space between them was steadily closing. "Am I getting too personal?"

"Yes, you are." Shay fought the heaviness she felt intruding on her breathing. "Why are you trying to get in my business?" *And why are you getting so close to me?*

Braxton came to a standstill when he was merely inches away from Shay. He gazed down into a face so lusciously caramel-hued, he imagined what it would taste like against slow, teasing motion of his tongue and lips. Was she as sweet as she looked? Would she taste like the strawberry fragrance that was intoxicating him at that moment?

"Why am I trying to get in your business?" he repeated her question.

"Yes, why?" Staring up in his face, she didn't know what was most gorgeous about him, his eyes, his lips, his skin, his bones. Everything was beautiful.

"Maybe I'm interested." His voice had lowered.

"In what?"

Braxton's lips didn't move. Rather than that, his eyes searched her face, until they ceased, burning motionlessly in her eyes. Much to his delectation, heated intensity stared directly in his eyes too. Only the sound of David and Christina in the hallway diverted Shay's attention to the doorway.

"Here she is," Christina declared. Her wide hips swaying, she sauntered into the lounge, tossing the wayward end of her shawl over her bare shoulder.

Following Christina, David split his gaze between Shay

and Braxton, inevitably settling on Shay. "We missed you. Are you ready to leave? It's about over."

"Sure—sure, I'm ready." Uneasily, Shay glanced at Braxton. "Good-bye."

He nodded. "Good-bye."

Thinking about having met Shay Hilton, Braxton drove unto the white-sheathed land surrounding his home. A blast of frost whipped him in the face when he opened the door of his old, red Mustang and stepped out of it. Making his way across the sprawling stretch to his front door, he sunk his black, shiny wing tips in the steadily piling snow as flakes falling baby-soft brushed his face, some clinging on his lashes.

He had never liked snow. He never understood the big deal people made over the first snowfall. It made traveling inconvenient. Plus, there was that slushy mess after it melted. Oddly enough, though, tonight it wasn't bothering him too much. The chill sweeping over his skin wasn't so cold that it was unbearable. Neither had the frigidity burned away his sense of smell, especially the scent he'd smelled all night—the strawberry fragrance she'd worn. Somehow, Braxton could still smell it. When he entered the warmth of his house it seemed to become more pronounced.

After hanging his coat in the vestibule closet, he headed upstairs to the master bedroom. But he knew that there was no way he would fall asleep right away. If he wasn't reminiscing about his short interaction with Shay Hilton, he was speculating whether she went home with that guy, the one with the glasses. Braxton recalled his mentioning that he was a doctor.

Gruffly, Braxton removed his tie. He shed the rest of his formal attire just as harshly. When he was down to his bare chest and snug black underwear, he plopped down on the bed, folding his hands behind his head. Why did he feel like something bad had happened to him? It hadn't. He just didn't get enough time alone with a lady that he was extremely attracted to.

Rolling on his side, Braxton wondered where she was at this exact moment. What was she doing? Who was she with? That doctor with the glasses? Were they dancing to a slow jam at his place? Was his head buried so deep on the side of her neck that he was kissing off the strawberry that had been sprinkled over her skin? Or were they making love? Braxton hoped not. That man wouldn't know how to make love to a woman like Shay.

Certain that he did know how prevented Braxton from sleeping. A toss here, a turn there and he finally gave up on getting a good night's rest. Shay Hilton wouldn't let him. Hence, he decided to be seduced by his lover. He got out of the bed, headed down the hall to his artist's studio and went over to the blank white canvas. Shay Hilton's eyes when she first looked at him. That's what he would paint. Even if that *something* he beheld in them was all in his imagination, he had to capture it.

With her arm latched around David's elbow, Shay escorted him off the elevator that led to her penthouse. Laughing and talking, they eventually reached her door. Shay turned her back to David, sticking her key into the lock. That's when she unexpectedly felt his hands on her shoulders. Curving around with a smile, Shay didn't feel so playful seeing how solemn he looked.

"What? What is it, David?"

He tapped the middle of his glasses upward. "I want to come in."

"You know you can come in." She shifted her weight off of her tired left leg to the right one. "You're always welcome at my place." She halfway grinned at how silly he sounded.

"No, Shay." Taking a deep breath, he glimpsed from side to side as if it would help him express what was bothering him. "I want to come in, and I want it to be different. I want more."

"More," she responded, lowering her head. With all her heart, she wished she could have made herself feel what he was feeling. *What is wrong with me?* She had even decided that tonight their relationship would take a turn in a romantic direction. Except now that it was time to follow through, something wouldn't let her.

Watching her reaction made David feel guilty. "What am I saying? You had a stressful enough night with Marquis. Now here I come nagging you. I'm sorry. I—"

"No, David." She gazed up at him. "You have nothing to be sorry about. We've been close friends for a few years, and what's the harm in your wanting a little affection? You're not trying to jump my bones. You just want something . . . some semblance of what naturally happens between a man and a woman who care about each other . . . a kiss, a caress. And neither of us is involved. No one that I've dated has really interested me enough for me to give myself emotionally or physically, and the women that you've dated haven't impressed you enough to want to make them your lady. So you have nothing to be sorry about. You're thinking that we could take things to that most intimate level since we get along so well and we're both unattached. You're human. And I do want more too."

"But. I hear a *but* coming."

"But I'm just not ready. I don't know what's wrong with me, David. It's me. It's not you."

David clasped her hands gently within his. "It's all right, Shay. I don't want you to think of me as another anxiety to add to your plate. Marquis is enough of a pain in the butt."

"Amen." Smiling, Shay squeezed his hands. "You're so understanding."

"How can I not be? I care about you. Whether we're lovers or not, I always want to be part of your life. I'd rather be a good friend in your life rather than not be in it at all. You're too special to lose."

"You're just as special to me."

"I'm glad." He unclasped his fingers. "Now I better head home and get some sleep. I have a long day tomorrow."

"Me too."

He pecked her cheek. "I'll call you."

David made wide, high steps back down the hall, his arms swinging lightly as he moved. Shay turned the key and the knob, grateful to enter her suite.

Letting the door slam behind her, her mind was so entrenched with varied thoughts, she was unaware she'd left the key hanging from the outside lock of her door.

On the other side of town, Braxton faced his canvass and painted Shay as she looked when he first saw her. It was the expression in her eyes that he was determined to capture. It was unforgettable. More than that, was how it made him feel. Like she was as attracted and somehow connected to him as he was to her. It was so strange.

Making delicate brown strokes in her pupils, Braxton felt almost as good as he did when he was making love. Almost. He loved painting. Ever since he could remember he had a natural flair for it. He could do it for hours and always finish with what his family saw as a masterpiece. Although they never encouraged his painting as a profession. "Do something with your life and lift yourself and us up," his mother and father stressed. "Go to college and be somebody," His mother loved lawyers, loved watching them on television, loved the respect they received, loved that they lived financially comfortable lives, so she suggested becoming one to her son. Being an artist was out of the question. Artists starved. Clarice Steele, a nurse's aide, and Braxton Steele, a postal worker, had worked too hard all their lives to see their oldest child grow up to become impoverished. Hence, Braxton's law dream was born.

During college, he became more dedicated when he met another aspiring lawyer, who truly inspired him. However, his art, his true love, was shoved aside as a hobby, so his family thought, so everyone thought. But he couldn't just paint anything. Braxton painted the most beautiful things, the moments of ecstasy he'd experienced in life. He would always have that moment with him to take out and look at it—that image of ecstasy, which he could keep forever, when having it in his mind wasn't enough. That's why now he painted the way Shay Hilton looked at him when she first saw him in the room.

While Braxton painted Shay, she snuggled her body into a lime, satin nightgown. Loving the way the fabric felt on her skin, she lit several strawberry candles on her bedroom night tables before diving onto her silken lavender sheets. Hoping the soft ambience would relax her into slumber, she cut off the lamps. Afterward she lay backward. Inhaling her beloved scent's sweetness immediately mellowed her into closing her eyes. But after ten minutes of trying to find the best position to help her sleep, she realized a good night's rest wouldn't come easily tonight.

How could it when so many thoughts were in her mind? If she wasn't thinking about her encounter with Braxton Steele, she was deliberating about what David now wanted.

And if she pushed those thoughts aside for merely a second, the ugly thought would invade the open space—Marquis. Why had he intruded on her happy night, forcing her to remember the horrible past? The past that was filled with Eric Lebleau.

Thinking back, Shay partially blamed the decline of her relationship with Marquis on his best friend, Eric. Eric had a big problem. It was falling in love with a woman who didn't and couldn't reciprocate his affection—Shay. Feeling unrequited love made Eric bitter. So much so that he lied to Marquis about having an affair with Shay. Shay had no doubts that Marquis believed her denial. Particularly so since he kicked his childhood friend out of his life. As well, her accidental pregnancy seemed to make him so happy, he quickly did something he claimed he longed to do anyway—put a huge engagement ring on her finger.

Yet on their day of wedded bliss when the minister asked Marquis if he took Shay as his wife, Marquis stared coldly into her eyes and barked, "No! I had no intentions of marrying you. This was all for fun. That ring isn't even real." He then peered into the audience until a scandalously dressed woman stood. As more than three hundred guests gawked in horror, Marquis left Shay's side at the altar, walking over to the woman. He kissed her, kissed her passionately, even nastily, ultimately announcing to everyone, "This is the woman I'm going to marry. Shay, you can be with Eric."

An indignity that no human being should have endured, it caused Shay to collapse. At the same instant that she was rushed to the hospital, Marquis left the church with his fiancée. Hearing the doctor say she'd *miscarried* caused a huge rift in her heart. She was so accustomed to suffering by then, only a few tears slipped down her cheeks when Marquis didn't visit her at the hospital, or call to check on the baby's condition and hers. Even when Rakim tracked him down to inform him that Shay lost the baby, the man to whom she had given all a woman could give hurt her further with his indifference.

Rakim treated him to a black eye, and days later ran into him at an auto repair shop and did it again. In any case, Shay hadn't seen Marquis again. She'd heard he went to California with his new lady. But she hadn't seen or heard from him again until this day.

With her pillow damp from the tears the memories invoked, Shay carried her head over to its dry twin. Some days she was still mystified that one human being could be that cruel to another. Had there ever been any indication that Marquis was such a monster and had she overlooked it because she was so in love?

Shay would have questioned how her spirit had risen from that low point to the high point where she stood now, but she knew God was the answer. Only God could have saved her from losing her mind or taking her life. Now she was grateful for the gifts that life bestowed upon her. Beauty existed abundantly in her world. Tonight, for instance, she had come across someone very beautiful. Physically that is. *He* just wasn't for her.

"I'm not going to let him get to me," she whispered, finally feeling drowsy. "I'm not going to think about him. He insulted me." But even as the whisper trailed with her into sleep, Braxton's eyes were searing into hers as hard as his lips were kissing her in the haziness of her dream.

If only the penthouse's front door opening slowly were a dream, too.

Thumps, banging, glass shattering, objects smashing. Shay could hear them all around her during her struggle to free herself from a locked closest. Flailing her arms and kicking to escape the closed confines, she struggled and struggled until she awakened. Relieved that she was dreaming, she began to panic when she realized she was still hearing the sounds. They were coming from the living room.

Her heart felt like a fist. A fist banging repeatedly to get out of her chest before it exploded. Still, Shay tiptoed toward the noises until suddenly they stopped. There was silence. Not a pin drop. Only the breaths of her suffocating fear. Was whoever broke into her home coming to get her? She couldn't stand there uselessly.

Lifting an umbrella that sat in a corner stand, she proceeded. At the living room entrance she bent her head around the wall and peeked inside.

"Oh, God, Please noooooooo!"

Screams coming from the next penthouse froze little Bobby Matthews until the sound stopped. Springing up in bed, he carefully placed his ear against the adjoining wall, listening for the least remaining sound. Hearing none, the four-year old soon dashed into his mother's room, dragging his Winnie the Pooh teddy bear behind him.

Her mouth gaped open, his mother slept. Soft breaths escaped as the side of her face engraved the stuffed cotton pillow. Tugging on her hip, Bobby's round brown face appeared frightened for his pretty neighbor. If something happened to Miss Shay, who would he call his girlfriend?

Lydia Matthews, a single mom and owner of a flourishing gift shop in mid-Manhattan's tourist district, treasured sleep and the few moments she had for it. So when she heard through her cloud of slumber, "Mama, Mama, I heard Ms. Shay screaming," Lydia's lids were too heavy to open.

Her thin hand simply patted the empty spot behind her

on the bed. "You can sleep with Mama if you want," she mumbled. "It was a bad dream."

"But I wasn't dreaming," he insisted, his doe eyes stretching with his adamancy. "Ms. Shay was screaming."

Sleep was conquering Lydia Matthews. Too deeply asleep to crack her eyes, she patted the mattress again. "It was a dream, baby. Dream . . ."

Sulking, Bobby relented, climbing into his mother's bed. Tucking himself and his bear underneath the thick African quilt, he looked over at the back of her head. Hundreds of small braids spilled in every direction along the pillow. "But it wasn't a dream. I think a bad man is there."

Three

Blood. Everything was broken. There was so much blood and everything was broken around Shay. Through the blurred images that gradually came into focus, she saw pools, smudges, streaks and droplets of red coating every wrecked item in the room. She viewed it all from where she lay on the floor.

Who in the world had gone mad enough to do this? And why was she flattened on the carpet? And whose blood was it? Attempting to sit up and examine herself for wounds, she found it too difficult to move. She was extremely weak. Was she stabbed? Shot? Dying? Fortunately, she didn't feel any stings or pain and she didn't think she was bleeding. Frantically, her eyes searched around the room. Was what she was beholding real? What had happened? She felt confused. She wasn't sure she was fully awake. But as her eye captured Marquis lying motionlessly on the floor, horribly bloodied and beaten, her mind became as acute as her eyesight.

"Oh, my God!"

Questions. A thousand questions ran through her mind as Shay tried to get over to him. She had to help him. A thousand questions that were running as fast as her heartbeat and as powerful as the alarm rising in her blood like lava in a volcano that was seconds from erupting. Nevertheless, her body was unwilling to obey her and hurry up over to Marquis before it was too late. Oddly, it persisted in feeling like it weighed a ton. It required every effort and muscle to move an inch. What had happened to her? To Marquis? In this room? How did Marquis get in there? Spotting the cracked front door somewhat answered the question.

All Shay remembered was peeking into the room, seeing him like this and racing into the living room to help him. What happened after that she couldn't remember.

Was the person who did this still in her home? Were they hiding? Had they knocked her out? Or had the animal attempted to kill her and failed? Vigilantly, Shay scanned the room. But it was when she gathered the strength to raise her head that she observed the strangest thing when she looked down at her own body. She was gripping a candlestick. Globs of blood were sticking to portions of it. How had it gotten in her hand?

"Police!" she heard. Her head snapped up to the officer making the command. He was opening the already opened door wider. "Put it down!" Hurriedly slipping on latex gloves, the cop cautiously approached Shay. His green eyes stretched on her as if she were a freak of nature before he glanced at his colleagues. "To think we almost ignored that caller." Several other policemen and paramedics crowded behind him. They trailed him to a point before dispersing throughout the demolished room. Their expressions varied from surprise to disgust to composure.

Immediately the gloved officer bent down, loosened the candlestick from Shay's fingers and deposited it in a plastic bag. As he sealed the top of the evidence container, he moved aside allowing two paramedics to attend to Shay. The other medics scurried to examine Marquis.

Uninvolved with the medics checking on her condition,

Shay was equally disinterested in the officer who inquired about who she was and what had occurred. Halfheartedly she responded to him. What was occurring across the room was all too consuming. Paramedics were desperately working on Marquis, constantly mashing his chest, until ultimately they shook their heads. One of them gazed up at the inquisitive cop. An odd look that further unsettled Shay was exchanged between them. She studied the scene as if she were viewing a tearjerker movie. It wasn't quite real. Especially when the medics carried a sheet over Marquis's toes to cover his body and face.

"He can't be!" Shay shouted, shoving the probing hands away from her. Somehow she regained her strength and raised herself to a sitting position. "No, he can't be!"

"What happened here, miss?" Patrolmen Todd Jamison asked.

It was one of many questions he'd asked since entering the crime scene, and one he'd asked repeatedly because the answer he received wasn't satisfying him. He believed this woman was lying about not knowing what had happened to her ex-lover. He disbelieved her speculation that she must have fainted when she saw the victim in this state since the medics could find no signs of injury or assault on her.

Hell, Jamison as well as the other officers witnessed this Shay Hilton clutching the object the man was bludgeoned with as they tramped in the door. Not only that, but an anonymous caller had stated that a man and woman were arguing and fighting at this penthouse, and the woman was raving that she was going to kill the man. The caller believed she carried out her threat, because they didn't hear the man's voice any longer.

Having removed the gloves from his fleshy hands, Todd tossed the latex inside the only undisturbed furnishing, a garbage can. "Can you just tell me the truth about what happened? Make it easy on yourself. We'll find out sooner or later."

Shay didn't hear him. Fending off the hands of the paramedics who tried to help her as she stood, she didn't notice Todd watching, watching even more prudently as she sauntered wobbily across to the body.

One of the officers blocked her path. However, Jamison, nodding that it was all right, made him step aside. He needed to assess Shay Hilton's reaction, detect if she was angry, sad, remorseful or stifling her joy. Studying her with his emerald eyes now narrowed, Todd Jamison was having all kinds of thoughts about this one. Despite nineteen years on the force, he was unlike many other officers. Often they were so accustomed to seeing the repercussions of violence they could leave it on the job as easily as they drove a car. Not Jamison.

Every murder was personal to him. As a child his best friend was lured into the woods and hacked to death. The killer was never caught. It became his life's mission to never let murderers get away. Especially one like this one. With her model's face and body that any man would desire, this was the type of woman who always overlooked him to get to more attractive or richer men.

Standing above Marquis, Shay peered down on the white sheet. She still felt like she was viewing a movie. "Please, get up. Please!" Her voice didn't even sound like hers. There were tears in her throat, and she could feel them making their way up to her eyes.

"Why did you strike this man so brutally?" Officer Jamison asked.

Again Shay didn't hear, didn't turn around to acknowledge him. She was concentrating on the sheet, reaching to pull it down. Another very slender officer, Patman, restrained her hand. Nonetheless, Jamison nodded to him also. Patman released her.

Shay peeled the sheet down to reveal the face. It looked like Marquis. A battered, bloodied, stone-still Marquis. Just hours ago, he'd stared into her eyes with fire burning in his, while his lips begged for her love. Now he couldn't look at her. He couldn't speak to her. He would never look at her like that, or speak to her again. Not in this lifetime.

"If you just wake up I'll forgive you."

Jamison stepped beside Shay. He gazed over at her doll-like profile. "Did he reside here?"

"If you just open your eyes, I'll truly forgive you."

Jamison sighed. "What was the argument about?"

"It was just that you hurt me so bad. So, so bad. You have no idea how much you hurt me."

"Answer my questions, Ms. Hilton."

"But I won't hold it against you. I won't hold the baby against you. I won't hold nothing against you. If you just . . . if you just . . ."

"If you don't answer them here, you *will* answer them at the station."

Fed up with the game this woman was playing, Jamison decided on his next action. Because Shay Hilton was beautiful, rich, probably smart, he knew she presumed she was spared the rules abided by those less than fortunate citizens. Tired of her, he unhooked his handcuffs.

"Sir, I have to speak to you for a minute," Patman said, stepping over to his partner of three months. He threw his head toward a secluded corner.

The two men shuffled to the lone area of the room. Patman's thin hand rubbed across his mouth before he spoke. "Sir, what are you doing?"

Jamison's eyes squinted angrily on the young face. "What do you mean, what am I doing? How can you ask me that? We walked in and saw her clutching the murder weapon. Plus, there was that call."

Patman rubbed his mouth again. It was a nervous habit he'd developed since being on the police force. "But, sir, we don't have any facts. We don't know anything about what happened here. She claims she doesn't even know what happened. All we know is this woman's name and . . ." He glanced at the award Shay received. He had picked it up off the floor and laid it on a shelf. "And that she's some hotshot magazine editor."

"We know enough." Jamison glimpsed at Shay. "I don't buy her act."

Patman took a deep, exhausted breath. "Sir, do you want a repeat of the Bolder case?"

Jamison looked off, seeing only a memory playing across his mind. It was a recollection he would have rather forgotten. Bolder was an assemblyman he'd arrested hastily after he was found in his car with his girlfriend shot to death. Bolder's gun was used in the homicide. Bolder maintained his innocence, claiming that robbers had grabbed his gun and pulled the trigger. Jamison saw things differently. But after only a fifteen minute interrogation Braxton Steele determined that the charges should be dropped against Bolder. A day later the district attorney even tracked down the true perpetrators. Jamison and Patman wound up looking like fools in the press. Their superior officer further suggested that the next time there was a doubt about a homicide arrest of an eminent figure, that they should let the district attorney's office make the decision.

"All right," Jamison said with an annoyed sigh. "Get Steele on the phone. Tell him to hurry over here."

Unfolding his cell phone, Patman nodded, then pressed a button.

"Hello," the sleep-husky voice answered.

"Steele, it's Patman."

"Why . . . are you waking me up?" Braxton slurred, sleep heavily muffling his words.

"Because chief said. . . . Oh, hell, we need you."

Patman heard Braxton yawning while he spoke. "Man, you guys are a pain in my butt."

"You have to get over here, Steele."

"Over where?"

"A crime scene at the Cliffside Towers. A homicide. The case is sketchy. We don't want to jeopardize it. We need you to question a suspect."

"What happened?" he yawned out.

"This babe . . . a real hot babe, oh, man. Anyway, she might have killed her boyfriend. An ex. Beat his brains out with a candlestick. She was holding it when we walked in."

"Doesn't sound like a nice lady," Braxton mumbled.

"She sure looks nice. So how long will it take you to get here? My partner is getting restless."

"You and Jamison can handle it." He sounded muffled. "I'm not getting out of my bed to get in that snow. I . . ."

"Come on. She's not cooperating. Plus, this one might get press. She's a hotshot editor or something."

Patman heard breathing.

"Steele? Steele, are you falling asleep on me?"

The placid, methodical breaths persisted.

"Steele, wake up! Steele!" Patman was yelling.

"All right," Braxton said, his deep voice becoming clearer. "You really are a pain in my butt. What time is it anyway?"

Patman glimpsed his watch. "It's 1:15."

Braxton noticed snow falling outside his window too. "Do you see what it's doing out there?"

"So I came out in it."

"I am not getting paid enough for this." Braxton cleared

the remainder of sleep out of his throat. "Now you said it's at the Cliffside Towers?"

"Yeah."

"What floor and suite?"

"The sixteenth. Suite L."

"And whose name is it in? The guards will ask."

"Shay Hilton."

"Shay what!" Braxton suddenly felt awake.

"Hilton. Shay Hilton."

There was silence.

"You got it? Steele? Steele?"

There was a click.

Jamison had begun the same round of questioning for what seemed like the hundredth time to Shay when something began to dawn on her: There was a matter nearly as serious as Marquis's death at stake—her freedom. In all the flurry of seeing Marquis laying lifelessly on her floor, she had thrust aside those questions that her own mind first asked about this horror. Adding to the puzzlement was a question: If she had fainted as she proposed to the officer, who other than Marquis had been there also? It made her feel so violated. And how did anyone get in her house in the first place?

Something told her to look at the door. "My keys!" she exclaimed, as she spotted them hanging from the lock. Mindlessly, she must have left them in when David escorted her to the penthouse. A dangerous habit, it wasn't the first time she'd done it. Glimpsing Jamison, she pointed toward them. "My keys! I left them in the door. That's how they must have gotten in my house."

As her eyes were compelled to rise above the keys, an unexpected presence filled the doorway. From Shay's perspective he seemed to obliterate everyone and everything in the room. A chill shivered over her at seeing Braxton Steele. She didn't know whether it was the way he was looking at her that caused it or if it was the fact that it hadn't dawned on her that the D.A. could be called in to interrogate her. Whenever a district attorney showed up at your door, she knew it wasn't to deliver a sweepstakes prize. Particularly since he'd heard you announce you could kill the man who now lay dead on your living-room carpet. Shay's eyes trailed Braxton as he inspected various areas of the living room.

Finishing his inspection, he pulled the sheet down that overlaid Marquis. Battered as he was, he now took a good enough look at him to discern why he looked familiar. He was an actor, Braxton realized. He had a movie on videotape at home with this guy in it. He hadn't blown up yet, but the brother had appeared in some exciting roles. Shaking his head at the shame of it all, Braxton then looked upward and paused with thought.

Shay couldn't tell what he was thinking, not even when his eyes clung to her. She was poised on the edge of the sofa cushion as if a frail wind would blow her off.

"Ms. Hilton, we meet again," he said, taking a seat next to her. He swiveled sideways to face her.

"I never thought we'd meet again like this."

Jamison stood above them. "You two know each other? Now that's interesting."

Braxton looked up at him, noting Jamison's bulbous nose first. "We met at an awards ceremony tonight." He gazed back at Shay. She was rolling her eyes up at Jamison, which gave him a chance to quickly roll his own over her. Dewy-skinned cleavage was spilling out of her low-cut nightgown.

Braxton raised his eyes to her face before she saw where he was looking. "Ms. Hilton received an award," he told Jamison. "She was one of the entrepreneurs of the year."

Disliking the tone of admiration in the D.A.'s voice, Jamison's scrutiny divided between the two. "Is that right?"

"Ms. Hilton is a very talented lady," Braxton elaborated.

Shay tried to smile but couldn't.

"And she's possibly a dangerous lady," Jamison added.

"I didn't do it!" Shay was glaring at both Jamison and Braxton, finally settling on Braxton. "As I told these officers over and over, I fell asleep. Alone! Marquis and no one else was with me. I just fell asleep." *Thinking about you.* "Then I woke up to all this noise. I walked in here and saw Marquis like this. Thereafter, I draw a blank. I must have fainted. The paramedics say I have no injuries or signs of being drugged so I must have fainted. I don't know how that candlestick got in my hand, but I mistakenly left my keys in the door. So that's probably how Marquis and that . . . that animal that did this entered my home. But after the party I had no contact with Marquis. You have to believe me. He had harassed me all day, but I swear I didn't touch him."

Braxton simply stared at her. He was struggling to see beyond the beautiful face and the tempting fruit below it to detect if Shay was lying. And how could he not take into consideration what she said earlier to the deceased. Braxton hated to bring it up. She looked frightened enough. However, with all those other witnesses who heard her say it too, the truth was bound to come out. It would be neglectful of his position if he didn't put it on the table.

"What about those parting words you gave him at the ceremony?"

Scowling, Jamison moved closer to them. "What do you mean, 'parting words?' "

Shay knew it was coming. She just wasn't prepared to hear it come from Braxton. The way he was looking at her made her feel like he just wanted to caress her skin from head to toe with his delicious lips. Then again, he was known to be a player. He probably looked at every woman that way. Besides that, she was no longer merely a woman to him. She was a suspect in a murder. He was likely her prosecutor.

"I know what I said earlier at the party. But I didn't mean it."

"What did you say?" Jamison inquired.

Shay ignored Jamison, preferring to appeal to Braxton. "I could never have done that to Marquis. I loved him once. I loved him like I loved no one else. I would have done anything for him. Anything in the world to make him happy."

Braxton pondered if Shay was the greatest actress in the world. She was sure making him believe she loved the victim. He would have loved for an ex to speak about him like that. "Why did you break up?" His eyes uncontrollably dropped to the plunging neckline of her lingerie again.

This time Shay caught the look. She glanced down at herself and was shocked that she was falling out of her negligee. Straightaway, she tugged the shoulders up higher. The neckline lifted. Feeling more comfortable, she went on, "Our breakup is a long story."

Braxton could still see enough to make him swallow the rush of adrenaline in his throat. "I would like to hear it."

"So would I," Jamison added.

Shay shot the evil eye up at Jamison again before softening her gaze on Braxton. His warm brown eyes looked sympathetic. At the same time, she caught them more than once sweeping over her body.

"Why are you holding back?" Jamison reacted to her hesitation to reveal her history with Marquis. "Why did you break up?"

Shay didn't offer Jamison the evil eye this time. Neither could she look at Braxton. Instead she peered deep into the past, sharing the wonderful beginning of her relationship with Marquis until the horrible end. Afterward, she recounted the two times she had seen him during the day.

"So you threatened to kill him?" Jamison concluded at the end of her story.

"No, I didn't," Shay argued. "I told him I *could* kill him!"

Jamison scratched the tip of his nose. "Sounds almost the same to me."

"Almost is key," she countered.

Jamison smirked. "Lady, don't get cute. I do have enough to arrest you."

Shay felt the air being sucked from her. "Look, I didn't do it!" She was appealing to Braxton. "You have to believe me. Yes, I was mad at him. But I couldn't kill him."

Jamison scratched his nose again. "Then why is the evidence stacked against you? One of your neighbors even called and told us a man and a woman in this apartment were arguing and fighting. That's why we came here."

Baffled, Shay looked from man to man. "But it wasn't me!" Everything was becoming stranger by the second. Could Marquis have been arguing with a woman in her home? But why hadn't she heard the argument? She heard the objects being broken and falling. Maybe there was no argument. Maybe someone was trying to set her up. "Maybe the person who called the police did it. Who called anyway?"

"A neighbor," Jamison responded.

"Who?"

"They didn't leave their name."

"Was it a man or woman?"

"The operator said it sounded like an old man, maybe a drunk too. That's why we started not to pay the call any attention. Good thing we did."

Suspicion narrowed Shay's eyes. "I doubt any drunks live in this building."

Jamison chuckled. "Why, because only high-class people like you live here?"

"Listen to me," Shay stressed. "Whoever killed Marquis could have put that drunk up to do it." Amazed at all that had happened and what was happening, Shay shook her head. The way Braxton started looking at her didn't assuage her emotions either. "What? Why are you looking at me like that?"

"Did you feel he killed the baby? And that's why you wanted to kill him?"

"Yes, when I miscarried my child, I thought he caused it. But I swear to you, I didn't kill him. I didn't!"

Making no comment to that, Braxton scribbled some notes on a pad.

Jamison was distracted by activity near Marquis. Curious about what he was staring at, Shay's attention wandered that way too. Chalk was being drawn around the body.

"I say we have enough for an arrest." Jamison steadied his gaze in Braxton's.

Shay switched teary eyes back to Braxton. "And you feel that way too?"

Braxton stood. "Get some clothing, Ms. Hilton."

"No, you can't!" Shay wiped across her eyes before any tears fell. "I didn't do it."

"Pack for a few days."

"I didn't kill Marquis!"

"You can't stay here."

"I swear I didn't do it!"

"This is a crime scene. And we have to let our forensics people do their work here. You have to stay with a relative, a friend or at a hotel."

Shay sighed. "Thank you."

Jamison wrinkled up his nose like a foul odor had entered the room.

Braxton tucked his pad in his coat pocket. "Don't thank me yet. Because you can't leave town. After forensics gets through with this place and the murder weapon is checked, it's a possibility you may be taken into custody—tomorrow."

"You're going to arrest me?" Shay's heartbeat seemed to pause waiting for his answer.

"If there are no other fingerprints on that candlestick, that is a serious possibility."

Braxton turned away from her. He couldn't talk to her anymore. He couldn't look at her anymore, not into her eyes, not at those lips, not at her body. He couldn't be tempted to compromise his obligation to his profession. Yes, Shay Hilton was so beautiful she could make any man crazy with desire. And yes, she had turned him on even as she sat there discussing a sick act she might have committed. And yes, he knew he was going to go home and imagine making love to her as he had all night. Regardless, he was an officer of the court. Being such, he had a responsibility to the people of the community to build cases against suspects of murder. He had a duty to prosecute them to the fullest extent of the law. That man, Marquis Jackson who was dead on the floor, could have been any man, his friend, his brother, his father. It could have been him.

Shay's eyes followed Braxton and Jamison engrossed

in deep conversation as they walked to the front door. Knowing they were discussing her fate made her feel like she were coming apart. How was she going to hold it together during this ordeal? How was she not going to lose her mind? She was actually being accused of a murder she had no part in committing. And Braxton had the nerve to glance over his shoulder at her precisely before walking out the door.

"Ms. Hilton," Patman said, jarring her from her thoughts.

"Yes?"

"We have to take your prints. After that, wherever you're going to be staying tonight, you better make preparations."

"I am. I have to get in touch with my brother."

"Don't move, baby. Please don't move." Rakim could barely squeeze the begging between his rapturous moans as Christina lay beneath him. Her gentle, addictive movements welcomed him deeper and deeper inside her until he could go no further and feel no greater joy.

Rakim had experienced many wonderful, exciting things in his life. He had traveled around the world, once even jumping from a parachute in Ghana, West Africa. He had looked up into the ecstatic faces of millions as he participated in a track-and-field division of the Olympic games. He had helped make his sister's dream come true, and now was fulfilling his own. He had even married a beauty queen and had been blissfully happy for a few years. Still, nothing ever, ever compared to being with this woman. Why hadn't he noticed Christina was his dream sooner? He had known her for years, since she and Shay went to high school. Now it felt like he was just getting to know her.

"I want to stay like this forever," he confessed.

Christina felt Rakim's tender touch cupping her face in his hands before his tongue slid beyond the warmth of her lips, kissing her deeply. With the same emotion, she enthralled him. If falling in love with this man wasn't heaven, she didn't know what was. She didn't want him to move either. The glorious sensation their lovemaking had delivered to them was a breath away from orgasmic. Then suddenly with his delicious tongue and lips caressing hers during the same moment that he began to sway his hips as if his muscles had lost control, Christina couldn't bear the joy satisfying her. Her screams blended with his utterances of unbearable bliss.

Breathless, Rakim flung himself beside Christina. She eased her head atop his chest and felt his strong arms slip around her shoulder. Smiling, she looked up at his pretty, big eyes gazing down at her while his smooth, chestnut skin shimmered with the musty oil of their love. Craving any part of him again, her lips brushed his chest and the saltiness of his sweat seeped against her tongue. She looked back up at his angular face. He was still staring down at her, his eyes silently whispering that no one could ever make him feel like she did.

For so long she'd waited for this—for Rakim Hilton to fall in love with her. From the moment Shay introduced Christina to her big brother after school one day, she was smitten. The feeling progressed to even more when she saw how considerately Rakim treated his sister and what an overall tender man he was. But he always saw her as Shay's little friend, his other little sister.

When he decided to marry a former Miss Black New Jersey, Janet Sheridan, and become a corporate attorney in her family's thriving banking empire, Christina knew that her dreams had died. She never forgot attending the wedding, hugging Rakim, dancing beside the blissful couple and crying all the way home that night.

So she was surprised when Rakim stopped by her home one night months ago just to talk about pursuing his real dream to get into criminal law—the dream that he was passionate about, that he went to college and law school for. She worked in a law firm, as a legal secretary. He asked her to keep him abreast of the firm's taking on any new attorneys. Now he had just returned from a trip where he represented the firm.

Rakim lifted Christina's soft chin, positioning her mouth upward so that he could taste her once more. When he let her go fully satiated, he just looked at her. Why hadn't he always seen her beauty? Not merely the pretty, round face with the exotic kitten eyes, but her caring about others, her strength, her pride of who she was, her honesty, her warm heart, her positive spirit, her loyalty for those she loved. The woman who had just made fire blaze through his blood had developed into one dynamic woman.

He saw Christina's eyes drifting close. "You better not go to sleep."

"Why not?" Chuckling, she faced him, forcing her eyes back open.

"Because I haven't seen you in days and once is not enough."

She laughed. "What are you trying to do, make me an invalid?"

"No way." He kissed her finger. "I need you nice and energetic so when we get married every night is like this."

Her smile lost a bit of its curve.

He noticed it. "What's wrong?"

She sighed. "I don't know. So much about life seems unfair. I loved you for so long and now that I have you, I can't really have you because your wife won't let you go. I guess that's my punishment for loving a married man."

Rakim sat up, causing her to sit up too. Gazing deep into her eyes, he shook his head. "Janet and I are not separated because you came along and stole me. We were separated and then you and I became lovers.

"And I left her and got this place not because I wanted to cheat, but because my marriage has been over for years. She fooled me. She pretended to be someone she wasn't. And I fell in love with that imposter. But day by day as I began to see her inside, the real her that she'd hidden, I fell out of love. And that's when I finally got the courage to leave."

"But why is she fighting the divorce so hard? She had to feel like it was over like you did."

"She's in denial. And she's also into appearances. Doesn't matter if she's really happy in our marriage. What matters to her is how it looks to other people."

"I think Janet knows."

"She doesn't."

"Rakim, she knows that we're involved."

"How could she? I told her the honest reason why we couldn't be together anymore, and believe me it had nothing to do with you. She didn't even ask if there was someone else."

"That's because she already knows there is."

"But how could she? We've been so discreet. I wouldn't hurt her that way."

"I know you wouldn't. But she knows. I can tell. When Shay and I were at lunch the other day she came in the restaurant. She spotted us and she came over. She was polite and everything. But at the same time she gave me the strangest look."

* * *

Janet closed her deep-set eyes for her tenth attempt to sleep that night. To her misfortune, her mind kept her awake with the same picture—her sexy, beautiful Rakim making love to that woman Christina. Janet was aware that something was going on between them even before the private investigator showed her the pictures. Every time her sister-in-law's friend was around her husband, Janet never missed that longing in Christina's little eyes and the softness in her tone whenever she spoke to Rakim.

Reaching for the lamp light in the dark, she turned it on, then sat up against the headboard. Grabbing the remote control, she flipped on the cable TV. There were many shopping shows on. Maybe she could find something nice to buy for herself and Rakim. A second into the program, she'd lost interest. Nothing she could buy could make her feel better. Her husband was in love with another woman. He had even left her for her.

"Janet," her mother said, drawing her attention to the doorway. Wearing a pink negligee the short, stout woman entered the room.

"Mother, why are you up at this hour?" Janet turned off the television. Preferring to reach for the latest Bloomingdale's catalog on her vanity rather than confront the pity in her mother's face, her russet nails began skimming the pages. She regretted telling her mother about her marital problems and the other woman. Normally she never confided in her. Except Rakim's abandonment had been too traumatic to keep inside. "You really should go home."

Victoria Sheridan strolled farther into the room. "I'm not going anywhere when you're in this state."

"What state?"

"Depression." Victoria relaxed near the footrest. "I will not go anywhere when you're like this."

"I'm not depressed, Mother." Janet laid the catalog on the spread.

Victoria's watery gray eyes set hard into her daughter. "He's not worth it. You were too good for him anyway. He had no class, nor wealth."

"Wealth!" Janet yelled. "Mother, it isn't money that I love and miss about Rakim."

"Oh, I know what you love and miss all right." Victoria tapped her ample bosom. "I know all about that."

"You don't know anything."

"I do. You think I don't miss your father's arms around me, God bless his soul. He was so romantic. Don't you know that I ache for that man's comfort? I may not be the newest model on the block, but my motor still desires tuning up. But your father is not here to do my tuning, so I live without it and go on."

"I miss everything about Rakim. Not just *that*. His smile, his kindness and so much I can't describe. If he came back to me I wouldn't do those things that I did that turned him off. I'd change for him. Be completely different. I wouldn't even argue with him anymore about leaving the company to become some lowly paid defense attorney. If that's what he wants I wouldn't bother him about it anymore."

"No, you wouldn't bother him. But it would bother you. You craved your equal, darling."

"He is my equal."

"He isn't! He had nothing when you married him. And once he gets out there in that coldhearted world, without you to lean on, he'll have nothing again."

"Are you still trying to say he married me for money? He didn't! He was the one who volunteered to sign the prenuptial agreement. Mother, his lawyers brought over the divorce papers and they state that he wants nothing but his freedom."

"He's just saying that now."

"He means it."

"He'll be crying for money once he gets further into the proceedings. But don't you worry, we'll fight and win."

The phone ringing brightened Janet's face. Only Rakim would call at such a late hour. Excitedly, she swiped up the receiver. "Hello?"

"May I speak to Rakim Hilton?"

Her expression dimmed at the unfamiliar man's voice. "Who may I ask is calling?"

"My name is Greg Forest. I'm another attorney at Rakim's firm. Is he back from his trip with the Chicago client yet?"

The question silenced her for a moment. Rakim hadn't informed her of a business trip. Neither had he told his firm about his new marital status or living arrangements.

"Are you still there?" the man asked among the sudden quiet.

"Yes, I'm—I'm here. He's not in right now. Can I take a message?"

"Yes. Tell him I was down at police headquarters seeing a client, and I heard the news about his sister. Is—"

"About Shay?" Janet's frown drew one on Victoria's curious face.

"Is he going to represent her?"

Janet looked confused. "Represent her for what?"

"You know? For the murder."

"Murder!" She nearly screamed.

"I thought she would have contacted Rakim, but maybe she's got the same response I did. I couldn't reach him on the cell phone."

Janet knew what Rakim being unreachable meant. Rakim always turned off his phone when they made love.

She resisted a sick feeling in her stomach. "So they're talking about Shay and some murder?"

"About arresting her in the morning for her ex's murder."

The man babbled on, but Janet had already decided what action she would take by the time the receiver attached back to its cradle.

"What happened?" her mother asked.

Janet was hurrying to her closet. She pulled out a knit top with matching slacks. "Shay's going to be arrested for her ex's murder."

"She what!"

"Shay is going to be arrested for her ex's murder."

"My Lord!" Victoria's hand slapped against her cheek. "She killed someone?"

"I don't know mother." Janet slipped the top over her head. "I have to get to Rakim and tell him this."

"Call him. Don't go where he is."

Janet slipped one leg in her pants, then the other. "He needs me."

"Did you look out there at the weather? You're going to wake your driver at this hour? It's suicide driving out there now."

"I'm not waking anyone." She didn't want anyone to know she was tracking down her wayward husband. "I'm driving myself."

"Don't!" She abhorred seeing her daughter this desperate.

"Rakim is really going to need me at a time like this."

"Like hell he does."

"Besides, he's not answering his cell phone. The other phone isn't in his condo yet."

"How do you know where he lives anyway? You told me he wouldn't give you the address of his place."

"No, he wouldn't give me the address." Janet began brushing her hair.

"So how do you know where he lives?"

"Because." She gathered the auburn tresses, placing a clip around it in a ponytail.

"Because what?"

She couldn't stand this interrogation. "Because I hired a private investigator!"

"My Lord!"

Ignoring her mother's gasps, Janet grabbed the first boots she reached in the closet. "I wasn't planning to do it." She stuck her foot into the slim, leather lining. "But he left me no choice."

"Don't go there, darling."

"This is an emergency." Of course she was going there. Nothing, not snow—not even an earthquake—would stop her. What better excuse was there to visit Rakim's place, catch Christina there and fling her out of his bed?

"Please, you mustn't go."

"I have to mother."

"Look at how you'll look to him. To them. There are so many other men out there who are your equal, who will worship a beautiful, refined woman like you."

"But I don't want them. I want Rakim."

"Please, I—"

"I know what I'm doing." Janet hurried to the door and fled into the hall.

"Don't go, Janet," Victoria warned, rushing to the doorway. "I forbid you to go!" Ignored by her daughter as she often was, Victoria heard Janet's feet padding down the stairs. Sadly, she flopped back down on the bed whispering, "He might be with that woman."

Four

Straining to see beyond the snowflakes crowding the windshield and the blades swiftly wiping them away, Janet leaned forward for a better view when she saw the condominium address she was seeking, 704. Aside from the storm dulling the allure of the complex, Janet could see that Rakim's new home was among a neat grouping of residences in a resort-type atmosphere.

A pool, a tennis court, basketball turf, a band shell, a closed restaurant and myriad deck tables made it look more like a retreat for vacationers rather than a place where people ordinarily lived. She could imagine how much fun it probably was in summer. To a couple it might be a honeymooner's paradise. Was that what it felt like to Rakim right then, right then with that Christina? God knew she hoped what she was thinking wasn't true. She prayed her woman's intuition was wrong.

Her doubts were stronger than her faith. A knot formed in her stomach at the mental picture of Rakim receiving and giving intimate pleasure to another woman. It all summoned an ache, a frenzy that hurried her out of the car. Oblivious to the snow pelting her skin, she headed across the courtyard until her boots squished into the welcome mat.

For a moment, as she faced the door she had to catch

her breath, temper the untamed rhythm of her heart and swallow the clumps of nervous saliva constantly replenishing in her throat. Feeling slightly calmer, she mentally rehearsed what she would say to Rakim and that wench if she saw them together. Surely, Rakim would come to his senses and realize what he was giving up.

With trembling fingers, Janet pressed the bell. However, just as she was about to touch it, a harsh thump against the other side of the door made her hand clutch her chest. Startled, she jumped back a bit as another thump and another hit the door. Following this, there were more thumps. Ones that sounded methodical. Janet was so terrified that someone had broken in and was fighting Rakim, she debated yelling out to him. Was someone beating him up?

Moans answered her question. Moans from a woman. Moans of ecstasy. *That damn Christina's moans.* Trailing them were Rakim's husk-filled utterances. "Oh, I never felt like this. Never. I love what you're doing to me. And I love you. Oh, I love you . . ."

Janet opened her mouth, gathering the wrath and pain inside of her to curse them both to hell. Puke spewed past her lips instead, the force of it bringing her to her knees. After she was finished, she struggled back to her feet, her stomach empty, her clothes soiled and her spirit so drained, she barely had the strength to tramp back to her car. Before she reached it, she turned around. Motionless, she stood watching the door of Rakim's new home. With the snow sliding down her warm skin, slipping into her mouth, she whispered, "This isn't over. This isn't over by a long shot." And then she thought of Shay—the supposed reason she was coming to see Rakim. Once Janet had adored her sister-in-law. Not now. Shay was Christina's best friend. Therefore, she was aware of what was going on. Janet was sure of it. She was probably all for it.

"To hell with Shay! She probably did do it. I could understand a woman being mad enough to kill the man she loves. Oh, how I understand that." Narrowing her eyes on Rakim's condo, she nodded. "I hope Shay goes to prison worse than the one you put me in, Rakim. Because that's sure what it feels like, like you put me in prison and threw away the key. Yes, go to hell, Shay. All of you are going to hell!"

Miles away on a dark, winding road, Shay felt like she was already in hell. Tormenting images of Marquis's body, all the blood, the likely courtroom she would face, the enclosed jail cell and even her execution in an electric chair caused her to see and not see. The moderate snowfall that accompanied her as she got into her car had burgeoned into a white whirlwind but she barely noticed.

A honking horn sent Shay's foot slamming on the brakes. Not paying attention, she'd almost run a stop sign. The blur of the car she nearly hit smacked her into reality. A raging snowstorm was descending on Englewood Cliffs. She was in the midst of it.

The person driving the vehicle Shay almost collided with cracked their window. Embittered eyes peered through the opening as a woman shouted, "Get off the road, you idiot, until you learn to drive!" Ignoring her, Shay pulled her vehicle on the side of the road. She had to get herself together. Fighting the demons in her overactive imagination, she turned off her car to conserve her small amount of gas. If only she could turn off her mind just as easily.

When was the last time she felt this down? And how did she get out of it? Get through it? Was it when Marquis caused her to lose their baby at the altar? Or was it during that other unforgettable season in her life so long ago?

At that time, Shay had just turned eleven and Rakim was thirteen when their parents left them at home one Sunday afternoon to go on a romantic date into New York City. Shay could never forget the loving way they looked at each other as they walked out the door that day hugged up like teenagers. They didn't arrive home at the time they specified to Shay and Rakim that they would. Nor did they return a few hours later than that.

Rather than hearing their parents laughing about their good time upon entering their home from their outing, Shay and Rakim opened the door to see two policemen. Sensitively they delivered the news that their parents had been killed in a car accident. A drunk driver was at fault. It was an experience that Shay wished no other child would have to endure.

Shay felt just as helpless and alone now. Was this a horrid dream that she might be convicted of murdering Marquis when she was innocent? Or was this all really happening to her? It *was* happening to her. It was as real as the tears she felt trying to burst from her eyes. No, she wouldn't cry. She couldn't because she wouldn't be able to stop. Shaking her head, she folded her arms across the steering wheel. Gently, she laid her face against it.

A knock startled her head up. The window had misted with the car no longer running. Beyond the glass was a fuzzy image of a man, which made her draw back. Who was he? What did he want? Headlights from a vehicle behind hers, which she assumed was his, illuminated the area surrounding her. Was she some psychopath's target?

"Are you all right?" he asked, and she immediately recognized the voice. As much as Shay was relieved that it wasn't someone about to harm her, she felt upset by this visitor. Like she was a criminal about to flee, she had been followed.

Her finger mashed the button that rolled the window down. She stopped halfway because of all the snow blowing inside her car.

Squinting from the pricks of flakes on his face, Braxton bent down to the window. Anger flashed in Shay's eyes, but he was more concerned with her being injured.

"Are you all right? I saw that near accident."

"Why are you following me? Why are you tracking me down like an animal?" His lips parted to respond, but she wouldn't give him the chance. "I couldn't reach my brother, so I was headed to my friend David's house." Being that Christina picked up Rakim at the airport, his whereabouts were questionable. On the other hand, David was headed straight home after leaving her. He never answered his phone after a certain time, but she was sure he was in his house. "I gave those cops the address." She sniffled to fight off the runny nose she felt coming on. That was all she needed when he was right in her face. "How dare you tail me like this!"

"Whoa, whoa," Braxton said, air blowing from his mouth, making her gaze linger there. "I wasn't following you for that reason."

"Yes, you were!"

"I wasn't." Bunching up his shoulders from the cold, he rubbed his hands together. Afterward, he abruptly walked away.

Braxton headed toward the back of her car. Since his vehicle was behind hers, Shay thought he'd left her alone. A surprise it was when her passenger door swung open.

"I'm about to freeze my butt off out there," he said, sliding onto her seat. Moving around so his long legs fit in the car comfortably, he closed the door. That's when he smiled over at her. He couldn't help it. There was something about the way her mouth balled up when she was angry that was so cute to him.

Shay wasn't getting the joke. Not even dimples like those would bend her lips up. Her eyes remained firmly fixed on his, until his staring back made her uncomfortable.

"I wasn't going to run. This harassment is totally unnecessary. It's ridiculous!"

"I wasn't following you for that reason. I was concerned about you."

"Concerned?" She gave him that *Oh, please* look.

"You're damn right I was concerned. When you left, I was still sitting in my car, waiting for the snow to lighten up. Then I saw you come out of your building, and you just looked so messed up. So messed up." Pausing he stared at her for a moment. She still looked so upset. At the same time, there was something so sensual about her face, he didn't want to stop looking at it. "Then you . . . you got in your car. So I started walking over to you. Thought maybe I should drive you wherever you were going. But you took off. I hurried back to my car and took off after you. I wanted to catch up and convince you to ride with me. This weather is no good when your mind is clear. But when one is as upset as you looked, you shouldn't be driving in this. I've been trying to catch up with you for miles, but in all this snow this is the first chance I've had. Can I drive you where you need to go? Is it far from here?"

Shay simply stared over at him. And this time when he stared back she didn't feel uneasy. She beheld warmth and something so inviting and safe, it was a struggle to look elsewhere.

She forced her attention ahead. Snow had nearly covered her view of the road. "Look, if you were concerned, I appreciate your concern. But I can take care of myself."

"It's no trouble."

"I'll be fine, thank you. Now I'm sure you have a nice cozy bed to get to. And I want to get to one too before . . . before . . ." She couldn't even utter aloud what the day might bring.

Braxton nodded. "If that's the way you want it." His eyes perused over her lush profile, before he opened the door.

Shay lay her head back against the headrest as soon as she was alone. Bizarre as it was, his presence had somehow filled every inch of air inside the car, and when he left she could still feel him all around her. Even amid the icy temperature freezing her senses, she inhaled a subtle masculine scent that lingered. Woods with pinewood trees came to mind. It was all so strange. And was he sincere? Was he truly concerned about her? Or was he just giving her a clever answer? Though she couldn't sit there and wonder too long. She had to get to David's place. Her body craved rest. Tired couldn't describe how she felt.

Turning the ignition key, she planned to put the windshield wipers on RAPID so they could clear the snow off quickly. None of the road was visible now. When the car didn't make the slightest grunt of engine, she tried the key again. Nothing. Once more. Nothing. Repeatedly she attempted to start the car. Nothing. Nothing. Nothing. A brand-new *expensive* car and it had stranded her like this.

Her toes were already numb. Desperate, she made more attempts to get the car moving. Eventually her toes' numbness progressed to aching. Her nose began to run. Worst of all, it would take hours for a car service to rescue her on this road.

Shay was aware that Braxton hadn't driven off yet. His headlights shined through the snow that had almost completely covered her rear window. Unlocking her car, she soon felt the blistering whips of snow and wind on her delicate skin. Making her way toward the old Mustang, she felt icy water seeping down into the foot of her boots, making her wish she had been thinking more clearly when she left the penthouse. If she had been, she wouldn't have worn boots that weren't waterproof. On the other hand, was she thinking clearly now by seeking help from a man who might attempt to imprison her?

Moments later, Shay couldn't believe she was riding with Braxton. Like before, his presence somehow filled up the air in the enclosed space. So much so, her awareness of it made her forget to give him David's address.

After quite a distance on the highway, Shay looked over at him. "David lives at 814 Mountainview Terrace. It's part of those new condos in back of the Richfield Mall."

"We're not going there right now," he said, concentrating on the road. "We're going to the closest place we can get to for shelter. And that's that little house down there." He tossed his head in the direction of a home they were approaching.

"Little house?" Shay stretched her eyes at the huge stone-built structure. "That's a mansion if I've ever seen one." She looked back at him. His skin was so Caribbean-tanned she wondered how it could look that way in such frigid weather. "You must know the owner."

"Very well." He turned onto the property.

"Who owns it?

"I do."

Braxton could tell by that circle Shay's mouth had formed, along with her silence, that she wasn't happy about being his houseguest. As he hung her leather jacket in the closet beside his parka, he observed her sitting on the couch. If only she understood.

He wasn't trying to forestall her from escaping his prosecuting clutches. Pure concern was one reason that made him pursue her. The combination of the hazardous road conditions and her emotional state was disaster waiting to happen. Even if she was furious at him, he was glad she was now safe.

Braxton wasn't sure about this case. He wasn't sure if she was truthful about not murdering her ex-lover. In fact, after what she shared about his mistreatment, he could hardly blame her. Braxton had been that enraged once. Sometimes when he allowed himself to think about the tragedy that got him so out of control, his blood would heat with that rage all over again. Yet he refused to allow it to take hold of him. If he did, it would consume him until he was useless. That all being as it may, whatever the day would bring pertaining to the murder, it would bring. But in these moments, there was the chance to be alone with Shay. He had a chance to get to know her, and see if her mind stimulated him as much as her body did.

Braxton sensed something intense lay beneath her surface. He could feel it whispering, calling something within him. All during their earlier encounter when their eyes would meet, he felt some connection. Being near her in the car, he felt it now too. Whatever it was, even if for these sole moments, he had to know what it meant. Why was it there? What was he feeling? How could he even describe something like this?

Sure, he had been strongly attracted to women before. He had fun dating them. There was an excitement in meeting someone. There was an excitement in getting to know them, even if in the end none of them turned out to be that special one. But this, this was different. Along with Shay's physical sensuality, which harshly stroked his, there was a need to be near her, to protect her, to comfort her and he didn't know why. A yearning to hear her voice because it had quickly become addictive to him. In some way there was a knowing of her, although they hadn't talked or been around each other long enough for him to truly know her. In a sense it was a knowing of her spirit—something about hers that drew him to it. He could almost compare it to when you meet a stranger that you feel so comfortable with it's like you've known them much longer than you have, and you may even tell them something personal that you wouldn't dare tell someone who you've known longer. But this knowing was something more. It made him feel emotional. It made him feel weak. It made him want her.

"Can I get you something?" Braxton stood above Shay.

Sitting on his plaid couch, she stood out no less than a giant peacock unexpectedly splashing its colorful presence among the earth tones in his living room.

"No," she said, looking past him.

"I have some spaghetti that I can warm up."

Still looking past him, Shay folded her arms. "I don't want any."

"Would you like some cocoa then? It'll warm you up."

She shook her head.

"Okay, well I'm . . . I'm going into the kitchen."

Braxton disappeared behind two swinging wood doors. Standing by a counter, he was pouring cocoa powder with marshmallows in two mugs when the doors exploded open.

Shay looked like she was about to cry. "You have no right to hold me like this! I wasn't arrested yet! You all said I had until the report came back! I have a right to rest at my friend's house. This is not right! You know it's not!"

Braxton hated the way she was looking and sounding.

He had no idea he'd upset her like this. "I'm not detaining you. You have to believe me."

"Yes, you are! You could have taken me to David's house."

"In this weather? He lives too far from where we were. I couldn't take you there now."

"Yes, you could have! But no, you want to keep your eyes on me. Make sure I don't make my getaway so you can make your big arrest for the press. Well, I'm not staying here! I'll walk to David's house if I have to. I'm getting out of here. I'm not arrested yet!"

She hurried into the living room, heading to the closet for her coat. Braxton caught her by the hand midway there. Swiftly, he curved her around, and before Shay knew anything, both of his arms were clutching hers. Firmly yet gently he held her. Firmly yet gently in a way that reminded her she hadn't been held by a man in so long. Firmly yet gently enough to let her know that she wouldn't have minded being held like this much more often. Further intoxicating her was that scent again—wood and pine trees. It seemed to come from his neck.

She was staring up into his face as intensely as he was staring down into hers when she moved back. Reluctantly, he dropped his hands at his sides.

"Just take me to David's. Just let me have some more of my life. A little time to myself before. . . ."

"You sound like you know how the report is going to turn out."

"I don't know! All I know is that I didn't kill Marquis, and someone did a pretty good job of making it look like I did."

"I want to believe you."

"Then do it!"

"But I know how it is!"

"You know how what is?"

As if the question triggered something, his eyes traveled beyond her, and Shay could see him thinking about something that had a powerful hold on him.

"What? What are you thinking? What do you know?"

"Nothing." He switched his gaze back to her.

"It is something." She searched his face. "What is it? What were you going to say?"

"It's nothing."

"Tell me."

There was an urgency in her tone, and with those eyes looking at him that way, Braxton found himself taking a seat on the couch, ready to share at least some of it. "I was going to say that I can understand a person being *that* mad."

"But I didn't do it!"

"Listen to me. You wanted to know what I was thinking and I'm telling you." He watched her come across the room until she was sitting next to him.

"Go ahead," Shay urged.

He took a deep breath, and looked off somewhere that seemed farther than the room. "I can understand being mad enough to kill someone. I've been there. Part of the reason I'm a prosecutor is because of the time I was *that* mad. Instead of killing however, I decided I was going to get them back through my skill as a lawyer."

There was something about what he said. Lowering her head, Shay thought back to an article she'd read about Braxton that related to this. Remembering it, she looked up. "In that paper called *High Profile* there was a story about you on this subject."

Braxton was stunned she knew about that piece. That was such a small-circulation paper. Hardly any of his friends had seen it. "You read that?"

I've read everything I could about you. "Yes, I—I read that the reason you became a prosecutor was because you wanted to get back at someone who killed someone close to you. Was someone in your family murdered?"

Braxton rubbed across his eyes, as if he were tired. "It's really getting late. It'll be day before long. Both of us should get some sleep. Let me show you to where you'll be sleeping upstairs." After standing, he extended his hand to her.

He didn't want to talk about it. Shay got the message. And too exhausted to get up on her own, she gripped his hand, letting him assist her up. Like his hold on her arms, his touch was firm and equally gentle. She could even feel it when he wasn't touching her. They were simply mounting the stairs.

"Cozy," she remarked, as they walked into a large, mostly russet-colored room. Strolling around it, checking out the bed, dresser and television that were the sole furnishings in the room, she was starting to realize something. "You don't like to decorate much, do you?" She had noticed downstairs that everything was very plain, and there were few furnishings. "But it is cozy." She started taking off her boots.

Braxton grinned. "I know what you're thinking. A big old mansion and it doesn't have a bit of style." Yet he liked it that way. It wasn't his idea to move into a mansion anyway. A little simple house would have been fine for him. A promise was what made him make such an extravagant purchase. A promise he'd made to someone special. "Well, I leave that decorating stuff to women. All I want is to be comfortable."

She looked around. "It's comfortable."

"I did have a decorator." He was always tickled when he thought of her. "But I put her special skills to use elsewhere. My sister, bless her sweet soul, she tried."

His humorous expression drew one on Shay's face. "What do you mean?"

"My little sister Tracey, she is an interior decorator. So when I first moved in here I gave her a shot. Boy, did she make it look *special* in here!" He shook his head with swearing conviction.

Shay was smiling. "What did she do?"

"What did she do! What didn't she do! The girl had this place filled with so many colors and stripes and flowers and zigzags and stuffed tigers and stuffed birds that every time I came home I had a headache. It was so psychedelic I was scared of my own house."

Shay chuckled. "So how did you change it without hurting her feelings?"

Pausing for a moment, he just had to enjoy that smile she had. "Well, Tracey . . . Tracey wanted to start her own interior design business and wanted me to finance it. Some of my brothers and sisters said that was crazy since they knew how my sister decorated, but the way I see it you have to support your family. When they have a vision, you may not understand it or see it like they do, but you have to give them your support. You never know how it might turn out. So I gave it to her, and Tracey is making money with her interior decorating business. Big money. That shows you there is a market for everything. I guess your passion for it just has to shine through."

Shay loved that he supported his sister that way. Rakim had done the same for her with her business. "But you still didn't tell me how did you explain not having the place decorated the way she left it."

Braxton was still tickled. "Oh, yeah. Along with the business funds, I threw in a mansion in California. I go visit her. She's never seen it like this."

"Ooh, that's cold," Shay teased. At the same time, she

was thinking what a wonderful brother he was. She was also wondering something. Since when did district attorneys make so much money? How did Braxton afford a mansion anyway? One for his sister too? And he financed Tracey's business too.

"I'll get it decorated," Braxton went on. "When I get married, I'll let my bride do whatever she wants with this place. I . . ." Shay's shocked expression interrupted his completing his sentence. "Why are you looking at me like I have ten heads?"

"Because," she said, raising her brows, "I guess I didn't take you for the marrying type."

"And why is that?" Curiously amused, he folded his arms.

"I don't know," she lied. She didn't want him to think she was interested in that gossip she'd heard and read about his love life. She plopped down on the mattress, making it squeak.

"Well, if I'm not the marrying type, why would I be such a big fan of your magazine? You sure do have a lot of information in there for people who want a long-term committed relationship."

Shay speculated. He had complimented her on the magazine at the ceremony. Nonetheless, she assumed he probably browsed through it once or twice or heard of it probably from one of his women. Never had he mentioned being a *fan*.

She looked up at him. "You're not a fan. How many issues of *Love & Relationships* have you read?"

"All of them." He approached the bed, halting his steps when he stood over her.

"No, you haven't." Staring up at him, Shay swung her legs to the side of her.

"Yes, I have." Glancing at her legs, he wished she was

still wearing that gown she wore at the ceremony. That split on the side was talking to him. "I can name some of your best editorials." He dug his hands deep in his pockets.

"Name them then." Anticipating his answer, she uncurled her legs, stretching them out in front of her.

As he thought, he glimpsed her feet. Round, neat kissable toes made him imagine things. He was indeed a foot man.

Bringing his contemplation back to the editorials, he said, "You wrote 'Keeping the Fires Burning,' 'Finding Yourself Is the Key to Finding Love,' 'How to Heal a Broken Heart' . . ." Braxton couldn't continue because the sadness on Shay's face halted him. It appeared when he mentioned the last title. "You wrote that one for your readers and yourself, didn't you? It was a way of helping you deal with what Marquis had done."

Shay lowered her head. For just a few moments she had pushed Marquis and the entire nightmare into the back of her mind. *He's dead. He's really dead. The man who made me wish I was dead not so long ago. He took my heart and he just threw it away.*

"Shay, I'm sorry." He drew her glistening eyes up to him. "I didn't mean to bring you down."

"Forget it," she said, realizing that was the first time he spoke her name. It sounded different coming from his lips. "I need to get some sleep anyway."

"Yes, we both do."

He hated to leave her. He wanted to talk and look at her some more, but both of them did need sleep. He thought about her bags that they'd left in the car. Snow and ice had jammed the trunk. "I guess you need something to sleep in."

"Do you have anything?"

A negligee that a date had left on purpose a few months

ago came to mind. That wouldn't have been right to offer Shay another woman's gown to sleep in. "Would you mind wearing one of my shirts?"

"That's good."

"Great, I'll go get one."

He headed toward the door, but feeling the sadness he'd brought to her, he curved around. He sensed she was still thinking about it, about Marquis. "I know it's none of my business. But it wasn't you who was the fool. It was him. Any man who would so brutally hurt a woman who loved him that much is a damn fool. Any man who would hurt a woman like you period is a damn fool. Too bad he realized it too late. It was him. It wasn't you."

Shay's eyes followed Braxton's broad shoulders and that urban cool swagger of his until he disappeared into the hall. She had to shake her head at what she was thinking. She didn't know whether it was because he was looking finer by the second or that he flattered her by naming her editorials or made her feel better by confirming her point that Marquis had been a fool, but she couldn't wait for Braxton to come back to the room.

After giving Shay his shirt, Braxton went downstairs to the kitchen. He still had a taste for the cocoa with marshmallows. Maybe Shay wanted a cup now too. Soon carrying the warm mugs back up the stairs, he walked carefully to avoid spilling the cocoa. At the doorway of the bedroom Shay was in, his feet came to an abrupt halt when he looked inside.

She was sleeping. Sleeping on top of the covers wearing his shirt. Indulging in an unhurried study of her pretty toes on up to her bared thighs, Braxton was reminded he was a legs man too. And if the sudden heat he felt was any indication, for legs like those he could definitely be the man.

Cocoa spilling down on the carpet from a tilted mug made him realize how he must have looked standing there drooling. If Shay woke up, she would have thought he was a pervert. Not wanting that, he wiped up the mess, turned out the light and headed down the hall.

Shay's personal waterfall was nudging her awake, forcing her to sit up half-asleep in the dark. At first, in that blurred consciousness of waking, she believed she was in her own bedroom. Reaching for the lamp and touching only air, brought her back to reality. She lay in a bed in Braxton Steele's house.

Shay sat up. There was a clock ticking somewhere in the room. It compounded the panic clambering up through her as her imagination tried to scare her again with what might happen during the day. Like a frightened child, she felt like running to her parents' loving embrace for their comfort, and their soothing words telling her that everything would be okay. Since that was impossible Rakim's arms would do.

Was he home now? She had unsuccessfully tried to reach him before falling asleep and left a message. Could he be reached now? It was too late. Contacting him could wait at least until it was daylight.

What about the other love of her life, Aunt Sarah? If only she could have talked to her mother's aunt, the beloved angel who had rescued them from heartless guardians after their parents' deaths, and raised Rakim and her in love. Then again, she couldn't worry her with this. A volunteer in the Peace Corp, she was enjoying her work in Africa. If everything was handled the right way, she would never have to know about it.

Determined not to surrender to the negative thoughts, Shay swung her legs over the side of the bed. Serenity, she was going to have some, even if for a moment. Neither would she succumb to that feeling she had before falling asleep. That one that made her want Braxton near. Again she had to ask herself, what was it about that man?

Now that they'd met in person, it was almost as if the fascination she had with him prior to their meeting had progressed to a spell. How else could she explain his convincing her to sleep in his bed for the night because he wanted her safe? And why, when he said he wanted her safe, did he make her feel like she was in the company of someone who truly cared? He couldn't possibly. They were supposed to be enemies. But opposite sides or not, how could she stop what she felt growing every time he was near? It was an attraction like she'd never known. His made-for-her-eyes face and make-a-woman-think-of-things body had made her close her eyes last night thinking of amorous scenarios between him and her.

Although it was more than Braxton's blatant sexiness that was getting to her. There was that something about him. At times during the evening and night when she looked in his eyes, there was something reflected from them that was somehow familiar but at the same time new and frighteningly exciting. It was almost as if she had a special view into his soul, and within it she recognized something that she felt an unexplainable connection to.

There couldn't be any connection, Shay scolded herself as she stood. Sure, she wanted to feel chemistry with a man—her Mr. Right. The mystery man that she envisioned side by side with her in the future. A player like Braxton couldn't be her dream. More than that, the man who could possibly prosecute her could be her worst nightmare.

As far as connections went, she had to be imagining it.

Reading all those wonderful romance novels had her placing herself between those pages, imagining that Braxton was looking at her like the hero stared at the heroine in her favorite story. That's what it was—imagination. What she felt from the look couldn't be as real as it felt either. She wouldn't let it be.

"I can't be attracted to that man," Shay whispered, making her way through the darkened room. She didn't know where the light switch was. She did remember the bathroom was on the right side of the room. "He can put my butt in jail." Fumbling along the wall, she quickly grasped the door's knob. She cursed when it wouldn't turn fully. The bathroom was locked.

Shay recalled that another bathroom was centered at the end of the hall. Feeling her way out of the room into the pitch-black hall, she stretched out her hands so she wouldn't bump into anything. At the same time, she hoped to touch the homely little lamp she'd glimpsed in the hall earlier. Awkwardly, her bare feet moved forward on the thick, toe-clinging carpet. Her hands extended in front of her.

Shay halted when she began feeling skin, skin covering muscles and muscles exposing hair. And while her feet ceased moving, her hands didn't stop feeling. Her fingers had no control as they probed, going from one shoulder to the great width that led to the other. Chest, chest and more succulent, muscular, warm chest, she glided over, unable to get enough. Down further she went on touching until she could feel his rock-hard stomach quivering and his excited breaths escaping with hers.

"Do you need anything?" Braxton asked.

Five

"What am I doing?" Shay questioned, snatching her hand back as she reached the elastic of Braxton's sweat pants. "Is what happened making me lose my mind? I didn't mean to touch you like that. I don't know what came over me."

"You didn't hurt me," Braxton said, his deep voice still husky with excitement. He hoped whatever came over her was the same thing that had come over him. The thing that was all over him now—wanting him as much as he wanted her. "I heard you in the hall and thought you may have needed something."

"I had to use the—"

"Shay I . . ."

There it was again. That way he said her name.

"I have a confession to make."

"A confession?" She felt him moving closer. She inhaled that sexy scent.

"And my confession is that I did bring you here to keep you safe, but also because I wanted to be alone with you. I wanted to get to know you. Shay, you intrigue me."

Shay was as flattered as she was stunned. "I intrigue you?"

"So much. . . . From the first time I saw your picture in the magazine and read what you wrote, I wanted to get to know you. In fact, that's how I wound up at the party. I read in a newspaper that you were going to be there, and I had to be there."

This was some news to her. Wishing it didn't make her feel as wonderful as it did, she also confessed, "I've been intrigued by you too."

"You have?"

"I've read every article about you, Braxton. Every single one. Probably seen every time you were on television too. If I wasn't going to be home and I knew you were coming on a show, I would make sure I taped it."

Braxton couldn't believe this. It made him feel so good that she had been as interested in him as he was in her. "This is deep. So you've been reading about me, I've been reading about you, and we've been fascinated by each other. So now that we've had a little time together, what do you think?" He couldn't help moving closer. "Are you still intrigued?"

Shay was aware of his closeness. His breathing filled the silence. His scent was ever so intoxicating. His skin was somehow burning into her fingertips. Fed from the excitement of it all, something maddeningly intense filled her. It had been a long time coming, but she was attracted to someone again. She was feeling those feelings that made a woman feel sensually alive and so attuned with her femininity. His kiss, she wondered how it would taste. His chest, her fingers ached to caress its hardness again. Her own body, she trembled for it to be touched by him. Overall, she wanted to be enraptured in romance. But why with this man? What was it about Braxton that ignited those sensations in her? A man she hardly knew. The one who was going to try his best to incarcerate her.

She eased back. "Braxton, what I think about you isn't important. What you think about me isn't important. If we were intrigued by each other before, we're on opposite sides now. In a little while, it'll be day, and what happens, that's what's going to matter. Not anything that we think . . . or feel."

Braxton knew she was right. More than that, he was surprised at himself. It wasn't like him to let a physical attraction cloud his judgments and actions. To think that in a matter of seconds, he was going to attempt to kiss Shay. And he would have been pleased to oblige her in anything else she wanted too. Was he losing his mind? He certainly had lost his perspective. He couldn't kiss or, worse, sleep with a woman he had to build a case against. This attraction to Shay, he had to let it go.

Trying to do just that, he moved across the hall where his sole lamp was located. After cutting it on, he forced himself not to look at her. He knew how she would look. He knew how she always looked. So succulent that he would want her. And after her touching him like she did, it would have felt like torture just to look right now.

Abruptly he began walking down the hall toward her bedroom. "I forgot to unlock the bathroom in your room," he threw over his shoulder. "I'll do it now."

"Thanks," Shay responded, unable to move. Staring at Braxton as he walked away, she had to bite her lip to stifle the hunger. Muscles like mountains stacked on top of one another, wide, sweeping shoulders and long lean legs that led to the cutest, tightest narrow buns, made her hungry—man hungry. It was too bad they were on opposite sides, because she really felt like being fed. *Umm, umm, umm.*

Janet knew Christina wasn't hungry anymore. Desperately, she wanted to erase the sounds in her head of Christina and Rakim making such ferocious love. If she could have, she wouldn't have done any of the things she did that turned her husband off. To turn back the hands of time—she would have paid any price for that magic.

Since she couldn't perform any of the feats that she wished, she tried driving away for the ninth time. "This is crazy!" she raved, when again the car was sliding so dangerously she couldn't get to the highway. Once more, she returned to the parking space in front of Rakim's condominium complex. However, she was too frustrated to sit in the car waiting for the snow to lessen.

No car-jacker, serial killer or psychopath madman was going to kill her, not while Christina lived and made love to her man every day. That would not happen. She was going inside Rakim's house to be safe, stay warm and get things straight as she had initially intended to. Once matters were settled Christina would be leaving. Not her.

Hearing a persistent knocking at the door, along with the bell ringing, Rakim wondered who the hell was coming to his home at this hour. It had to be late. Much too late for company. No time for glancing at the clock in the study, he had to hurry to the door before this person waking him up woke up Christina too. After what happened between them during the night, he wanted his baby to rest, especially since he wanted a replay of every second of their lovemaking.

Opening the door, his large eyes stretched. His body froze. His tongue wouldn't move to form a comprehensible word. Instantly he recalled how Shay used to always scold him about opening the door without asking whom it was. It was a bad habit that he now sorely regretted.

Missing the warmth of Rakim's body entangled with hers in the bed, Christina wakened as well. Other than Rakim not being snuggled with her beneath the cotton spreads, there was also a chill running through the house. A window must have been opened somewhere. Searching for the mystery of the wind and her missing baby, Rakim, she eventually found him in the vestibule. He was facing someone outside the door. Oddly, he was looking like Satan had come to visit.

"Who is that, honey?" she asked, his weird expression drawing her to where he was.

Once standing in the freezing doorway, Christina watched deep-set eyes peeling over her big-boned frame from head to toe. Her heart jumping from the shock, she felt self-conscious in her sheer, pink gown with nothing underneath.

"Have you been keeping my husband warm during this cold weather?" Janet asked. She flashed a chiclet-white smile that seemed brighter than the snow to Christina. "Have you?"

David posed a question too. Why did he have such a headache? He had taken a pill hours earlier, had dosed off listening to his beloved Rachelle Ferrell CD for the third time, and now a dull ache persisted in bothering him. Believing that not obsessing over the pain would possibly make it go away, he tried to busy himself with work. The last time he had this sort of headache that had been the remedy.

Inside his home office, David shuffled about, finally settling at his desk. On it he found plenty of things to do. One set of documents required him to check with his answering service. He picked up the phone and attempted to do just that. There was no dial tone. Incensed, he slammed the receiver down on the cradle. Yet why was he so furious? It really wasn't because of the service being out of order. It wasn't even because of the headache. It was Shay.

Why didn't she want something more between them like he did? What was it about him that didn't qualify him as a lover? Was it the nerd in him again?

As a child, growing up in an affluent and loving family, David should have felt wonderful about his life and himself. His mother was a housewife, devoted to her family. As well, she was gratefully involved with organizations and community activities that bettered life for all children. His father was an esteemed, much-sought-after neurologist. Along with his brothers, David's father, Thurston Robertson, also owned a highly successful medical supply company.

David could have emulated his father's career in neurology. In school, his grades certainly revealed he was intelligent enough. However, with each day, he seemed drawn to another area of healing, psychology. Other than a keen interest in every aspect of the field, he desired to understand himself.

His two brothers and himself just didn't seem to fit in with other kids. Although all the children in the private schools he had attended came from wealthy families, the Robertson boys were set apart. Everything about them was subject to ridicule: their looks, which weren't in vogue; their lack of athletic ability; their overly proper English; their bungling dance steps; their goofy gaits. Altogether, their peers considered these the attributes of a nerd. Psychology helped David understand he wasn't a nerd. He was rare. He had other capabilities that would one day be appreciated, cherished, enjoyed and utilized in the world. He was a treasure.

Why couldn't Shay see that? Since he had become a man, throngs of other women had. David was assured it wasn't because of his success either. Women had truly fallen in love with him. Not David the psychologist, but David the man, David the lover. As one who studied the science of the mind, he recognized genuine feelings. Love had even fluttered his own heart on several occasions.

All in all, after the inquest of time that all relationships endured, it was clear that none of these ladies was the right one. Hence, David simply dated, searching for his dream. Yes, these women proved to him that he wasn't a nerd anymore. They confirmed he was wanted, lovable, desirable. Despite it, so much of the boy who'd lived in him long ago lived in him now. That was apparent in how wounded he felt by Shay tonight.

Deep down he knew she wasn't feeling for him the reservoir of passionate emotion he felt for her. Furthermore, he was never comfortable when she went on those occasional dates. What would he do if she started getting close to another man? What if she needed some hot loving from him? It had been a long time since she'd been with a man. How long could she hold out? More than that, how could he handle it if he weren't the one receiving not only her sexy body but her heart forever? David couldn't even stand her looking at other men. Like tonight at the party for instance. Never had she looked at him the way she looked at that D.A.

Did I really mean it when I said I could be her friend even if we weren't romantically involved? Be her friend even if she overlooked me to get to another man? Could he accept just friendship? In his mind, David knew that would have been the mature thing to do. In his heart, he knew that would be a bitter pill to swallow. Maybe that was why he was so angry and still had a headache. Perhaps it was because of what she had said to him at her door. Could he go on like this, wanting to be part of someone's life when they didn't want him to be part of their life in the same way? Sometimes it made him feel so bad it was almost like living in hell.

In contrast, the one who paced in a black room felt they had taken a flight to heaven during the night. Something amazing had been accomplished. One more amazing indiscretion was to come. "Shay, oh, Shay," the voice whispered.

Six

"Are you all right, Janet?" Rakim was just as shocked to see how bad Janet looked as he was to see her appear at his doorstep. Her coat was soiled, with a repellent odor. Her eyes were so bloodshot he wondered if she'd been crying.

"I'm fine," Janet spat, her stare blazing into Christina's as she sauntered inside the condo.

Stumped, Rakim spread out his arms. "Then why are you here? At this hour? And how did you know where I live?"

Taking a seat, Janet was still gazing at Christina as she spoke to Rakim. "I'm here because of your sister."

"What about Shay?" He came closer to Janet.

"What happened to Shay?" Christina echoed his concern.

"She's going to be arrested for murdering her ex."

"What!" Rakim grabbed his head. "Arrested!"

Janet went on to explain the call she'd received from Greg Forest. She summed up the truth with a lie. "I hired an investigator tonight so I could find you and tell you this. You weren't answering your calls."

After assessing that the road was too treacherous to drive to Shay at that instant, Rakim rushed to the phone. Receiving a busy signal rather than a dial tone didn't deter him in persistently trying to reach his sister.

Imagining what Shay must have been feeling,

astonishment and worry overcame him. He couldn't bear his sister enduring something else that would attempt to destroy her. First, there had been the devastation of losing their parents when they needed them most. Then there was living with relatives who loved them no more than they did a stranger in the street until Aunt Sarah had rescued them. Following that, was that nightmare with Marquis. Hadn't Shay suffered enough? Now this murder thing. *God, please don't let the Devil give my little sister any more grief.* Certainly, he believed Marquis deserved exquisite torture after hurting his sister so. But as far as Shay killing him, he knew she could never kill anyone.

Across the room, Christina stood worried about the best friend she had ever had. In the tenth grade she'd met Shay. That afternoon she never knew what an important role her friend would play in her life. A boyfriend had just dumped Christina after she'd given up her virginity to him two weeks earlier. Leaning against the iron schoolyard gate, she couldn't stop crying. She couldn't stop hurting no matter how bad she wanted to.

Having been stared at for a while by Shay, Christina soon had company. After introducing herself, Shay kept asking her what was wrong. Christina repeatedly lied that it was nothing. Except while they were standing there, Christina's ex walked by. He was hugging another girl, not even glancing at Christina. Finally Christina broke down, telling Shay about her heartbreak. Shay told her he wasn't worth her tears. She assured her that there were other fish in the sea. In fact, she claimed to know a boy "way cuter than him and sweeter too." Christina thought she was just talking. Until Shay took her home.

While Christina's brow furrowed, Janet continued to glower up at her. Whatever Rakim saw in her Janet couldn't see it. Though she did notice that her husband's mistress's penny-colored skin glowed. It sickened her that Rakim's lips and tongue kissing Christina's skin was probably what made it look that way. It made her suffer more looking at the sheer nightgown.

Christina was a thick-boned woman, with large breasts and wide hips bared through the gown. Seeing the traps she used to seduce Rakim, the infirmity Janet felt quickly grew to rage. She balled up her fists so she wouldn't slap all the sex Christina received from Rakim out of her.

"You didn't answer my question, Christina. Have you been keeping Rakim warm during this cold?"

Christina's baby-doll lips moved. The words were just stuck somewhere inside her guilt and embarrassment. She found no pleasure in being the other woman. It didn't turn her on in the slightest to know that she was making a man so much happier than his drop-dead gorgeous, successful wife. Rakim and Janet were separated, Christina always reasoned with herself. It was over between them, Rakim assured her every day. He'd even filed for divorce. She was there when he did it. So why now did she feel so low?

"It goes against everything in me to be with a man who's married, Janet. I wasn't raised that way. I didn't mean to hurt you. I—"

"Oh, stop that ridiculous lying!" Janet laughed out. "You love the idea that you, a plain Jane, took away a man from Miss New Jersey. Now how did you manage to do that? Giving it to him down-and-dirty style?"

"Wait a minute!" Rakim shouted. Already frustrated with not being able to reach Shay, he slammed the useless phone down, then rushed over to Janet. "I thought you came here to tell me about Shay. Not to talk to Christina like that."

Fighting back tears, Janet's eyes cut from Rakim to Christina. "I was just trying to find out how whores steal husbands. Is the secret down-and-dirty style?" She leered at Christina. "Is that how you got him?"

Wildly, Rakim was shaking his head. "This is not cool. Not cool at all." He looked over at Christina. "Could you let me speak to Janet alone?"

Christina felt strange about doing so. She nodded anyway. "If that's what you want."

Both watched Christina walk away until she closed the bedroom door behind her.

Rakim's attention shot back to Janet. "Down-and-dirty style, Janet. You know something about that. You sure like it down-and-dirty in the dark."

"I know I do! With you!" She sprang to her feet in front of him. "You're my husband!" With one fist she beat her chest. "Mine! Mine, Rakim!"

"And you've always been ashamed of me!" He leaned over in her face.

"I'm not ashamed of you!"

"Then what is telling everyone that I graduated from Harvard Law? What's wrong with the city college I went to?" He threw his hands up, stressing his point. "And what's with telling everyone that my parents were lawyers too and that I grew up not far from you? What's wrong with saying that I grew up in Jersey City and my parents were factory workers?" With an aggravated sigh, he turned away.

She shuffled around in front of him. "Because I was trying to help you. A corporate lawyer with Sheridan Banking has to have impressive credentials to attract clients and business associates."

"I don't care about that! I never cared about impressing people like you do."

"I just wanted you to go to the top!" She pointed upward, emphasizing her point. "Winners want winners around them. It's how the game works. You know that. Rakim, this is the kind of world we live in."

"That's the kind of world you live in." He set his eyes hard in hers. "And I want no part of it. My world is simple. I want to do defense law. I want to help brothers and sisters struggling to make it pull themselves up."

"We were helping them. We gave to those causes."

To that his wide mouth twisted in a smile. "You say *those* causes just like you say *those* people. You write them a big check for a tax write-off and to look good in the society pages, but you don't give a damn about them."

"They don't give a damn about themselves. But I'm willing to change if it'll make you happy. I'll even spend more time with you and stop going to every society function."

"No, you won't. Because your family will pressure you to go for the business and they come before our marriage."

"Not this time they won't. I've learned from all this, Rakim. I deserve another chance." She stared across at him, her hazel eyes begging as much as her voice. "It won't happen again."

"It will happen, Janet. Everything is for appearances, for your family, for the success of Sheridan Banking, for the sake of having a Ferrari newer than your friend's. I'm not made that way, and it became real old being around that environment. Just like it became real old being a corporate attorney. I let you talk me into working for your family, doing a kind of law I had no passion for, and it's robbed me years of doing what I always wanted to do. No more."

"If we love each other, we can work it out." Moving close to him, she cupped his face within her slender hands. "And I know you still love me. I can see it."

Looking down at the beautiful face he once adored,

Rakim did feel something for her. It probably was love. He would probably feel love for her the rest of his life. However, he wasn't *in love*. There was such a big difference between the two. The difference he discovered with Christina.

Gently, he removed Janet's fingers from his face. "I'll always care about you, Janet."

"Care?" She felt like freeing the tears she'd fought since she'd entered the house. It was getting harder with each second to hold them back. But she wouldn't let herself look so pathetic. "Rakim, you have to feel more than that. You just don't want that whore to hear it. I know she's listening!"

"Stop it!"

"It's true. She is a whore. Her whoring is the reason we're not together."

"That's not true! We're different kinds of people. That's all there is to it. Too different. We were having problems long before Christina became part of my life."

Janet shook her head. "No! She made her move when she knew you and I were having problems!"

"I don't want to talk about this any more. I have too much to think about with this situation with Shay. Now I'm going to go get a few hours of rest. Hopefully the snow will be clear soon and I can go see my sister." He started toward the bedroom.

Janet grabbed his arm, forcing him to face her. "You are not going in that room to sleep with that whore!"

Christina had heard the insults one time too many. She raced out of the door, charging in Janet's face. A sour odor she smelled since Janet first entered the house made her squiggle her nose up.

"I am nobody's whore!" Christina told her. "I was invited here. You weren't!"

Janet smirked. "I am his wife. You aren't."

"Let's end this right now." Rakim stepped between the two.

Christina glared beyond him at those evil hazel eyes. "He doesn't want to be with you anymore." She squiggled her nose more at that acrid smell. "If a man handed me divorce papers when the relationship was obviously miserable, I'd sign them in a heartbeat and keep on stepping. You can't make a man love you when it's not there."

"You don't know what's in his heart!"

"It's not you."

Janet's tiny nostrils flared. "It is me! He married me. Did he marry you? You knew him way before I did. Did he ever look twice at you before? No. Because you weren't his type. You weren't good enough. And you're not good enough now. You're a distraction. A side dish. A last resort when the real thing is unavailable."

Sweat popped on Rakim's forehead at that one. He thrust his hands out each side to keep the women apart. "This really has to stop."

"I don't care what you say," Christina addressed Janet. "You're just hanging on, making yourself look like a fool." But even as she spoke so confidently, Janet's painful insights crept into the corners of her mind. Why hadn't Rakim noticed her before? "I have more pride than to be with a man who doesn't want me." Her small eyes squinted with her intent. "But you just hang on." That rancid stench made her wrinkle her nose more. "You know you're not happy. You just don't want to tell everyone that your marriage is over. That's what you really hate. Telling everybody that your fairy tale isn't a fairy tale at all!"

"You shut your mouth! You don't know anything about me!"

"On the contrary . . ." Christina placed her hand

against her hip. "Rakim has filled me in. In fact, we talked about you while we were laying in bed tonight."

Rakim stretched his eyes at Christina going there. More sweat popped on his forehead. "Look, this—"

"Well, you better remember that last conversation in bed," Janet interrupted him. She laughed wryly. "Because that is your last one. I am sleeping with my husband when he goes back in that bedroom."

Christina inhaled. "Not smelling like that you aren't. You need a bath."

Her jaws clenched, Janet stepped up in Christina's face. "I threw up for your information." She couldn't possibly tell her why. "That's why my clothes are soiled. What's the excuse for your face and body? Why are they so uninteresting, so forgettable, so aver—

"Janet, don't." Rakim cut her off. "Just tell me this. Are you all right now?" Although they weren't going to be together, he would always care about her welfare. Equally, he would always want the best for her. "Do you feel better? Did you eat something that didn't agree with you?"

Janet looked at him warmly for his concern. Feelings were still there, and she was ecstatic for Christina to see them. "I'm fine, except for wanting to be alone with you."

At that request, Rakim took the back of his hand to his forehead, wiping off the sweat that felt like it was drenching him. During the same minute, Christina turned away from Janet, heading toward the window. Posing in front of it, she couldn't believe she had let Janet agitate her so, reducing her to such behavior. If she kept entertaining this woman with gibes, sure enough they would be rolling on the floor in a catfight. No, she wasn't going to argue senselessly over a man—not even Rakim. Neither would she ponder what Janet claimed about her being Rakim's second choice. She knew where she stood with him. This bickering was silly.

Christina whirled back around, fastening her eyes on
Rakim. "Honey, I'll sleep on the sofa."

Janet gawked at her. The nerve of her calling her husband *honey.* "You belong out the door."

Rakim watched Christina roll her eyes at Janet instead
of responding. For her tact, he had to smile at her. "I'll
be the one sleeping on the sofa, young lady. You can go
back to my bedroom, and . . ." He gazed at Janet. "And
you can sleep in the guest room."

As soon as Braxton woke, the brightness coming from
the window lured him to it. "Goddamn!" he swore, looking out of it. That snow from yesterday was nothing compared to what he was looking at now. The amount of it
had doubled. He had never seen so much snow. Never
even imagined it, especially when spring was merely
weeks away. Worse, the flakes were still coming down.

In his fascination, his gaze wandered everywhere, soon
catching sight of the telephone poles. The lines were
coated with ice. He went over to his phone and picked it
up. There was no dial tone. Braxton strolled back toward
the window. Marveling at the billow of white, he knew it
would be impossible to go out of the house or call anyone.
A grin spread across his lips because of what that meant.

He shouldn't have been glad he was stuck in the house
with Shay. After all, his case was being delayed. Added
to that, the two of them were on opposite sides like she
pointed out. Even so, that episode in the hall last night
had been so *interesting* he couldn't help hoping for another day alone with her. What would it bring? He just
wouldn't let things get that *interesting* again. He couldn't.
There was too much to lose. They would be housemates
today. That's all. What's more, he would start the day off
right by doing something she would like, treating her to

his cooking skills. His housemate had better get her stomach ready for one delicious breakfast.

Having heard her walking overhead when he was downstairs in the kitchen, Braxton knew Shay had woken up. And he knew it wasn't being a gentleman or a good host, but he couldn't help himself when he stepped toward the partly opened door and peeked through the cracked space like a peeping Tom. Clutching a tray of bacon, sausages, eggs, sweet rolls, grits and orange juice, he was hoping to find Shay in something much less than his shirt.

It nearly shocked the tray out of his hands when he observed that his wish was almost reality. He guessed she'd just finished showering. Wrapped in a white towel that extended across her torso and down to the bottom of her buttocks, her back faced him. Braxton cursed that the towel wasn't a little shorter, so that he could see her buns. Still, he had a good view of their perfectly round shape through the snug white towel. Beautiful, he thought, and was reminded that he was a butt man too.

Suddenly sensing Braxton behind her, Shay swiveled around to catch him conveniently fixing the food on the tray. When their eyes met, she saw the mischief in them, and it was clear he'd been standing there watching her for a while. She knew she should have felt discomforted by that. Instead, she found it as much a turn-on as the thoughtful deed he'd obviously done.

"Is this what I think it is?" she asked, her gaze shifting to the tray. "You made us breakfast?" The delicious combined smells of the sweet rolls and the bacon made her deeply inhale. "Oh, my goodness, if that tastes like it smells . . ."

"I hope you like it." Uncovering the food, he let his eyes wander over her. Obviously well rested, she looked so seductive to him. In their exotic naturalness her eyes,

her lips, everything about her seemed exquisitely designed
for his eyes. "I just put a little bit of this and that together.
Used some of those skills my mom taught me."

"Looks like your mama taught you well." Shay was
standing in front of the tray, marveling at it. "I'm so hungry too." She glanced up at him but found his eyes looking
into hers a little too hard. She quickly switched her attention back to the tray. "Thank you."

"You're my guest. I had to feed you. You're not a vege-
tarian, are you?"

"Actually I do like to eat healthy foods, and I try not
to eat red meats." She was still lusting over the food. "But
sometimes I get that taste for something I have no business
with and the next thing I know my face is all in it."

"I know what you mean."

"My Aunt Sarah, she throws down like this. I was raised
on this kind of food."

Braxton was still captivated by her, wishing he could
move things with his mind. If he did possess that power,
that towel would have definitely loosened and fell. "That
looks good on you." He threw his head toward the towel.

Smiling from the compliment, Shay looked up at him,
really looked at him this time. Oddly, he had that tanned
look again in the room's brilliant light, and wearing a black
tank top with matching sweat pants, he was so sexy everything else in the room blurred away. She wondered how
she would get through this day without letting her eyes
drift over his body—without letting her eyes drift like his
eyes were occasionally drifting over her.

The heated, wandering looks made her feel something
more than other men did when they stared at her. Those
men would make her feel attractive, but regardless of how
attractive the man was, she felt nothing back. This was
different. She had to quell the waves of arousal that were

getting stronger with each moment spent around Braxton Steele. "I hope you don't mind me helping myself to your towel," she said, pinching one of the sweet rolls.

"You can have as many towels as you like." He liked the way her face tensed up as she tasted the bread. Was he that good of a cook? "And I'll get you a new shirt to put on today, with some of my jeans to go with it." *But if I had my way you would wear only your birthday suit.*

"Mmm, this is good." The buttery, sweet, breaded taste felt like it was seducing her tongue. She pinched another piece.

"I'm glad you like it that much. Hope you'll enjoy the rest of my hospitality. We're stuck as you've probably seen."

"I know." She was chewing. "I peeked outside."

He studied the sinuous motion of her lips. "And the phones are down."

"Yes, I tried to call my brother." Then pausing, her expression dimmed. "I bet you're disappointed you can't make contact with the station."

"Disappointed?" He smiled, but his eyes only held intensity. "No, I'm not disappointed. To tell the truth, I'm glad we can't go out. I'm glad we're alone." He was silent a moment, his gaze steadying in hers. "And if my guess is right, I think you're glad too."

The words made Shay confront last night. She lowered her head, as she stopped fighting thinking about it. It was all she thought about since she woke. All the while she'd been standing there with him, she'd tried to pretend it hadn't happened. To think she'd almost touched his most intimate place because she couldn't control her desire to feel him made her wonder if this Marquis tragedy was making her lose her good sense. Was she having some sort of breakdown?

Sensing he'd made her uncomfortable, Braxton switched his interest to the food. He inhaled the bread's sweet aroma. "This good grub is going to get cold if we keep talking."

Shay perked up as she faced him. "Where are we going to eat it, in here?" She glanced at the bed since there were no tables and hardly anything else in the room.

Braxton thought for a moment. "How about in front of the fireplace downstairs?"

"So your Aunt Sarah used to throw down in the kitchen?" Braxton remarked as he relaxed on a blanket across from Shay, enjoying the breakfast feast. Watching the vibrant embers play across her skin, to him they cast a sensuous copper-orange hue on her as if she were basking in the throes of a sunrise.

"She used to throw down all the time." Shay sipped some orange juice, then set the glass back down. "Aunt Sarah was the second guardian who raised me and my brother, Rakim, after our parents passed away."

"Oh, I'm sorry to hear that your parents passed."

"Yep, they're gone," she acknowledged but refused to be sad. She smiled thinking about her aunt. "She was really nice to us. Still is, even though she's miles away and a volunteer in the Peace Corp."

"She sounds dedicated." He bit a piece of bacon.

"Yes, she is. But if we need her, or anything, she's there." She glanced at his mouth. His lips were moist from the greasy meat and moving torpidly as he munched. "She ah . . . she's my great aunt and she had her old-fashioned ways, but she's my heart. The only things we had conflict about was how much we should go to church." She saw those dimples instantly dent his cheeks.

"So you had that problem too?" He swallowed the bacon and went for a roll. "My mama made us go a lot too."

"Really?" His mouth caught her attention again.

"Oh, yes. My mother loves her God. I do too now, don't get me wrong. But my mom would have me and my brothers and sisters going to church twenty-four hours of the day if she had her way."

"My aunt is the same way. And I do love the Creator myself, but I can't go all the time. And when I can't, I just have to serve him in the way I treat people, in the way I live my life."

Gazing at her fondly, Braxton nodded. "I usually make it to service every Sunday, but I totally agree with you in serving him in the way you treat people and live." His keen instincts never led him astray about people. Although they hadn't told him if she murdered or not, they were telling him she meant what she had just said. "So you mentioned having another guardian before Aunt Sarah. How were they? Did they treat you and your brother good?" He hoped she hadn't been abused, because that could have led to what happened with Marquis Jackson. But to that question, Braxton beheld a strange look from Shay. "I shouldn't have asked you such a prying question. We don't really know each oth—"

"No, it's all right." There was a warmth about him now that made her want to share the experience with him. "When my parents first passed away, the only relative we had was my mother's cousin. She had a husband, two kids and an all right home."

Braxton could tell by her tone that something had been awry. "Were you abused in any way, Shay?"

Once more he said her name in a way she'd never heard. "No, I wasn't. Not physically that is."

"But mentally?"

"I don't know what you would call it."

"Call what?" He came closer to her.

"Just not being loved." Shay made a dry chuckle as she looked beyond him, thinking back. "I remember the first Christmas with them; we didn't get any presents. Their kids had all kinds of new things under the tree, toys, electronics, clothes, everything, but Rakim and I, nothing. Instead my mother's cousin looked through her kid's closets and gave us their clothes that they didn't want anymore. That was Christmas for us." Shay sadly chuckled again. "They never bought us anything. They gave us small portions of food. They never talked to us. They never hugged us. They just had us there for the money. They didn't care if we lived or died."

Feeling each breath of her pain, Braxton shook his head. He wished he could have traveled back in time with a power that would have prevented it all from happening to her. "I'm glad your aunt rescued you. I know she's proud of the woman you have become."

Braxton and Shay talked more as they washed the dishes in the kitchen. They discovered that both of them had grown up and lived in various areas of New Jersey, finally settling in Englewood Cliffs. Both had also struggled financially before their careers took off, refusing parental help, and they shared some of the rough and amusing times of those days. Finishing the dishes, they were enjoying the conversation so much, they returned to the blanket in front of the fireplace.

"So what made you start a magazine about love and relationships?" Stretching his long body across the afghan, propping his elbow on it and resting the side of his face in his palm, Braxton gazed up at Shay. The flames were making her skin shimmer more by the second, and it all made him wonder if the covered parts of her body looked as sexy in firelight. "There has to be something that sparked the idea of a love and relationships magazine."

The question made Shay's eyes scatter about the air as brightly as her abrupt smile. "My parents. I have so many happy memories of them."

"They had a good relationship?" He watched the excited glow of a little girl come to her face.

"Did they." She shook her head. "They were really in love. It was the real thing, right before my and Rakim's eyes everyday. They were so nice to each other. They were always joking and playing and smiling at each other. They were always doing sweet things for one another. They were best friends too, always talking about their dreams and working toward them. Now, they did argue some. My daddy used to love to play numbers and horses, and my mama was always after him about wasting money. And there were other little minor squabbles, but they worked through them, and they never argued in front of me and Rakim."

"So how did you know they were arguing?"

"Because we always eavesdropped at the door." She chuckled with Braxton. "But I'll never forget that last time they went out on that date." Shay looked off into the memory. "He was just looking at her in that way." Shay switched her gaze back over to Braxton.

He was looking at her in a way. A way that made her unable to resist looking back. When Braxton's eyes slid down to her lips and her own glided toward his, Shay felt a surge of heat sweep through her.

"I bet you think I'm corny," she said, gazing off into the fire. "Getting so caught up in my parents' romance that I made a career of it." She wiped at some moistness on her forehead.

Feeling a heat of his own, Braxton sat up to get more comfortable. "I don't think that's corny at all. I like it. That's a beautiful way to spend your life, focusing on loving relationships, finding them, making them even better. It's real beautiful." Pausing, he rested his eyes on her mouth again. "And who better than you, someone who saw and was part of the experience of real love, to show others what it's supposed to be about. Plus, you probably have it in your own life."

Shay had to smile at how slick he was. "Are you trying to find out if I'm in a relationship?"

"No." Braxton scratched the back of his neck. "I was just making an observation. I know that the doc is your man." His tone was playful.

"David is not my man," Shay said with as much playfulness as came from him. "Are you in a relationship with all those women you're famous for being with?" She hadn't meant to mention the women, but he caught her off guard.

Braxton raised back, looking surprised. "I know you said you read about me but that too?"

Her fingers rubbed back through her shag, her attempt to appear nonchalant. "It's your business who you date."

"True. But would you like it to be your business?" He stared at her. "Do you care?"

To that, Shay's eyes clung to him, wandering over him softly. "I can't afford to."

Reminding himself of their situation, Braxton nodded. "You're right. And it's flattering to know that you've been reading about me. But just to set the record straight, I do date, but not as many women as the press has me dating. But I do date occasionally. Although, I'm not in a committed relationship."

She pretended that the information didn't phase her. "Do those women know you're not committed?"

"Of course. I'm honest. They're dating other people too. Now back to you, what's going on with you and the doctor?"

"We're friends."

"Just friends?"

"Just friends."

Braxton recalled how the man who defended Shay at the party looked at her, how protective he was of her. "You may feel that you're friends. But he doesn't feel friendly. He wants some."

Shay's brows raised at his rawness. "And I want a friend, and that's what he's been."

"So there must be someone else?" *I hope it's not serious.*

"No, there is no one," she said, feeling odd that she was telling him this.

"You don't have a man?"

"No, I don't. I date, but I haven't found someone that. . . ." She searched for the right words. "I haven't found someone that touches my heart and soul in a way that no one else ever has."

"That's exactly how I feel," he thought aloud.

She was shocked. "You do?"

"Most definitely."

That made her just look at him a moment, wondering if he was just saying what she or any other woman wanted to hear. At the same time, Braxton was silently watching her, amazed that they had that in common. But as he watched her, her playful air suddenly transformed into sadness. He understood why. "I think you let what Marquis did stop you from loving another man. Don't give him that right. You're missing out on so much."

Shay looked down, weighing what he said, before giving him her attention again. "Until you've been in love like I've been in love and hurt from it like I have, you have no idea what's been going on inside me."

"I do know."

"No, you don't, Braxton. You think you know, but you don't. It's easy to tell yourself, let's get over him. Let's love again. But it's hard to feel the actual love when your heart has been scraped out, dug out, shot out, burned out, kicked out, cut out by someone who you thought loved you." Pausing, she closed her eyes. After taking a deep breath, she opened them. "It's not that easy to recover and move on when you thought the person was so much a part of you, it was like you breathed one breath together. You can't help who you fall in love with, just like you can't help feeling the ache of that love when it is no more."

Braxton pondered the deepness of her words for several moments, until his reflection carried his attention to a painting on the wall. Andrea was sitting in a patio chair. She was also staring down at him at that moment.

Shay followed his line of vision until she stood and strolled toward the portrait. "She looks happy," she remarked.

"Yes, she does." Braxton walked up behind her, joining her in admiring the portrait.

Shay stepped aside, looking at another work, a portrait of a black family at an outdoor gathering. "So you're a fan of his too?"

"Of who?" Braxton looked up proudly at the colorful images she was staring at. "You've seen this artist's work before?"

"Of course. My brother's mother-in-law has his work all over her house. Rakim and I tried to get some of his portraits but people buy them as soon as they hit the galleries."

"He is kind of interesting," Braxton commented, smiling up at the work.

"Kind of." Shay stepped even closer to the canvas. "He is something else. I'm not even a great art lover and I'm into this guy." She squinted her eyes to see the inscription. "Yes, that's Ecstasy's work. I'd know it anywhere."

Braxton's big grin felt like it would break through his face. "I have several of his pieces."

"I can see that." Shay strolled around, admiring all the works. They were all beautiful, and all depicted some type of happy scene. "You know what I like about this artist?"

"What?"

"He captures those moments in life that you just want to hold in your hand. You know what I mean?"

"Oh, yes." He was standing directly behind her.

"Those moments that feel so good, it's like magic is happening just then. And you're just floating and you know that one day when you look back, that's going to be one of those moments, those images in your brain of ecstasy that you want to remember forever or wish that you could live all over again. Those moments that are the most beautiful and precious and that make you feel so incredible that you wish time would stand still. They are the moments that we all live for and hope for and dream of. I think that's why he calls himself Ecstasy. He probably feels that our purpose on this earth is like I feel, to pursue happiness and give it to others. It's that simple. But he's not weak. He's his own man, and the way he does his thing, his good things are on his own terms. What do you think?"

Shay turned around, and she had never seen Braxton's face look like it did then.

Neither happy nor sad, he looked vulnerable as he stared at her. "I believe you have looked into that artist's soul. I believe you know him."

Shay stared back at his handsome face, her eyes lingering on his lips. So tempting they were, she dragged her attention back to the portraits. One in particular caught her eye. It was of a man holding a baby up to a dark sky. "Now that one looks as if he's saying a prayer for the baby."

"He is. I'm certain of it."

Shay swung around. "How do you know that?"

"I know the artist."

"You know Ecstasy?"

"Yes, I do." Braxton looked up at the work. "That was painted when his nephew was born and his brother held the baby up to the sky and prayed for him. He was as happy as his brother was. A miracle had fallen from the sky into all their lives."

Shay was touched, not by the story behind the painting, but with the emotion Braxton told it. "No one has ever seen Ecstasy. All anyone knows is that he is a man. That's what my sister-in-law Janet and her mother said. They say he's real private about his identity. So how do you know him?"

"It's a secret."

Shay smiled. "You can tell me, can't you?"

"It depends."

"On what?"

"What do you want to do to get the information?"

"What do you want me to do?"

Straightaway, he looked at her lips. Heated from the look, her eyes drifted toward his too.

"What a CD collection." Shay said, turning away from temptation. She walked over to what appeared to be hundreds of CDs.

Braxton strolled behind her, loving how thrilled she was. "So you're like a kid in a candy store when it comes to music too, I see."

"I *love* my music." Shay picked up a handful of CDs and took them back over to the blanket.

Braxton grabbed one, put it in the player, and before long Deborah Cox and R.L. were powerfully crooning why they couldn't be friends. "Love this song," he swore and noticed Shay tensing her face up the way she did when the roll tasted real good to her.

"Ooh, this is the jam." She gladly watched him sliding next to her on the blanket. "They're not singing. They're *sanging.*"

The stirring ballad was a prelude to a sharing of thoughts about music, about movies, sports, spirituality, philosophy, morality and so many other ingredients of life that they had in common. The more they talked, the more they wanted to talk, needed to talk, loved to talk. On the rarity that they couldn't agree on something, their differing opinions and arguments were exhilarating, intelligent and incredibly fun. Never had Shay found a man so in tuned to the way she thought, the way she lived, the way she was. Never had Braxton been with a woman that knew his soul the way this beautiful creature before him did. The high between them was such that it felt addictive. Against the backdrop of lowly played romantic song after romantic song, intensified by the seductive flames of the fire lighting them and everything in the room with a glow only made for lovers, they easily fell under the spell of it all. If their laughter and teasing of each other weren't indicative of only those feelings a desire for each other stirred, their looks into each other's eyes and the arousal moist in her and firm on his body would clarify any confusion.

What was felt between them reeked so powerfully in the air that when Shay glimpsed the sun setting outside the window, it was a welcome distraction.

"Where did the time go?" she asked, looking up at the sky. Hues of orange and red were melting into the sooty blue.

Braxton shook his head, watching the dusk. "They say it flies when you're having fun."

Shay stood to go over to the window. A pain in her leg

made her bend down to clutch it. "Ouch, I must have been sitting too long. I have a cramp in my leg."

"It hurts bad?"

"Not too bad," she said, touching the spot. "That happens sometimes to me when I sit in one place a long time."

"And we have been sitting here all day. But I have something for it."

"What can you do?"

"I can make it feel better." Painstakingly he prodded the spot, but the jeans wouldn't allow his fingers the access they needed.

"Would you mind doing something for me?"

"What?"

He looked up at her. "Could you take off the pants? I'll make it better. I'm an expert at this stuff."

Shay thought for a moment. The shirt covered her bottom. "Sure."

Standing above him, Shay unzipped the dungarees. Slowly she slid them down her legs, while Braxton divided his attention between her eyes and legs. When they were completely off, she still stood while he remained on the blanket. Gently he began massaging her leg, before increasing the pressure slightly.

"Ooh, it's beginning to feel better," she moaned. "You're good at this."

Braxton stopped and gazed up at her. "I'm good at a lot of things."

At that, Shay just looked at him but didn't comment.

He concentrated on the massage again. "If you lay down I can do it better."

Hesitantly, Shay nodded. "Sure."

Braxton watched her lay on her back before him. "Comfortable?"

"Very." She stared up at him as he began working on

her again. Was she in heaven? Was the sexy Braxton Steele actually doing this to her?

In silence and for several moments, he massaged, occasionally glimpsing Shay's face and finding the crystal brown depths that he could never get enough of looking into his eyes.

"Is it gone yet?" he asked. She was so beautiful it took every effort for him not to kiss her.

The cramp had been gone before she lay down. "Not yet."

Braxton wasn't even massaging the same leg. That little liar, he thought. He massaged higher, moving from her calf to her thigh.

Shay's eyes fluttered close. "Umm."

Braxton was enjoying the expression on her face. He wanted to give her much more to moan about. His fingers wandered dangerously to the top of her thigh. "I can massage anywhere else you need it."

Shay's eyes opened. Braxton was looking down at her, openly staring at her body and it turned her on. Too much. She raised herself to get up.

Braxton's chest coming down on hers from the side forced her back down. "We can't go on denying it," he whispered.

"Braxton, we can't." She tried to push his chest. Like steel, it wouldn't budge.

"One kiss." He stared at her mouth and swallowed. "One kiss . . ."

His face was so close to hers, she felt like she were dreaming. Her raging heart let her know she wasn't. "What about our situation?"

"Maybe tomorrow there won't be one." His lips brushed hers. "I don't believe you did it."

Shay didn't know what made her feel more excited—his

believing her or the feel of him. She was trembling with heat. "You mean that?"

"Oh, yes." He kissed her closed lips, then did a slow dance with his mouth along her neck.

Her eyes slipped closed. "Or are you saying that to get some?"

"No, baby." He laughed a little as he found her lips again, kissing them with gentle teasing pecks. "I mean it." He couldn't stop kissing her mouth. "Delicious. You're delicious." He couldn't believe he was with Shay like this. "I'm going to make sure the real killer is caught."

"But you can't. . . ." She could hardly talk because his lips on hers felt so good. "You can't guarantee me that." She opened her eyes.

He raised back, staring in her sparkling eyes. "I can guarantee that I'd never hurt you. I'll only make you feel better than you've ever felt in your life." He caressed her plump mouth with his fingers before replacing it with his lips.

"Stop," she slurred, loving his lips on hers. *How can this be happening?*

Braxton deepened the brush of their mouths until they were swaying to a sweet rhythm more sensuous than the one he'd imagined Shay and he could create. It was only the heat coming from the fireplace that thwarted his tongue from plunging beyond her lips. They had came too close to the flames.

Braxton pulled Shay back. "Another few inches and we would have been in another kind of fire."

Shay stood. "It was a sign we shouldn't be with each other. Nothing can happen between us, Braxton."

"But I meant what I said." He came to his feet. "I don't believe you did it. We'll work it all out at the station tomorrow. I will find the killer. He was alone with you in that penthouse and could have killed you too."

"That is frightening to think about."

"I know your heart now. I know you couldn't have killed Marquis."

"And I hope you mean that."

"I do."

"But I still can't be with you."

"Why?"

"Because. You have no guarantee that you'll clear me. You may be prosecuting me."

"But what did I just say to you. I'm going to help you, Shay."

"I have to help myself."

"Why are you so afraid of me?"

"Afraid of you?"

"Yes, you're afraid of me. And it's not about the case either."

"What else could it be but the case?"

"It's something else."

"I'm *not* afraid of you."

"Then why do you look like you want to run?"

She couldn't tell him the truth. He would think she was insecure. "I don't want to run. I—I just wanted to go look around, and—and give myself a tour of your house. Do you mind?"

"Yes, but no tour without me. I'll show you around."

The final room Braxton escorted her through was his bedroom. Shay found it to be the coziest room in the house. Full of that wood and pinewood fragrance, it had the same earth tones as the other rooms. On the wall was one of those paintings by Ecstasy—featuring the same woman who was in the living-room portrait. There were also more furnishings complimenting the atmosphere than in the other rooms. There were also roomier closets. She peeked in one of them. The red silk teddy that she saw in it made her close its door quickly.

"What's the matter?" Braxton saw a funny look on her face.

"Nothing." Folding her arms, Shay strolled and scanned around the room.

"Yes, it is something." He started to open the closet but remembered before opening it what was inside it. It was a previous date's negligee.

"Seeing that nightie bothered you, didn't it?"

"Why should I care if a woman's teddy is in your closet?"

"But you do. That's why you can't ease up just a little. That's why you can't trust me that I'll clear you and that there won't be a situation to overcome between us. Because you're afraid that I'll hurt you if you let go and hold on to me. You believe that stuff you read about me and those women, and you don't want to get hurt again."

"I don't feel like getting into this type of conversation with you. What you do is your business, Braxton. We hardly know each other." Shay began walking past him.

He grasped her arms, forcing her to look at him. "We know each other very well. You know it and I do too. The length of time that we know each other doesn't matter. It's the *way* we know each other that counts. I'm feeling something very special with you, Shay."

"How do I know you don't say that to every woman you're with?"

"Because I don't. I haven't said that to a woman in years. Only to a woman I once loved. But she's gone. And you and I are here. We're *alive*. Alive in a way that both of us haven't been in a long time."

"I can't get involved with you, Braxton." Again she tried to bypass him.

He wouldn't let go of her arms. "You're already involved." He stared in her eyes. "I see it. You see it in me."

She managed to free herself and backed up. "We can't."

"Shay, I won't hurt you. We will work the murder situation out. I'll clear you. I'll find the killer. Just give us a chance." Staring in her eyes, Braxton came toward her. "Please. Because . . . because what we're feeling is so rare. And you thought you would never, ever feel it just like I did."

"No." She was still inching back until she couldn't go any farther. Her back flattened against the wall.

"Yes. You know I'm right. I know Marquis hurt you. I know how much. You would get up in the mornings thinking about how wrong he did you. The betrayal was so baffling. The hurt was like a toothache that wouldn't go away. It was just there. Just there. You would think about him, what he did, all of it, all day long. You would try to get it out of your mind, busying yourself with your career, with anything to help you get some relief, but when your head would hit the pillow at night, you couldn't sleep. You couldn't because you were still trying to figure it out, trying to understand what went wrong." He watched a tear stroll down her cheek. Ever so tenderly he stroked it away. "You wondered whether you were pretty enough, sexy enough, smart enough, together enough. You just wondered whether you were enough period. Or if it was him that was all screwed up.

"You wondered sometimes if God was punishing you. After all, your baby . . . he was taken from you. You wondered how God could bless you with such a gift, give you something so precious just to take it away. It wasn't fair. But no matter how much you screamed about it, no one could answer you. No one could soothe you. No one could know the depth of your agony." He stroked another tear. "You wondered what you had ever done in your life to deserve such hell on earth. You were crying all the time, even when you or anyone else couldn't see the tears. You wondered over and over when would it end, this feeling. This awful feeling. How could you make it go away? What could relieve it? But there was nothing. It was just there. Lingering.

"You felt alone and you felt so empty. And you tried to find another man to fill that hollow space inside, to remove that loneliness. But no one could ever fulfill you. They all left you feeling as empty and alone as you were on your own. There was no one. All there was was the pain Marquis left. You wondered and wondered when the day would come when God would send you someone to make you forget him. To forget it all. But most times you tell yourself there is no such person. Well, you're wrong. Your prayer has been answered. I can make you forget him in your mind, in your heart and in your body."

Not knowing how he knew those things about her, Braxton eased his face toward Shay's damp face, pressing his lips and body against hers. The knowledge of how she felt, he couldn't question it. He knew that some things weren't meant to be questioned. Some things human beings instinctively knew. Like he knew he'd been sent to her, just as he knew she had been sent to him. "You feel so good," he breathed, feeling her softness against him. He couldn't believe this was happening. "So good, Shay. I wanted to be this close to you for so long. I wanted to kiss you for so long."

"Oh, Braxton," Shay whimpered, feeling his sweltering lips brushing across hers, feeling his rigid masculinity pressing into her stomach, it all filling her body with a tempest of heat. Acutely she felt a need for him in her intimate place, especially when his tongue gently pried her lips apart and his arms came around her, holding her so close.

Seven

"Yes!" Jamison exclaimed to himself "We have her right where we want her!" He was standing in the station, above his desk, poring over the forensics report. He was so grateful the snow had stopped, the plows were functioning perfectly and he was able to get to the place he loved more than anywhere else—the police station. His work was his entire world. "Now Steele can stick it to her real good!"

Slipping himself out of his parka, Patman walked up, catching the tail of his partner's words. "What did you say, sir?"

Gleefully, Jamison shook the paper. "No other prints were on the murder weapon but Shay Hilton's." He had been so anxious to know what was in the report, he'd headed straight into the office as soon as he entered the station. He hadn't even taken off his coat. "She did it!"

"We'll see." Patman scanned across his cluttered desk as he settled behind it. "We have to see what Steele comes up with."

"Steele heard her say she could kill the poor sap at a party." Finally he unbuttoned his coat. "Don't fall for her looks, Patman." He tossed his jacket on a rack beside them. "She wouldn't look twice at guys like us. Thinks she's too good."

"You think so?"

"I know it. I can tell. Just don't feel so sympathetic toward her. A beautiful woman has destroyed many men."

"I won't, sir. I just want to make sure we don't wind up looking like we did before."

"That won't happen." Jamison plopped down in his chair and reared back smiling. "This case is going to get us in the headlines. Did you know that poor sap was an actor?"

"I heard it the same time you did."

"Isn't that something? Now I never heard of him either, but lots of other people have. Boy, the headlines are going to be something else, a fancy magazine editor kills an up-and-coming actor. We're going to look good, kid. Real good."

Patman looked worried. "You sure?"

"Never more sure of anything in my life. Now, could you get Steele on the phone while I go alert the wire services and the press. Hope the phones are working. Then I'm going to go get a warrant for Ms. Hilton's arrest."

Grateful that his headache had subsided, David was watching his favorite evening news anchors, when he was flabbergasted by the sight of Shay's face flashing across the screen. He hurried out of his recliner, moved closer to the television and turned up the sound.

"Some very disturbing news just coming in. One of the magazine world's hottest editors is going to be arrested this evening for the murder of her ex-lover, actor Marquis Jackson." A picture of Marquis's face appeared beside Shay's. "The successful entrepreneur, who received an award at a ceremony last night, threatened to kill the deceased there and allegedly carried out that threat some time after midnight, bludgeoning him to death. Mr. Jackson was in town for a visit. He recently appeared in the suspense flick—ironically titled—*The Last Breath.* We will keep you updated on this story."

"No way!" David yelled at the television and was so in shock he couldn't move immediately. Soon realizing Shay needed him, he hurried into his bedroom, to his closet. He had to get dressed and get to her fast. He could only guess how distraught she must have been. He knew she hadn't killed anyone, and it enraged him that someone believed she did. She couldn't have. It wasn't in her nature. However, to kill Marquis, to rid the world of such a worthless excuse for a man, it was in his nature.

As for killing, Rakim sat at the table of his dining room, amazed that it had arrived at the dinner hour without Christina and Janet killing each other. From the time they woke Janet had argued with Christina about her man-stealing ways. And as much as his beloved had tried to dismiss his wife's tirade, there were occasions when Christina was so insulted that the two women nearly came to blows.

Rakim felt fortunate that the snowplows had reached his area and knew it was simply a matter of moments before they all could leave the house. The problem was, would Janet give Christina flack over riding with him to the police station? What if both wanted to ride with him? How could he break up a fight if he was driving?

From where they were seated on opposite sides of the table, both women picked at the food Rakim had prepared. Rakim sat in the middle, not out of any male feeling of superiority, but just to make ensure things didn't get violent as they had nearly reached several times during the day.

"Any one want any more potatoes?" Rakim asked, before raking the last helping on his plate.

"No, thank you, honey," Christina answered, smiling at him.

Janet hated with a passion Christina calling Rakim that. "So you realized you shouldn't be eating any more of those," she remarked with a simper. "If my hips were as atrocious as yours I wouldn't eat any more fatty foods either. There is nothing that will turn a man off more than big, lumpy cellulite hips. One day he'll just look at those things and get a soft-on."

Rakim wiped a bead of sweat on his forehead. "Would anyone like punch?" He raised the punch bowl.

"Excuse me, honey." Christina tapped the pitcher aside to get a good look at Janet. "Let me tell you something, missy. The biggest, lumpiest cellulite in here is stuffed all through your stupid head. Not a bit of sense is in there if you think the desperate, ugly way you've acted here at Rakim's home is going to make him want you or even love you again."

"He does love me." Janet leaned across the table, stretching her lengthy neck as far as it would go. "And you'll never have *it* again."

Rakim shook his head. "Come on now. You have to stop this."

Christina chuckled at Janet. "Honey, you're too late. Last night when you were sleeping, I joined him on the sofa and had *it* then."

Rakim grabbed his head. "Chrissy, come on now." He couldn't believe his classy Christina went there. "Please let's change the subject. Okay?"

Christina wasn't given the chance to respond. Before anyone knew anything, Janet leaned down by her foot and up a boot flew in Christina's face. It just missed her eye.

Christina was across the table like a swift wind. She began dragging Janet by the hair with one hand. With the other, she smacked and punched her.

Janet was screaming her lungs raw. "Get her off of me! She's hurting me so bad!" Her arms were swinging, her legs wiggling, but she found no escape from Christina's clutches. "Get some help! Call the police! She's trying to kill me!"

Rakim managed to seize Christina's hands. "Chrissy, stop! You don't want to do this. You might hurt her bad."

Grateful to be free, Janet got out of the way, stepping as far back as she could. She was hurting so badly all over that her eyes filled with tears. Her nose was even running. "You animal!" she yelled, swiping her hand above her lip. "You're a savage!"

Christina rolled her eyes, turning away from Janet and easing into Rakim's waiting arms. Embracing him, she shook her head. "I can't believe I was fighting her like that. But she made me so mad. I have never had a fight as a grown person. This is crazy."

"I understand." Rakim stroked her back. "This has been an unusual situation."

"Get your hands off him!" they heard from behind. But when Christina swerved around, more than an angry mouth greeted her. Janet hit her in the face with the boot again. She'd hoped to knock Christina out. She was surprised instead, when Christina didn't fall or nurse the brutal hurt. She went after Janet.

Rakim watched the two women tied together like a ball of yarn, rolling on the floor, fighting for what it seemed like was the only breath left in the world. Several times he attempted to separate them. Unfortunately, his most successful attempt resulted in his flying across the room. He didn't know which one put him there. Worse, he saw things get much more dangerous when each began grasping whatever object was in their reach and throwing it from their respective sides. The horror of horrors came when Janet's boot smacked the chandelier. The hinge that held the chain and was attached to the main piece loosened. The chandelier would fall at any second. Both women were beneath it. He didn't think he'd be able to get to both women before it dropped.

He shoved Christina out of the way right before he heard the smashing of glass and metal behind them. He thanked God when he looked back and saw that the fixture had missed Janet.

"Whooh, that was close," he remarked, rushing over to his wife. "You're all right?" He touched her arm.

She shoved him off as if he'd burned her. "Don't touch me."

"Janet, I could only push one of you out of the way at a time."

Her eyes lunged at him. "And you chose her."

"I didn't want either one of you to get hurt. You know that."

"But you chose her. You would save her life before mine." Dazedly, she looked around the room. "What does that mean?"

"Janet, you know I didn't want you to get hurt."

She couldn't look at him, couldn't look at Christina. She looked all around them both. "My mother told me you would ruin my life. She told me our relationship would never work. She told me you would destroy me." A crooked smile crept across her lips. "And you have. You chose her life over mine. Hers over mine." Still looking bewilderedly at the room, she shook her head. "Hers over mine."

Christina's kittenish eyes met Rakim's. Except she

didn't know what to say. Neither did he. Sighing, he laid his head back against the wall and merely thought. Today, and last night had been a mess, a catastrophe. He could have done without this aggravation. The sole drama he craved was in the courtroom, establishing the innocence of a client. He needed to save everything within him to help Shay fight this murder rap. Poor Shay, he knew she was probably going through hell at that moment.

Shay couldn't stop herself from putting her arms around Braxton as his tongue played with the opening of her lips until they parted. Oh, God, thank you, thank you, oh, thank you, her insides cried as she felt his sexy deliciousness inside her mouth, while holding on to the muscular arms and shoulders she had only dreamed about touching. What a man, she thought, as the erotic swaying of his tongue beckoned to the core of her femininity.

She felt her secret place becoming as wet as a waterfall. The sensation intensified with a rush of pleasurable feeling that summoned for the intolerable joy that her body knew only he could fill her with. Anxious to delight him with the same potency, Shay matched the sensual thrusting and winding of their tongues with an untamed need to taste him, never getting enough. When had anything ever felt this good to her? Never, ever, her kisses answered to him. Never had she been kissed like this. Never had she been kissed by a man like this one.

Kissing her, Braxton felt at times like he was already where he ached to be, inside her warm sweet walls, and within them she was pulling him deeper, and he was about to explode. That was how good it felt to be this intimate with her. The joy of it all caused him to push his covered erection deeper and deeper against her.

The more the amorous gift of her kiss tantalized him,

the hotter he became. No kiss had ever felt so good. No woman had ever turned him on this much. He had never felt so wanted. He had never wanted a woman so much. In his quest to taste more of her sexy lusciousness, he kissed her harder. He held her tighter, loving the feel of her head laid gently in the crook of his arm. This was a moment he would have to paint, because if he didn't, he would think his mind had only created how gratifying it was. He was actually kissing Shay, holding her. If only he could have made love to her. He wanted to please her so bad. He wanted to feel deep inside her, as deep as her heart would hold him.

Desiring more, his fingers wandered up under the shirt, caressing around her panty line. Braxton halted his movements when he felt her tense up.

He raised his head back, making her lust-drugged eyes part. "Baby, you can feel how much I want you. My body isn't shy when it comes to you. But I'll go as fast or as slow as you want. I just want to be with you, Shay. In whatever way that may be."

"Braxton, you can tell that I want you too. But it's been a long time." She looked down and saw him tenderly holding her hands. She smiled up at him. "I haven't been intimate with a man since Marquis."

Tilting his head, Braxton brought his hands up to her face, cupping it as if it were breakable glass. He was happy about that. "That's all right. Actually, I'm glad. If you do choose to be with me whenever that may be, I guarantee that I won't take that lightly. I'll appreciate it. I'll treat your love like the precious gift it is." Kissing her hand, he stared in her eyes. "I want to make you so happy, Shay. Just give me a chance. I want to share so much with you. So much."

"I want the same." She closed her eyes and opened

them as he kissed her hand again. Everything he did to her drove her crazy.

"I want to show you something."

"What is it?"

Taking her hand, Braxton guided her out of his bedroom and down the hall. They stopped in front of a mysterious room that he had avoided showing her in the tour. After twisting the knob, he opened the door, spreading his hand out for her to enter. "I've never showed anyone this. But I feel I can share this with you."

"Oh, my God!" The astonishment of what she was beholding made Shay clutch her cheek, the beauty of it drawing her into the room as if she were being carried on a magic carpet. Once standing in the midst of it all, the striking paintings surrounding her made Shay feel like she was in another world, an enchanted one. She noticed there were several pictures of the woman in the portrait downstairs. "Is she the woman you were in love with?"

"Yes."

"She sure looks happy in these pictures too." She wanted to ask more about her but decided to wait until he told her about the mystery woman.

As she circled his studio, viewing the numerous portraits, Braxton simply observed her until she stopped at his most recent portrait. "Ain't she fine?"

"It's me! It looks so real. And I'm wearing the gown I wore at the ceremony." Captivated by the image, which looked as lifelike as she did, Shay knelt to read the inscription. "You're Ecstasy!" she burst out, turning to Braxton. "That's how you knew about the father and child in the painting downstairs. That's how you can afford to buy your sister and yourself a mansion. Your paintings sell for hundreds of thousands of dollars."

Loving to see her this excited, Braxton came close to her and the painting. He gazed at the beautiful face he'd drawn. "I do try to capture the images of ecstasy that we all are striving to experience, just like you said earlier. Whether it be a family scene, a baby smiling up at you or even a beautiful woman's eyes when she sees the man who's going to fill her with passion like she's never known." His finger caressed the softness of her cheek. "Each time I feel something that makes me feel ecstasy, when I get the chance, I paint that scene just the way it was. That way it's with me forever. I can take it out and look at it and be there all over again. It's like some force compels me to capture those moments of life that makes us feel so happy we want to hold on to them forever. And one of those moments was in the ballroom when I looked in your eyes." Braxton saw them looking at him in that same way and had to place his mouth against hers. "What are you doing to me?" he breathed.

Shay felt a feather-light pressure on her lips. "The same thing you're doing to me. Braxton, if you love painting as much as it seems like you do, why are you so secretive about your identity? Umm." His lips felt so good to her.

Ever so faintly, his mouth was caressing down the length of her neck. "Because no one understands."

"Umm. I understand." Titillated by his mouth on her neck, she reared her head back, wanting more. "I really do."

"I am my own man." He was kissing his way back to her mouth. "Always have stepped to my own drumbeat and don't give a damn what anyone thinks about it. But my family . . ." Lightly and with pecks, he was enjoying her plump lips again. "My family has such expectations. They're blue-collar workers who worked their butts off to send me to college and give me a better life. It meant everything to them that I became this successful lawyer. They are so proud. I'm the first college grad in the family. They don't know anything about artists, except that most of them die poor. They know my future is secure in the law but art. . . . My mother would worry herself into a stroke if I told her I'm making my living as an artist. It would break their hearts if I left the law to pursue what they feel should be a hobby."

But Shay could hear his own heart breaking with his words. Staring into his handsome face, Shay held it gently. "So you've been thinking about leaving law?"

"Every day of my life. I enjoy it, don't get me wrong. But the feeling, the passion for it isn't strong like it is for my art."

"Then you're in love with it." She fingered across his strong mouth. "So in love with it you could do it for hours and hours, losing yourself in it, finding yourself in it. In your heart you know it's your life's purpose. It's a high like no other to you. Except for sex." She smiled at him.

"You got that right." He grinned. Yet he was amazed. "How do you know those things about me that you just spoke of?"

"Because I just feel like I know you, Braxton. Just like you told me things earlier that made me know you know me too. And I can understand not wanting to hurt your family or let them down. But you can't live their dreams. You have to make you happy. You're a damn good lawyer, but from what I see you're a phenomenal artist. And if creating these works makes you as happy as it does, why is there a choice? You should get up everyday, bouncing out of bed with excitement to do your work. That way you give the world the best of you. God didn't put us here to be miserable. He wants us to seek happiness. To create those scenes just like you do in your paintings."

She was so awesome he raised her hand to his chest. "Feel my heart."

Shay felt a pounding like a crazed machine. "It's racing like you've been running."

"I have. I've been running toward you my whole life, from out there in that big old universe, but I just now caught up with you. No one has ever encouraged me to go after what I truly wanted like you have. Not even . . ." He glimpsed Andrea's portrait across the room. "Not even a woman I loved. She made me promise to be the best lawyer in the world. As wonderful as she was to me, she believed art should be left for a hobby too."

"And you fulfilled the promise to her. Now it's time to fulfill a promise to yourself."

"I'll seriously consider what you've said."

"I'm glad." Her gaze caught a picture of that woman. "Braxton, would you paint me? This is ecstasy we're experiencing. I'm sure there is ecstasy on my face. I see you've done quite a few paintings of that woman. I bet she's the woman you were committed to." She tossed her head toward Andrea's portrait.

Braxton's interest never moved from Shay. "I'd love to paint you."

"Is this okay?" She ran her hand down his shirt.

"It's gorgeous on you. Get on the couch."

Eagerly, Shay did just that, soon stretching out in an ultra seductive pose.

His dimples were grape-deep as he moved toward his easel and paints. "This is going to be hard. Painting you looking like that."

"Why?" she said, changing to different poses, trying to find the right one.

"Because you look so good, I'm going to want to jump on you."

Shay blushed, then revealed her perfect pose. Clutching the arm of the sofa, she sprawled across it with the shirt unbuttoned so that her bra and cleavage were revealed. "How do you like this pose?"

Braxton looked, and kept on looking. "I like it too much. This will be only for our eyes."

"Anything you say," she laughed out, watching him gather his brushes and paints.

Braxton began the portrait. Shay decided to be quiet so he could concentrate. But suddenly after brushing merely two strokes he rushed toward her as if he were saving her from something.

"What's wrong?" she said.

His lips and body smothering hers answered before his voice did. "Shay, you're so beautiful, Shay. So beautiful." Fascinated with her lips, his fingers cradled her face and before long, he thrust his tongue into her mouth as forcefully as his erection bore into the warm flesh of her stomach.

"Oh, Braxton," she whispered, closing her eyes, tasting him, wanting him, feeling him. She put her arms around his shoulders and soon screamed out, "Oh," when his head eased lower and lower, discovering her chest. Kissing the tops of her breasts, he also reached his hand lower and stroked the outside of her panties. "I know you feel so good," he moaned. "Baby, I want to give you ecstasy."

Her hand reached under him, rubbing the huge bulge that was prodding into her flesh. "You are already."

"Can I make love to you, Shay?" He was pinning her hands above her head and trying to kiss her breasts out of her bra.

Shay felt his teeth lightly scraping her cleavage. "Oh, Braxton . . . please. . . ."

* * *

Hours later, Shay lay snuggled next to a sleeping Braxton in his bedroom. They had snuggled, talked, did some light petting and kissed during the night but didn't make love. Still wearing his shirt, while he was still clothed in his sweat pants, she sat up, wondering why such circumstances had to exist between them. Not only was she wondering about the affect the murder situation would have on their relationship but a tiny part of her was wondering if she could fully give herself to Braxton. She knew she was being cautious because of what happened with Marquis. But how could a woman learn to give to one man after she'd been hurt so badly by another?

As they kissed on the studio sofa during the night and later in his bedroom, she had tensed up again, fearful of making love to him. It was her mind and the memories of Marquis's betrayal that prevented her. In her heart and body she was more than willing. She desired Braxton more than she ever had any man in her life. She would say a prayer that everything would work out, and she would feel the joy she knew he could give her.

Pondering this, Shay heard him breathing gently beside her. She couldn't see him because it was so dark in the room, but she couldn't help just touching his bare shoulder. It had been so nice to just lay on his chest, snuggle, talk and kiss the night away. His patience was a good sign to her.

Feeling a need to go to the bathroom, Shay stood and headed toward it. Except the ring of a phone in the hallway stopped her tracks. Braxton continued sleeping as the phone rang, but curious Shay was lured outside the room, toward it. Instinctively, she knew it was someone from the police station calling about her. Who else when it was after midnight and before daylight? Unless it was a lover. She was standing by the phone stand when the answering machine came on.

"What are you getting, your beauty sleep, Steele? This is Jamison. We've been trying to reach you for the longest, but your doggone phone must have been out of order. I want you to get down here. Fast! We got that editor where we want her. The forensics report makes her look as guilty as sin. But we haven't arrested her yet. She wasn't with the doctor she was supposed to be staying with or even her brother. Both those guys have been down here raising sand at the station. So get down here. We're putting out an APB. And if someone's been helping her hide from us, they're going to get it good."

When Braxton woke up, he wore a smile. He hadn't just been dreaming about Shay. She was actually with him. In his bed. Feeling as silly as a kid, he turned toward her side of the bed, planning to tickle her. "Good morning, beautiful."

When there was no response, Braxton sat up. He felt the bed where the covers lay bundled high beside him. Feeling nothing, he pulled them back.

"Shay?" he called and repeated doing so throughout the various rooms he searched for her in. He also peeked out the window and saw that the snow had stopped. Much of it had been cleared away by the plows. He hadn't heard a thing that was happening outside. He had been in an entire other world with Shay.

Finally Braxton returned back to his room. Plopping on the bottom of the bed, he asked, "Where the hell is she?"

The knives were all bloody when the hands lined them along the rusted table in the basement. After their use, the owner didn't want to clean them off. They had to always be that way, soaked with her blood. She wouldn't ignore her special friend anymore.

Braxton rushed in the station house, fighting off myriad reporters in front of the entrance. Jamison's desk was the first place he headed to. "That commotion is your fault!" he blasted, leering down at him.

Jamison shuffled papers in front of him. "What has your pants on fire?"

"The press! We don't need them breathing on down our backs right now. To do our jobs thoroughly, we're going to need as few distractions as possible."

"What do you expect from them? A rich magazine editor killing an ex who is an actor is big news."

Braxton looked disturbed. "You must have gotten the forensics report."

"Of course. Didn't you get my message?"

"No." Wondering where Shay was, he had been too worried to check anything or do much else. Yet as the hours drifted by with no sign of her, he thought he could at least do some good by coming to the station. He was desperate to hear the good news that another set of prints had been found on the murder weapon. "So how interesting did you find the report?"

"Very." Jamison walked over to a nearby file cabinet. "She did it." He tucked a folder inside the metal drawer and slammed the door. "Hers were the only fingerprints on the candlestick."

Braxton looked off, his mind racing. His head snapped back to Jamison as he saw him plunking back down in his chair. "You should have waited until I investigated this further before calling the press. What if the woman is innocent?"

Jamison reared back, studying Braxton for a moment.

A lazy smile, complete with a furrowed brow spread across his face. "She isn't getting to you, is she Steele?"

"Loose ends, that's what gets to me, Jamison. Have you considered that Marquis Jackson's prints should have been on the candlestick too? Surely he had to have grasped it at least on one occasion during the altercation, trying to avoid the blows."

Jamison looked perplexed. He hadn't thought of that. Regardless, he was certain Shay Hilton did it. "You shouldn't be grasping for straws. Let the defense do that. Unless something is making you want to switch sides?" Jamison raised a brow. "And speaking of defense. Here comes her attorney." Jamison tossed his head in the corridor's direction. "They've all been here for a while."

Rakim, Christina and David were hurrying toward Braxton.

Rakim was the first to reach him. "I'm Shay Hilton's brother. I'll also be her attorney. They say you're the prosecutor in this case."

"I am. But I'm still looking into things."

"What kind of things?" David inquired. "Shay couldn't kill anyone."

Braxton watched the doctor's eyes shrink to slits behind the glasses. "I haven't even had a chance to see the forensics report."

Rakim stepped up closer in Braxton's face. "And what about this APB they've just put out on my sister? I want it called off! Right now!"

Braxton spun toward Jamison. "You did that?"

"Look, Steele, no one knows where she is. She wasn't where she was supposed to be. I had to."

"She could get killed!" David yelled, glaring at Braxton and Jamison.

"But she won't," Patman assured them, walking up

among the crowd. "Our officers are specially trained for this."

Christina sucked her tooth. "Pleeassse."

"She's being hunted like an animal," David stated. "And I demand it be stopped!" This time the angry slits behind the glasses were only targeted at Braxton. That was until a headache David felt coming on distracted him, making him rub the side of his face.

"And where is she?" Rakim thought aloud. He wondered if was she hurt. "Where has she been for the last few days?"

Braxton opened his mouth to speak.

"I was stranded in the storm." Shay's voice turned them all around. "You'll find my car on highway 97." She stepped toward them. "I wasn't trying to run. I was just trying to stay safe." She stared at Braxton. "And warm."

Eight

The standard procedures of a suspect undergoing a felony arrest were so degrading and unbelievable to Shay, it felt at times like she were outside of herself during the unfolding of it all. Later, as she sat on an unsheathed cot in a gray, tiny cell, only then did what occurred to her actually have its evolution in her consciousness.

She had actually been arrested, fingerprinted, photographed in mug shots and experienced every other humiliation that those accused of murder were subjected to. She knew it had happened to her, was happening to her, though somehow a part of her refused to believe it. After all she'd accomplished to make a success of her life—college, career, starting a business, dutiful daughter, sister and friend—it was in a jail cell for those not civilized enough to reside with decent people, where she wound up. How was Rakim going to make these people believe she didn't kill Marquis when a murder weapon said she did? How was Braxton going to treat her now?

"Shay?"

Shay's heart jumped not just because she was startled, but because she was so excited to see Braxton approaching the cell. Reaching it, he gestured for the guard at the end of the corridor. A red-haired woman with a stern expression soon stuck her key in the lock. He stepped beyond the bars.

He kept an eye on the guard until he was sure that she returned to her post, then he gave his full attention to Shay. "How are you?"

She couldn't show how hard her heart was pounding. "Just wondering how I got here, that's all."

He searched her angelic face. It was as if sunlight poured over her skin rather than the dullness that reflected from the concrete gray walls. "You look as beautiful as you did by the fireplace."

"Too bad I don't feel like I did then."

Leaning back against the bars, he stuck his hands deep in his pockets. "Why did you leave like that?"

"Because I heard Jamison's message." She had hated leaving him. "And, Braxton, I just don't want to complicate the situation."

"You couldn't even leave me a note? I didn't know if something happened to you or what. You know, I was about to tell them you were with me. But I do believe your telling them that you were stranded in your car is for the better. They would probably take me off the case. And I can help you more if I stay on it."

She was so relieved he hadn't changed his mind about her. Even so, the fear of her fate felt like it was drowning her. "What's going to happen to me?"

Such little-girl fright was on her face, Braxton was tempted to reach down and swallow her in his arms. Except a glance outside the cell showed the guard wasn't as distant as she was at first. "Just trust me, Shay. I'm going to clear you."

"You said that in the house. But now we're here, and I've been arrested for murder because they have evidence. Braxton, you can tell me the truth if you don't believe me now. You can tell me if you've had a change of heart. I can take it. Plus, my brother's going to help me. He promised me he would. He's always been there for me. I can count on him. Can I say the same for you?"

"Mr. Steele, Judge Ornwell would like to see you," the guard said, appearing unexpectedly.

Locking gazes with Shay, Braxton hesitated in making any motion.

"Sir," the guard jarred his attention. "He said it's about this prisoner and it's urgent."

Shay found herself in a courtroom some time later. She was relieved to see Rakim and Christina at her side. David was also seated among the spectators, whose faces she avoided. What she wasn't happy or prepared to see was Braxton's confident, almost arrogant strut across the courtroom. More than that, it felt like he was burying her alive when she heard what came from his mouth.

"The facts of this case are that on the ice-cold day of February 27, 2000, Shay Hilton harbored just as much coldness in her heart for Marquis Carl Jackson. He turned up in her office early in the day after deserting her at the altar three years earlier.

"At that same altar he caused her to lose her baby, had no interest in her well-being and immediately took up with another woman. So when he turned up at the awards ceremony on that night of February 27, his presence again reminded her of what he did to her. That overwhelming hurt that she felt all these years, built up into an uncontrollable rage. I myself heard her scream out at the ceremony that she could kill the now-deceased Mr. Jackson. A roomful of others can testify to hearing her too.

"And later that night when Officer Todd Jamison and a crew of officers turned up in her penthouse, they discovered that is exactly what she did—kill him. She killed him! Shay Hilton, a respected, award-winning magazine owner, whose magazine upholds the institution of love, was filled with hate and killed the now-deceased, Marquis Carl Jackson. Beat him with a candlestick over and over and over until there was nothing but blood and his breathless body. The officers even saw her holding the candlestick that he was bludgeoned to death with. Marquis Jackson wanted to reunite with Ms. Hilton. Ms. Hilton wanted to rid him of her sight forever—and that's what she did. And my assisting counsel and myself are going to prove it."

When bail was mentioned, Rakim held Shay's hand before standing up, addressing the court. "There should be no bail amount set for my client. She should be released on her own recognizance. Shay Hilton is an upstanding member of the community, has never been arrested before, hasn't even had a speeding ticket. She was a successful journalist, providing informative commentary for magazines and newspapers. As well she is now the editor and owner of a highly successful magazine about love and relationships. On the night in question she was even honored at a ceremony for her outstanding achievements. Not only is her magazine full of useful information, but it also provides a substantial amount of jobs for the Englewood Cliffs community. Ms. Hilton would never risk the distinguished life she has built here by fleeing the state or country. Proof of that is her turning herself in to the police station."

After scrawling notes with his veined, freckled hand, Judge Ornwell waved the two attorneys toward the bench. Engaging them in a whispered dialogue for several minutes, he soon allowed Rakim and Braxton to return to their respective seats.

Once they faced him again, Judge Ornwell cleared his throat. "Shay Hilton, please stand."

Trembling, Shay raised up from her seat. *Oh, God, please help me.* She knew she would die right there if he denied her bail.

Judge Ornwell peered at her over his glasses. "It is in the judgment of this court that Ms. Shay Hilton be released under house arrest until and during the trial for the murder of Marquis Carl Jackson. She will not be allowed to leave the town, the state or country."

Succeeding embraces, Rakim, Christina and David immediately ushered Shay to the exit on the side of the courtroom to avoid the press. Before she headed out of the door, her eyes met with Braxton's. He had done his job well. Too well, the emptiness inside her was telling her.

Braxton was still watching the door Shay walked out of when he felt a tap on the back of his shoulder. He turned around.

Jamison was squinting at him angrily. "You know darn well you did a half-ass job! What's going on here? This case isn't at all like the Bolder case. You're not going to find someone else who did it. The evidence is there! Right in your face, Steele. You heard her with your own ears threaten the deceased with murder!" Jamison became annoyed that Braxton was turning away, packing his briefcase. He walked around in front of him. "Myself and the other officers saw her with the murder weapon when we walked in. She probably would have done him again. To top it all, hers are the only prints on the candlestick. What more proof do you need?"

Not looking at him, Braxton continued tucking the documents away. "If she's guilty, justice will be served. I'm only after the truth."

"Huh," Jamison sighed. "The truth is that woman

should be locked up and you had the power to put her there. Why didn't you? House arrest, my foot! With all that dough she has, she could be in China before the trial starts."

"Go do your job, Jamison." Braxton was closing his briefcase.

"I did do my job! I arrested a murderer! You better do better at the trial. You're getting sloppy, Steele. Real sloppy."

Braxton left Jamison standing there fuming. Getting a kick out of leaving him with no one to argue with, Braxton began striding down the aisle, headed out of the courtroom. A man stepping in front of him prevented him from leaving.

"Mr. Steele."

"Yes?" Braxton faced the serious expression of a man wearing an expensive blue suit and with his hair styled in a ponytail. The hair reminded Braxton of the murder victim's coif.

"My name is Eric Lebleau."

Braxton narrowed his eyes, trying to remember where he heard that name before. "You know Shay," he said quickly. He recalled that name in the story Shay had recounted about Marquis and her.

Eric's countenance grew curious. "She spoke of me to you?"

Braxton studied him. "Yes, she did. Told me and an officer that you were the reason she had problems with Marquis."

Eric's lips twisted sourly. "I regret so much that I did that. I was just in love with her, that's all. So in love and I couldn't handle the rejection."

"Wasn't Marquis your best friend? That's what I gathered from the story."

"Yes," he sighed. "We were tight. Knew each other since we were kids. Even dressed and wore our hair alike as you can see." He touched his ponytail. "We did everything together. Did everything to help each other. But when he brought her into our lives, all that went out the window. All I wanted was his woman."

Do you still want her and have you killed for her? "Wow, what a wonderful friend you were."

Eric looked down for a long while before meeting Braxton's scowl. "I know I was wrong. A strong faith in God now helps me see that. But man to man, can you help who you fall in love with?"

Straightaway, Braxton's mind filled with Shay. Was love what was happening to him? He couldn't stop thinking about her, thinking about the woman, not the defendant. He couldn't stop wanting her. He couldn't wait to be alone with her again.

"I guess you can't help it," Braxton answered, "but you can help what you do about it, if the circumstances are such that it would hurt people. But I don't have time to stand here and converse about your morals. What do you have to tell me? Anything relevant to this case?"

"Yes. Shay couldn't kill anyone. That's not in her nature. She loved Marquis too hard to kill him. She's that type of woman. She just loves hard. Any man who is lucky enough to have that love, should know it's a gift."

Since she didn't want to return to the penthouse and was restricted from doing so, Shay needed somewhere to stay. Rakim begged her to stay with him, but she couldn't impose. Although Christina and Rakim were still pretending with her that they were merely close friends who worked together, Shay knew better. What's more, she also knew they were probably using his new condominium as a prehoneymoon suite. Hence, she couldn't intrude.

Neither did she accept David's offer to hang out at his place. There was one special home she wouldn't have minded being in the atmosphere of again. Since that was impossible, she decided to rent a house. Located on the outskirts of town, the house was, Rakim believed, a great hiding place from everyone. To ensure that no one knew anyone was staying there, everyone agreed to park their cars at a distance.

Feeling bewildered by all the traumatic events, Shay let Rakim and Christina make her new living arrangements and assist her in settling in. David stuck by her side for every step, but had to leave her new abode early for a meeting with a client. He promised to visit later.

All in all, by twilight, Shay found herself settled into her new home, but feeling none of the comfort that the love of family and the lenient house arrest should have brought her. She felt dispirited, empty and oddly alone. Not just because of the unfairness of the Marquis nightmare but because of Braxton as well. In the courtroom, she had been mystified as to what he was doing. Was he trying to hurt her or help her? Was what he'd felt for her in his home wearing off? As he dazzled the court, dangling her life as his trophy, it sure seemed that it had.

At the same time, so many other things disputed that he felt that way. He seemed sincere when visiting her in the cell. Then there was the way he looked at her in the court. It filled her with such warmth. Was she just feeling what she wanted to feel? Above all, there were the memories of being with him in his house, his touch, his kisses, his words that touched her soul. And what about that painting, that image of ecstasy that he'd drawn of her? In the portrait her eyes were filled with such emotion. The same emotion that she swore she always beheld in his. Was this all in her mind? Or had she and Braxton begun to touch each other's hearts?

"We're going to the store and get you some groceries," Rakim said, coming out of the kitchen.

Christina was right behind him. "There's nothing in there, hon. The fridge is empty."

Shay sat up from the white sofa cushions where she'd been laying. "I don't feel like going shopping. I'm not in the mood to get harassed."

Rakim pinched her chin. "You're not going. Me and Chrissy are going to go get you some good munchies down at the supermarket at the mall."

Christina fluffed a pillow behind Shay's back. "You just rest here."

"Thank you guys." Looking up at both of them, Shay grabbed each one of their hands. "I don't know what I would do without you. Rakim, I'm sorry this happened. I . . ." Shay felt the tension behind her eyes and knew she couldn't hold the tears back any longer.

As if his sister were about to splinter into a thousand pieces, Rakim raced to her, squeezing her tightly in his arms. "It's all right. I'm going to get you out of this. You know I'll never let you down. You know that. Hold on. Just hold on a little bit longer."

While Christina and Rakim were out shopping, Shay was determined to put herself in better spirits. She was checking out the house and found that she really liked the way the white, beige and pastel pink hues splashed over ultramodern furnishings. It made her feel cozy. Exploring her surroundings further, she saw a pile of garbage. It was all those empty boxes from the Chinese food they'd ordered and ate while getting her settled in. Unlike the other scentless rooms, the kitchen smelled spicy and lived in because of the food's lingering smell.

Opening the front door, Shay lugged the sack of garbage down the pebbled walkway. After depositing it, she took in the view of the darkening sky and took a deep breath of the cool night air. It was astounding to her that a few days ago there was a blizzard. Now much of the snow had melted. Odd too, the air seemed much warmer than it should have for this time of year.

A rustling in the tall bushes to her right distracted Shay, luring her gaze in that direction. "Christina, Rakim, are you two over there? Are you smooching? Because I know the real deal. You two are much more than friends."

When no one responded, Shay assumed it was a squirrel, cat or dog. She went back inside. Heading toward the stairs, a knock brought her back toward the door.

"Who is it?" she asked. There was no peephole or nearby window.

"It's me" a muffled man's voice answered.

Rakim must have forgotten the key, she thought, opening the door.

Shock raised her brows beholding this visitor. "Braxton."

"Hello, beautiful."

The way he was looking at her truly did make her feel so beautiful. It made her feel as if he in his heart believed she was incredibly beautiful. But didn't his courtroom performance prove he was merely being charming and deceitful? "So the judge told you where I would be undergoing my house arrest?"

He hated that sad tone in her voice and hated even more that he'd put it there. "I know what you're thinking. You're thinking I was a little too good in the courtroom. But I had to show that I'm seeking the truth, which is my job. And in seeking that truth, I'm going to help you."

"Help me! You didn't sound like you were helping me in that courtroom today. You sounded like the enemy about to slaughter me." Turning her back to him, she shook her head.

Gently by the arms, Braxton curved her around. Looking in her eyes, he detected her weakness, the same aroused weakness he felt for her. "I'm not the enemy. I wouldn't have risked coming here tonight if I was. I had to see you." He gazed at her lips. They were in that angry circle. "I had to assure you that I'm working to clear you. I want to find out who was in that penthouse with you and Marquis. They could have killed you too. I'm seeking truth. And the truth is you didn't kill Marquis Jackson. If you were striking him why weren't his prints on the candlestick as he tried to defend himself? What I interpreted from the forensics report I read is that Marquis was bludgeoned at your penthouse, then the killer wiped his prints off of the candlestick, then smeared Marquis's blood back on it, then placed your hands around it. It also doesn't make sense that a woman of your average size could beat a man so brutally. The force of the blows and your estimated strength just doesn't add up. You didn't even have any wounds to indicate that he may have struck you back."

"That's all true!" Shay looked enlivened. She even smiled for the first time since he entered the room. "You've really looked into this, haven't you?"

"Yes, I have. I told you I'm going to clear you. Someone framed you and I will find out who. Just bear with me. It may look like I'm on the other side, but I'm on your side, and the side of the truth. Just don't stop believing in me."

"I won't." It made all this difference in the world that

he told her all this. He really did care. It made him look even more beautiful to her.

"I missed you," he confessed. "My house hasn't been the same since you left it. When I get a chance, I'm going to paint all that sugar we had in the house."

Shay was glowing. "I missed you, too. I wish I could stay there."

He chuckled. "Jamison would go straight after my disbarment if I did that. A suspect living with the prosecutor." He couldn't resist placing his hands on her shoulders. Even there, she was so beautiful, so soft, so womanly.

She paused at the sweet feeling of him touching her again. "You could get disbarred for doing something else, couldn't you?" She was looking at his mouth, hungry for it.

"Like what?" he said, his eyes lingering on her lips too. "Doing this?" Still holding her shoulders, he bent his head and placed his mouth ever so carefully atop hers. Their wordplay aside, Braxton knew kissing her was an offense of his oath as a prosecutor, but God help him, some things were worth risks. The taste of her, the smell of her like strawberries and the feel of her as he brought his arms around her were wonderful enough for him to have died for.

Feeling her head being swayed by the potent force of his mouth against hers, Shay thought that his deliciousness was worth dying for too. Life had been unkind to her lately, but she had to admit she was receiving a gift that was so much of a blessing, nothing in her life had ever felt better. Except maybe if they were to make love.

"Braxton, I'm aching to feel you," she managed between the powerful force of his lips. "I don't want to hold back anymore. I'm so ready for you. I want you."

"You want what!"

Shay was startled away from Braxton by Rakim's enraged voice. Not only had he entered the house with

Christina, but David had happened to return at the same time also. All three stared openmouthed at Shay and Braxton.

"What the hell are you doing?" Rakim dumped a bag of groceries on the couch, freeing his hands as he charged at Braxton.

Shay jumped between them. "Rakim, I have to explain something to you."

"There is nothing to explain!" He frowned, looking over her head at Braxton. "You're always in the papers with the ladies! But this one, you are not going to have!"

"Let me explain, man," Braxton tried to reason.

"Explain what! You can't keep your hands off the women, not even one you're legally supposed to keep your hands off." Rakim tried to come at Braxton again.

Shay's outstretched arms kept them apart. "Rakim, Braxton and I are working together."

"What?" Christina came closer to the commotion. "You are working together?"

"Shay, he's running a game on you," Rakim stressed. "And I won't stand for it."

"I'm not playing any game," Braxton insisted. "I'll tell you my plan if you give me a chance. All I want to do is help Shay. I know she's innocent."

Rakim waved his hands. "No, no. You're definitely up to something, my brother. But I tell you one thing, failure to act in your capacity as a prosecutor is a disbarrable offense."

"I am acting in my capacity as a prosecutor," Braxton corrected. "I'm seeking the truth."

Rakim's eyes narrowed. "Are you going to find it by kissing the defendant in your case?"

"Let me talk to him," Shay appealed to Braxton. "We'll talk later. I have your numbers."

Rakim shook his head. "What has he done to you?"

"We've come to know each other," Braxton answered. "We know each other in a way that is so rare. And I won't rest until I find out who really killed Marquis Jackson and clear your sister of these charges. I'll leave because Shay wants me to. But I'll be back. And I'm going to have something that's going to help her." Tenderly, he gazed in Shay's eyes. "I'll call you tonight."

Braxton left the house. Knowing he had to be discreet, he scanned the area to detect if there was anyone who could see him. Grateful that there wasn't anyone, he strode a great distance from the house quickly to the hidden area where his car was parked. Hurrying toward it and glancing around, he contemplated his moves in the investigation. First was visiting Eric Lebleau. After court, Braxton had done some checking on him. Some interesting information had turned up. He would have shared it with Shay but didn't want to get her hopes up without something substantial that would have linked Eric to the murder.

Reaching his wheels, Braxton bent down to get inside. However, a familiar face his eye happened to capture halted him. From across the highway near a grove, David had been watching him. He was standing beside what must have been his own car.

From Braxton's view, David didn't look happy. Nevertheless, Braxton didn't have time to entertain him with a sparring match as he had Rakim. He had things to do. He had to catch a killer. Intent on doing just that, Braxton sped off in his car.

"Where's David?" Shay asked, noticing that he'd vanished from sight. Suddenly it dawned on her how hurt he must have been seeing her kissing Braxton. "Oh, no, he must be so mad."

"He left," Christina told her. "And he didn't look happy. He went outside right in the middle of that little . . . mess."

"It's a mess all right," Rakim said, gawking at Shay. "What is going on? How do you even know that man well enough for him to have his lips on you?"

"Calm down," Shay insisted. As much as she loved her brother and as wonderful as he'd been to her, sometimes his protectiveness did get on her nerves. Now was one of those times. "Braxton rescued me when I was stranded in the storm."

Rakim eyed her suspiciously. "What do you mean *rescued* you?"

Shay took a seat, telling Rakim and Christina about how she and Braxton wound up together in his house and how they became friends. Because of Rakim's distrust of Braxton, she excluded any hints of a romance between them. She concluded by saying that she wholeheartedly believed Braxton was on her side.

"That's bull!" Rakim swore. "He was trying to keep you from escaping so he could make his big score."

"He wasn't. He really wanted to help me."

"He wanted to help you all right. Help you get out of your clothes, then help you go to jail!"

Huffing in frustration, Shay ran her fingers through her hair and shook her head. What could she say when he wouldn't listen?

Rearing back, eyeing Rakim, Christina propped a hand on her hip. "Now why do you have to go there? You're not listening to her, Rakim. The guy might be on the level."

"You're buying his act too? He's trying to get what he

can, and he's trying to win the case by all means necessary. I really should tell the judge about all this."

"And how will that help your sister?" Christina pointed out.

Shay couldn't believe he was acting like this. "That would make it worse for me."

Rakim knew they were right. "All right. I won't tell anyone. But I don't trust him, and you're not going to see him again."

Shay raised her brows at his nerve. "You don't tell me what to do."

"I am now. I'm not only your brother but your lawyer. And if I'm going to get you out of this madness, then you will do as I say."

"I will not if that means staying away from Braxton."

Rakim widened his eyes. "Listen to you. What has that man done to you?"

Christina could only imagine. She couldn't wait to get Shay alone to talk. "Ease up, Rakim."

"No! I'm not letting you see that man!"

"You're not letting me? You're not telling me what to do! You're not my father."

"I still know what's good for you."

"No, you don't!"

"Shay, you're getting into a mess."

"You're one to talk. What about your mess?"

"What mess?"

"The mess you're in the middle of, the one with your wife and my best friend! I know what's going on, Rakim!"

Shay saw the awkward looks on Christina's and Rakim's faces and immediately regretted getting so emotional she didn't think about what she was saying. "I'm sorry. I didn't mean to judge you two. But I do know that you're involved. And I'm glad you have such deep feelings for each other. I just want things to be straightened out with Janet. As much as I love you both, I feel for her too." She looked specifically at Rakim. "I really feel you should get a divorce and work on being friends with her as you depart. It's not good to leave things so ugly when you and someone have shared a portion of your lives together, not if you can help it. Believe me, I know. Besides that, if you don't part the right way . . . well, I just get a bad feeling about it. Something doesn't feel right about it."

Rakim's expression softened. "I have filed for divorce. And I won't take lightly anything you've said."

"I'm glad. For both of you."

"And I'm sorry I came down so hard on you. I just don't want your life to be ruined over all this."

"I know."

"Shay, I don't want you to get hurt again."

She hugged him. "I won't."

Separating from her, he pecked her on the forehead. "I'm going for a walk. I need to think about some strategies for the case."

While Rakim was out, Shay lounged upstairs in the bedroom to meditate. She was too wound up to sleep. When Christina sashayed in with a slice of pineapple cheesecake for both of them, it made Shay feel all the better.

Handing Shay her portion, Christina joined her on the bed, sticking her fork into her first chunk.

"Mmm," Shay cooed, chewing the scrumptious dessert. "You bought this at the mall?"

Christina swallowed the piece she was munching on. "I bought two of them. The other one has strawberries on it."

"Ooh, girl, you sure know what it takes to make me feel better."

"I bet somebody else knows better." Playing with her fork against her tongue, Christina gave her a cunning look.

Shay grinned. "I don't know what you're talking about."

"Oh, yes, you do."

"I don't know a thing." Shay was steadily nibbling.

Christina leaned toward her. "You got some, didn't you? And it was *real, real* good, wasn't it?"

Shay laughed. "I didn't."

"Yes, you did. I can tell." Christina's little eyes shrunk smaller as she scrutinized her. "And after it's been so long, you needed some."

Shay was cracking up. Christina always made her laugh. "No, honestly, I didn't."

Christina shot her a furtive look. "For real?"

"For real." Shay picked at the pineapples, plunking a snippet in her mouth.

"Now fine as that man is and as much as I can tell something hot is going on between you two, why didn't you? Is it because deep down you don't trust him?"

Shay looked at her sincerely. "I'll put it this way. We kissed and kissed and I've never been kissed like that before." She paused, remembering how good it was. "We touched." She tingled, recalling the tenderness and sensualness of his stroking her. "And we talked until it was like we shared one soul. Never have I felt like I've known someone my whole life, but on the other hand, I'm just beginning a wonderful adventure into that person, discovering him, and him discovering me, the best of me, the best of him, and bringing out the best in each other."

"Wow." Christina was resting her chin in one of her palms, forgetting all about her half-eaten cake.

"And we even slept in the same bed together, but I wasn't ready. Maybe deep down I just needed to be more sure he was the one."

"Are you sure now?" But Christina already had her

answer in the way Shay's eyes responded to the question. They were glistening. Wet with excitement and emotion.

"I'll admit that I was a bit confused. But I'm not anymore." Shay could see him right at that moment. She could feel his heartbeat the way it had beat against hers.

Shay wanted to share the thrill about Braxton's art. But since he wasn't ready for the world to know about his talent, she would keep his beautiful secret. Although she did tell Christina many wonderful things about their short time together. The conversation was lengthy and their chatter eventually led to other topics, such as the nightmare of this Marquis murder. When Shay was almost in tears, Christina thought of something she believed would make Shay think of something besides her own problems. She told her about Janet's unexpected visit to Rakim's condo, complete with all the dramatics.

Concluding the story, Christina sighed. "And when the snowplows had cleared the streets, we all went out to the cars. She got in hers, and Rakim and me got in his, and both cars drove their own way."

Shay was placing her empty dessert plate aside on the night table when Christina finished. "Janet must have wanted to run you over with her car after all that."

Christina nodded. "I bet she did. It was a real mess."

"Sounds like it was. But, Chrissy, why didn't you tell me?"

"About me and Rakim?"

"Yes. I thought I'm your best friend."

"You are."

"Then why didn't you tell me you and my brother were lovers? I already knew. I wasn't blind to what I was seeing. But I wanted you two to tell me."

Christina hunched her shoulders. "I guess I was embarrassed about. . . ." She searched for the right words.

"You mean after all those talks we had about us never messing with another woman's husband. Women should never do that to each other. It's so wrong we're above it."

"Yes. But I really shouldn't be embarrassed. Rakim was separated before we became intimate. Separated and had filed for divorce."

"Then you have nothing to feel bad about or worry about except. . . ." Shay didn't want to put a dark cloud over their relationship, but there was something that just didn't feel right. She had talked to Janet. Her love, or whatever it was she felt for Rakim, was such that it was kind of frightening.

"Go ahead and say what you were going to say," Christina urged.

"It's nothing."

"It is something. Shay, what were you going to say?"

"I don't want to put anything negative over your romance."

"Girl, will you just say it."

Shay took a deep breath. "Okay, it's nothing more than I said earlier. I think Rakim should straighten things out with Janet and part with her on good terms. I know now that it's very important how you break up with someone you've spent a portion of your life with. You don't just discard them, slap their dust off your hands and walk away. There is a human heart that has been handed to you gently, and you have to hand it back, just as gently."

"I guess that's a love lesson you learned."

"Oh, yes. And I want Rakim to heed it. Especially since I heard what happened at his house. I know that he really needs to get things straight with her. Because if he doesn't, he won't have any peace. Janet won't give him any."

Nine

Reliving the unforgettable scenes she'd endured at Rakim's house, Janet stood on her terrace, staring into the dark. Shortly after returning home from what had to be the most agonizing hours of her life, she sought seclusion there. For hours she'd been standing in one place, gripping the railing.

Victoria, who ordered Janet's maid and chauffeur to leave early because she couldn't bear them seeing her daughter on the verge of a breakdown, had consistently attempted to get Janet to come inside. Janet wouldn't stir in the slightest. It made Victoria grow more worried with each second. Janet hadn't changed the clothes she'd worn out the other night. She refused to eat. She wouldn't even share with her what happened once she confronted Rakim and his mistress.

Janet's expression cried to her mother what her voice couldn't. Never had Victoria seen her child like this—so helpless. If only she had a clue how to remove her suffering, she would have paid every million she had.

Earlier in the day, the air had been peculiarly warm for this time of year. That was why Victoria wasn't firmer about Janet coming in the house. However, early evening had brought with it a chill that was sure to wreak sickness on her body as much as Rakim had done to her mind.

"Please come inside," Victoria pleaded. Fumbling with her hands, she eased behind her much-taller daughter. "If you still don't want to eat, let's at least have a cup of your favorite herbal tea. I have that hard-to-find brand that smells like rose hips, but tastes like sangria. The one that relaxes you."

Janet didn't move, not even to acknowledge her mother's presence. "I don't want anything."

"Aren't you tired of standing here?"

"No."

"Aren't you getting cold?" Victoria was. She pulled her shawl higher on her firm, thick shoulders.

"I'm not cold, Mother."

"But it's getting colder out here. You're going to get sick like this." She reached up to tug her daughter's collar upward but was astounded by the condition of her hair. "Oh, Lord! Oh, my Lord!" She had noticed Janet's hair was slightly disheveled when she returned to the mansion. The missing clunks of hair she had not seen.

"Did he strike you? Beat you up? Pull your hair out of your head?" Victoria was shaking she was so furious. "Answer me!" She dug her fingers in Janet's upper arms, wrestling her around until they faced each other. "Darling, what has he done to you?"

Janet dropped to her knees as if she were about to say a prayer. Screams wailed from her instead.

"Mother, why! Why doesn't he love me anymore? If he really loved me he could forgive me for my faults. Why! Please, tell me why he doesn't love me. Not anymore. Not anymore."

Getting on her knees, a position her limbs had been too stiff to perform in years, Victoria Sheridan didn't cry outwardly with her daughter. Holding Janet as tight as her strength would allow, her tears remained inside. They were sealed within the ice-cold malice she harbored for Rakim Hilton. She didn't know why Rakim felt no love for her exquisite jewel anymore, the most precious dream she'd ever had come true, her only child. But she did know one thing. Rakim Hilton would pay for Janet's suffering. He would cry, too.

Rakim and Christina rode down the lonesome highway, their Mercedes's taillights illuminating the nightfall like Christmas lights. Shay watched from her walkway, feeling alone when there was no longer any sight of them. It had gotten colder, she thought, rubbing the sides of her chilled bumped arms. She hurried back down the pebbled pathway to her door. A rustling stalled her from going in the house.

Shay's eyes clung to the bushes the noise came from, the same place it had came from before. This time Shay plodded up to the area, searching for the little critter that adored the land around her new home so. Footprints were what she discovered in the stubborn, leftover snow. Not an animal's imprints but a man's. They were big enough for a man. They could have been Rakim's, Braxton's or even David's. All of them were at the house during the day. So why couldn't she help wondering if they were someone else's?

Shay rushed in the house, locking the door behind her. When she was finished, she examined the door, inspecting if it would be difficult for an intruder to open. Fingers mashing into the back of her shoulders made her jump around.

"Oh! Whooh." She exhaled, seeing David. "You scared me." She laid her hand against her heaving chest. "For a minute there, I thought that the person who killed Marquis was coming to get me too. But I'm sure it was someone just after him. If he was capable of treating me the way he did, who knows what he did to other people."

"Yes, who knows."

"But how did you get in here anyway? You surely didn't pass by me."

"I came in the back door. Rakim or Christina must have had it opened and forgot to lock it. Do you have a problem with my being here?"

"No," she said, noticing an unpleasantness in his expression that matched his voice. His overall demeanor was frigid. She could guess why.

"David, I'm so sorry if you seeing me and Braxton kissing upset you. I would never hurt you intentionally. I care about you so much. I love you like my own bro—"

"I could care less about you and him," David cut her off. "When I heard what sounded like a family squabble between you and Rakim, I headed down the road where I parked my car. That's why I left. The alarm had been giving me trouble, and I thought it would be a good time to check on it. And I just stopped by anyway to see if you were all right. I told you I'd be back after leaving my client."

"Yes, I'm fine," she said. Although observing his eyes, she questioned whether he was feeling well. Beyond his glasses they appeared almost squeezed shut, much like he was in discomfort or extremely angry. "Are *you* all right?"

"Great."

"Good. But about Braxton, I—"

"I don't want to hear it, Shay!"

"Okay. I just want you to know that you mean the world to me. I would do absolutely anything in this world for you. I don't want what you saw to interfere with our friendship. And you said it wouldn't. You said that if I had a relationship with someone else, you would still want to be in my life. What we have is so special you can't throw it away."

"I won't."

"Do you mean that?"

"Yes, I mean it. I mean it! I mean it! I mean it! *How could you screwing a jerk ruin our friendship?*"

Shay winced, stunned at the outburst. Where had those nasty words and that rage came from? It certainly hadn't come from David.

"Forgive me," he apologized. "You know I would normally never say anything like that to you. It's just that I've been getting these headaches lately. I had them last year, and now they've come back. They've been . . . they've been stressing me. I'll see you later." Swiftly, he unlocked her door.

"Hope you feel better," Shay yelled to him. He was hurrying away, and she knew she should have gone after him. Oddly, she felt afraid to.

It was astounding that David could blow up at her like that. It also hurt her. For she truly did love him. How could she not after he'd been so kind to her? When she told him she loved him, it wasn't a lie to assuage him or lessen her feeling of guilt about not loving him like he loved her. This was all a matter of the love lessons that her mother once enlightened her about. Shay was too young then to understand the wisdom. Now she fathomed it all too well. "You can't tell your heart who to love," her mother's soft voice stroked her. "It does the choosing. Who you fall in love with, you can't control."

Moments later, Shay's bare feet thumped across the cool, slick tile of her bedroom's bathroom. After turning on the water, she squirted a strawberry bath splash under the running stream. Instantly, the fruity scent became so potent she wished she could taste the air. Delighting in the immense powder-room space, mirrored walls and peach colored Jacuzzi, Shay shed her clothing. Carelessly, they sailed to the floor.

When the fragrant strawberry foam was about to spill out of the tub, Shay twisted the crystal knobs, turning everything off. Intending to luxuriate in every second of this private indulgence, she languidly dipped her body within the glittery white bubbles. Before long, they tickled her chin.

"Oh, this feels too good," Shay purred, closing her eyes. The moment was so blissful that the episode with David began to dissolve from her mind. Even the Marquis tragedy began to coast distantly in her thoughts. Because she felt this pampered, soft and relaxed, her emotions conquered her being, willing her to think of solely one beautiful creature.

"Braxton, I wish you were here," she whispered. "If I could just see you or hear your voice, I'd be all right."

As if he'd heard her, the phone began ringing. Located in the hallway, it startled Shay. It was the first time her new phone line rang today. Although she didn't want to get out of the warm, soothing water, her anxiousness to talk to Braxton overrode it. It could have been him. He said he would call. Dripping, she raced out of the tub.

"Hello?"

She heard nothing.

"Hello?" She greeted the caller more loudly in case they hadn't heard her.

Again, no one spoke.

"Hello?"

Getting no response again made her slam the phone down at the annoying caller and dial *69. The number came up unavailable. She hated when people had nothing better to do than play on the telephone like that. It was such a waste of precious time. Someone had aggravated her like that over the last few months at her office. Each time she dialed *69, their number would turn up unavailable then, too. Never had it happened at her home. Her office number was listed in the magazine's masthead, and that's probably where they saw it. Her phone number at the penthouse was unlisted. For this one, she'd requested the same. So how did some stranger get this one? It could have been a random caller who happened to dial her number. Or could it have been someone else—someone who knew exactly who he was calling?

And she never did determine whose footprints were outside by the bushes. There was no need for anyone to be near those bushes. It was well away from the walkway.

A little too much imagination started messing with the calm the bath had bestowed on her. What if that was Marquis's killer checking to see if she was home, so he could come and get her? Maybe he thought she'd seen him or her. What if those footprints outside were his? Could he get in her house?

After concluding her safety check and finding everything secure, Shay was grateful to return to her cozy bedroom. Having lost the mood for a bath, she headed straight for the dresser to find something soft and sheer to sleep in. As she wiggled a tiny nightie over her head, feeling the soothing fabric caress her skin, she heard the knocker on her front door. Since Braxton was going to call her, it couldn't have been him. Rakim and Christina had keys. Unless it was David returning, she doubted anyone else would visit. Fearing the visitor, she slipped on her kimono. Cautiously, she headed downstairs to the front door.

"Who is it?"

"It's me."

Shay swung open the door and beheld a much-desired gift waiting on her doorstep.

After kicking the door shut, Braxton hugged her so tight Shay didn't know whose heart was pounding so frenetically. There was solely one beat.

"I couldn't stop thinking about you," he professed, leaning back to look at her beautiful face. It always looked so sensual to him, the look of her lips, eyes and skin, like she was always ready for love. He hoped tonight to give her that love.

So glad to see him, she couldn't stop smiling. "You've been on my mind all night too."

He breathed in her delicious fragrance. "Oh, God, you smell good." He had to find out if she smelled that sweet all over. And if she tasted as good as she smelled.

"You always smell good." She inhaled the woods and pinewood scent that she always smelled all over him and all over his house.

"I have some news."

"What?" She could tell by the look on her face that it was something good.

He shared with her about Eric Lebleau's appearance in the courtroom and that he'd done some research on him. Braxton had discovered that Eric was a financial assistant to a minister as of a month ago. Interestingly enough, he handled the church's business affairs, not only at a church office, but at his private office, a commercial property in the same building Shay's penthouse was in. What's more, security traffic sheets showed Eric in the building during the time of the murder.

Shay was shocked. She never knew Eric had an office in her building. After the eruption between Marquis and him, he'd left Englewood Cliffs and moved to Maryland.

"Security also provided me with a copy of all the records during that night," Braxton went on. "Seems that Marquis paid off a guard, with money and an autograph, stating he was your brother surprising you. That's how he allowed him access upstairs to your place. Otherwise, they would have intercomed you. And entry was easy, since your keys were in the outside lock.

"But also, as unprofessional as it is, security would not notify the tenants when someone was visiting that they'd seen before. Of course, since all the heat has come down about this murder, everyone will have to sign in and the tenant notified even if the person is a well-known face visiting the building."

Shay was shocked. She'd never seen Eric in her building. She thought he was still in Maryland. "So you think Eric might have done it?"

"It's a possibility. From what I gather, he and Marquis had no love lost between them."

"But Marquis said that Eric called him to his bedside when he thought he was dying and told him the truth. Would he have done that if he were planning to kill him? Plus, he's supposedly religious now."

"Hey, who knows what goes through a guy's mind when he's insanely jealous over a woman." He thought about David. That expression of his when he watched him from the grove was unforgettable.

"Eric was quite—"

"Obsessed with you?"

"Yes."

Braxton elaborated on his investigation of the murder with his other findings. He'd also come across that Marquis had a falling out with his agent in California, a man whose gangster family had threatened him more than once. Further, there was the woman he'd abandoned Shay for at the altar, Vanessa Collier. On several occasions the

Los Angeles police had been called to the common law couple's home for violence—her violence against Marquis. Braxton added to his discoveries the medical examiner's findings, showing several inconsistencies that questioned whether she could have committed the murder. Braxton handed Shay a forty-page report he'd compiled.

She was ecstatic he'd put forth so much effort to help her. Most of his day had been devoted to her. She was on his mind as much as he'd been on hers. Did this mean his feelings were as deep as she was realizing hers were? "Braxton, I can't thank you enough."

"Don't thank me yet. I still have work to do. I have to see Eric. He wasn't where his secretary said he should have been according to his schedule. But I will catch up with him. I'd like to see his alibi."

"I feel so secure with you on my side. I really believe you will find the killer."

Tilting his head, staring at the face he couldn't get out of his mind, he cupped it in his palms. "I will. I promise I will. But for now, let's forget about all this. Let's concentrate on you and me."

She slid her palm across his chest. "I think that's a wonderful idea." She could feel the prominent muscles through his jacket and shirt. "I'd like to concentrate on you all night. Think you can handle that?"

"I know I can. Did you mean what you said earlier?"

"What did I say?"

"That you wanted me?"

Turned on by the heated look in his eyes, she moved her hands from his chest down to his writhing stomach. "I never meant anything more."

Crushing his lips against hers, Braxton picked Shay up. Smothered in the glorious feeling of his brawny arms, she soon felt his tongue swirling in her nectar. The desire in her sensual core rose to an unbearable peak with each erotic maneuver that they endowed the other with. She had to have him. Had to have him, her body cried with soaking need, as she felt herself being carried up the stairs.

Happy he found her room quickly, she was laid gently on the bed. Aching for him to satisfy the hunger that he caused, she watched him standing above her at the side. Silently staring at her, he quickly removed his jacket and shirt. When he lifted his T-shirt over his head, her breath thickened at the broadness and musculature of his chest. That I'm-going-to-drive-you-out-of-your-mind way he was looking at her heightened her arousal for him.

His pants couldn't come down his legs soon enough. Sexy, athletic thighs and legs made her fingers tremble to touch them. Instead, she restrained herself with patience. It was lost when his tiny black briefs came off.

Shay's mouth opened as wide as her eyes. Braxton was blessed. *Extraordinarily, extraordinarily* blessed. "Braxton, you're so gorgeous."

Painstakingly, he assisted her out of the kimono that hid too much of the enticing body. "You're so gorgeous too."

His eyes scattering all over her clad in the little teddy, he looked even more beautiful as he slid next to her. The expression in his eyes made her feel more womanly, feminine and sexier than she'd ever felt.

"I want to be inside you so bad, Shay."

Thrilling her with quick, tiny kisses on her face and neck, his hands fondled a stimulating trail down to the top of her short negligee. He swiftly lowered the straps, and the sensual deftness of Braxton's fingertips carried her further toward that daring cliff of sexual hunger. She could tell by the way he did just that, that his eyes didn't merely promise that he would drive her out of her mind.

He was already doing it. It had been so long since she had such an awakening as a woman, since she had desired to feel a man within her, since she felt that the man she was with had touched her soul. Never had she known a man like Braxton. It was so wonderful to be laying within his arms. This was one of those moments to capture, an undeniable image of ecstasy.

"Braxton," she whimpered, rubbing his back and swaying as her freed breasts were kissed so amorously by him. "Oh, baby." It felt so good that she couldn't be still. Delirious, she squirmed and stroked him wherever the maddening sensations would allow her hands to roam.

His chest—she couldn't touch enough of it. It was so sexy. He was so masculine it was overwhelming. His entire body—her fingers went wandering over it. They ceased when it she reached his stone-stiff erection. Incredibly long as he was, she took her time in pleasing him.

"Oh, God," Braxton cried out, loving her touch. When he felt it was becoming so unbearably pleasurable that he might release his joy without even giving her himself, he maneuvered out of her grasp and completed undressing her.

Kissing her as he slid off her teddy, he was more excited than he had ever been, when he beheld her full nudity. "You're so damn beautiful," he breathed, staring at her. Perspiration was popping all over his body. "So, so beautiful." Merely looking at her made him feel like he was on fire.

Shay loved the lust beaming from him at her. She loved turning him on. She loved even more when he became bolder in loving her. Reaching up, squeezing her nipples, his head swayed across her stomach as he kissed lower and lower. Biting her lips from the rapture and anticipation of what was to come, she soon felt the sweet pressure of his mouth against her soft folds. She screamed and raised her hips from the surprise of his tongue, then the excruciating pleasure he began delighting her with.

"Braxton," she called out in sweet agony. "Braxton, you're driving me crazy."

"That's what I'm here for," he breathed between kisses of her soft place. "I'm here to make you happy. And I'm about to make you happier."

He rose, bringing his sweaty face level with hers. "I know it's been a long time since you've been with a man. Are you sure you want me to. . . ."

He couldn't finish speaking because her suddenly caressing his hardness felt so good. He tensed his face up as if in anguish. "Oh . . . do you still want . . . oh. . . ."

"Yes, I want you. Please, love me."

Kissing her deeply, Braxton shifted his strong body atop the softness of hers. Shay weakened with each kiss, feeling her lower body moistening like cream with desire. Then finally, Braxton played with her tiny opening, caressing it, squeezing it and sliding his fingers inside before easing her legs apart.

With the tip of himself he penetrated slowly, carefully, kissing her face, her neck and breasts to lessen any pain that she might experience. But witnessing her reaction, as he felt the indescribable sensation of finally being inside her, Braxton was assured he wasn't hurting her. Erotically swaying her hips, Shay was welcoming him deeper and deeper and deeper inside her love. Feeling he could go no deeper, he finally lost control, moving gently at first, then as if he would never get enough of what had to be a gift of ecstasy unlike any other. Shay was the most precious gift he'd ever received. Never could he let this woman go. He had to have her all the time. This maddeningly good loving and this woman, her heart and her soul.

"You feel *so* good," he moaned, thrusting forcefully. "Oh . . . I can't take it! What are you doing to me?"

"Braxton, I love it too." She could hardly catch her breath. She could hardly open her eyes she was drowning in such pleasure. Putting her arms around his neck, she pulled him deeper and deeper. Moving, giving as much as she could give, she became hotter.

Braxton began to shake, his muscles seeming to be in near convulsions. "Oh, God. I'm coming, baby. I'm coming hard! Oh, God! Oh, God! I . . ."

Shay held on, feeling every bit of the earth moving as he did. Never had she felt such ecstasy. Never had she felt so loved. Every fiber of their passion screeched that they were made for each other. In their bodies, in their souls, and Shay knew, in her heart. She hadn't said it, but she was so in love with Braxton, she ached when he finally let go of her. He seemed to feel the same. Though he hadn't said it. So did he? Did he love her too? And not just the passion that just transported them to a place she had never known, but did he love her?

"I love you, Shay," he confessed, as if he heard the question in her mind. Sweating and breathing hard, he stared in her eyes. "I love you so much. My heart is just so full." He touched it, then placed her hand against it. "I love you. Not just your sweet love. I love that a whole lot too. Boy, do I love it." His dimples pinched his cheeks, then faded with his seriousness. "But I really, truly love you. I love you so much, Shay."

Tears seeping into her eyes from the emotion she felt from him, she held his face in her hands. "Baby, I love you too. I'm deeply in love with you."

After making love several more times during the night, Braxton was still sleeping when the sunrise brightened the bedroom with its vibrant yellow cast. For someone facing a murder rap, Shay found herself bouncing up into a sitting position with energy that she hadn't felt since she was a teenager. After staring over at Braxton for a long while, admiring how fine he was and wondering how she got so lucky, she sprang up from the bed, geared for action. She felt like climbing Mount Everest. She felt like skiing down the tallest slope on earth. She felt like doing cartwheels. She settled for going jogging instead.

Surely a bit of exercise on and near her property wouldn't hurt, Shay thought, heading outside. Besides no one lived in the vicinity. The nearest home was about a half mile away, which was good for her. Until this case was over and she was cleared as a suspect, she had to maintain a low profile.

Breathing in the fresh morning air, she was appreciative that only snippets of snow were left. Equally, she was happy it was another day like the previous one. Again, it was much warmer than it should have been. All she wore was a body-clinging black knit jumpsuit with a light gray sweat jacket.

Shay proceeded to do her stretching exercises to warm up. Extending her right leg outward as she flattened her palms against a tree trunk, she quickly felt stiffness in the muscle and in her side. Extending her left leg she felt the same. Did this mean she was getting old? No, she consoled herself.

The fault lay in working those twelve-hour days at the magazine. Putting off exercise, she had just let herself get out of shape. Surprising to her, people were always asking her beauty secrets, complimenting her on how great she looked and wanting to know how she maintained her figure. Right now her limb's inflexibility confirmed the adage that looks were deceiving.

Shay did some more warming up before she took off for her jog. Getting winded soon after running further admonished her that she needed to take better care of her one and only body. Nonetheless, there was also more motivation to look good other than her health and vanity. Now she had someone to look good for.

Mentally re-creating the real life fantasy that happened to her last night, Shay couldn't stop thinking about it. It was the man in the fantasy that still had her heart beating in triple time. Braxton was everything she dreamed of and more. Greatest of all, he loved her. He really loved her. She could feel it in every drop of air between them that he did.

The scenes in her mind's eye had her smiling, but she was so ensnared in her musings, Shay found herself lost in the woods. Turning from side to side, undecided about which direction her house was in, the sudden sound of footsteps behind her swung her around. Her heart did a jump seeing who it was.

Ten

Shay was frozen staring at the unforgettable person before her. She'd never forgotten the face. There were days when she had memorized its every detail like her own. There was the strong jaw, the compelling eyes and the shrewd smile that looked like she was always making fun of you. There was even her body that had too many curves.

When Marquis left Shay at the altar that day long ago, preferring to stride over to the woman wearing too much makeup and a too-tight dress barely covering her bottom, Shay actually questioned if her mind was playing tricks on her. What was happening at that moment was too horrible to have happened to anyone. So how could God let it happen to her? What sin had she ever done to deserve this kind of punishment?

Shay heard that the woman's name was Vanessa Collier. After all the dramatics, Shay vowed to leave Vanessa and her torturing memory in that church. Vowing was easier than doing. For too long when she woke up, thinking about Marquis, she was also thinking about Vanessa Collier. What magic had she cast on Marquis to make him so cruel to her? Was she perfect? Did she do everything perfectly? Was she a better lover? Did he prefer her body's shape to Shay's? Was her career more exciting? Was she more exciting? What did she do that made it so fun to be with her? What was it she did to make him so happy? After all, he had not only left his woman, but killed his baby as well.

The questions went on for months. Fortunately, though, Shay did see their importance lessened. In the wind of time, her life had no room for them. They were replaced with other important matters. As for Vanessa and the pain her mere name invoked, Shay packed it away with those love lessons.

Now Marquis had returned, and it was clear the magical woman had no magic at all. She had merely been a pawn in Marquis's web of deception. In his fit of jealousy, he had used her and played her so well. Shay could feel he was speaking from his heart when he cried that he never stopped loving her. The love was in his eyes, in his voice, in the dramatic rise and fall of his chest. It all proved how he felt about her, how he'd always felt about her. This woman's mere presence proved it.

"What are you doing here?" Shay asked. "Why are you following me?"

Vanessa's bright red lips curled in that smile that made it seem like she was looking at a joke. "I wouldn't say I was following you. I just came by to visit."

"At this hour in the morning? How do you know where I live? I'm sure you've heard about the case through the media. But there are only certain people that know where I'm staying during this case. Only the authorities and my family."

"Well, you have your brother to thank for that. He's obviously looking for suspects for Markie's murder. He found out I was in town, then tracked me down at my hotel. I guess he was trying to catch me early before I went out. And, yes, I was in town during the time of the murder. I followed Markie here from Cali. I even followed him earlier that day when he came to your office. He was so mad at me when he saw me in the lobby. Well, anyway, as for how I know where you live, I suspected that when your brother left me, eventually he would wind up meeting with you. So I followed him until he led me here."

"My brother?" Instantly Shay imagined Rakim seeing Braxton in her bed. She had to get back home. Fast. "Get to the point, Vanessa."

"Oh, you do know my name. I guess you would have found that out since I was part of a big event in your life. If you really look at it, I was part of your wedding."

"What is it you want from me? Why did you track me down here in these woods?"

"I don't want nothing from you. I just wanted to thank you."

"Thank me for what?"

"For killing him. I had come here to do it myself. But you beat me to it. Couldn't believe it when I heard the news. As soon as that snow let up, I went out and partied."

Shay studied that bizarre smirk, debating if she was serious. "Well, I have news for you. I didn't kill him."

Vanessa laughed. "Don't act like that. Be proud of it." Suddenly her smile transformed to a snarling scowl. "You rid the world of one no-good bastard!"

Wondering if Vanessa was the one who did it, wondering if she was perchance the one calling her and hanging around the house, Shay wanted to get away from her as soon as possible. What was more, she was praying that Rakim hadn't run into Braxton at the house.

Eagerly, she turned away from her. Again, Shay searched each direction, trying to figure out which one led to her home.

"It's to your right," Vanessa informed her. "Your house is to your right."

Skeptical if she should trust her, Shay followed her directions anyway. All the while she was looking back to see if she was behind her. Amidst the forest Vanessa had disappeared.

Arriving at her opened front door, Shay heard the arguing reaching all the way outside. Inside the house, she saw Christina barely keeping Rakim and Braxton apart. Evidently Braxton had just gotten out of bed. He was clad in only his pants.

"Shay, I told you to stay away from this guy!" Rakim yelled at her. "I can't believe I walked in here to see him in your bed. This is ridiculous! Have you lost your mind!"

Braxton gazed at her. "Baby, I tried to explain to him. He won't listen."

"You damn right I won't listen. What you're doing to my sister is foul!"

"Being in love with her is foul?"

Rakim looked like he was about to give birth. "You don't love her. All those women you have, you don't know the meaning of love."

"I have one woman and that's Shay, your sister. I love one woman and that's Shay."

"And I love him too." Shay tapped Christina aside, switching places with her in front of Rakim. "Rakim, if you really love me, you'll just be quiet and listen for a minute. Braxton is not the enemy."

"He—"

"Please! Just listen."

Rubbing his hands across his head, Rakim took a deep breath. She proceeded to tell him all the findings Braxton had uncovered to clear her. Braxton backed up what she was saying by handing Rakim the forty-page report.

"I haven't even given it to my assistant counsel," Braxton told him. "You're the first attorney who has seen it."

Looking stunned, Rakim pored over the documents. He found them so interesting he settled on the couch, utterly engrossed in them. When he finished reading, he found Shay, Braxton and Christina in the kitchen. Shay was telling them about the encounter with Vanessa Collier, the phone calls and the footprints. Braxton's worry and speculation about all this was interrupted by Rakim coming toward him.

Rather than extending his fist, he offered his hand to shake. "Brother, I misjudged you. I truly, truly misjudged you."

"You're damn right you did."

"You really have put a lot of energy into finding a suspect other than my sister. You've covered much more ground than I have."

"I'm a veteran at criminal law. You're a rookie. We forgive you, baby."

Shay and Christina chuckled. Rakim and Braxton laughed with them.

Rakim rubbed his hands together. "So we have some real suspects to go after. Eric Lebleau, the agent and I see you mentioned Vanessa Collier in the report. Now, I met with her this morning."

"So have I." Shay couldn't shake off how weird she was. "I was just telling Braxton and Christina that she just popped up on me in the woods. Said she followed you here."

Rakim's eyes widened. "You're kidding?"

"I wish I was."

Following more talk about Vanessa, Christina and Shay left the kitchen. Braxton and Rakim remained where they were, discussing the case. Since they'd been informed that the trial would begin in three weeks, both men were determined to work quickly and thoroughly. Even so, in light of hearing about Vanessa, the calls and the footprints, Braxton had become as concerned about Shay's safety as he was her exoneration. A few times during her jog the phone had even rung. Whoever it was hung up as soon as the answering machine came on.

"I think you should work with the information I gave you for a few days," Braxton proposed, "while I work here at Shay's for a while. I need to stay with her. Not just because I enjoy her company so much, but something about this Vanessa woman and those footprints doesn't feel right to me."

Rakim nodded. "I know what you mean."

"And what about these calls? We have to get a tracer on that."

"I'll take care of it." Rakim sighed. "I guess this all means that there is the possibility that the killer might think Shay knows his identity."

"It's going to be real interesting to find out what happened that night."

"Someone definitely tried to frame my sister. They killed him, heard her, hid, saw that she fainted, then put that candlestick in her hand."

"Could be." Braxton speculated. "I hope we're on the right trail. I really do."

"We have three possible suspects. Vanessa has no solid alibi. She said she was in her hotel. But no one can verify that. As for the other two, I can't wait to hear where they were." He noticed that Braxton was deep in thought. "What other trail do you think we should be on?"

"I'm not sure. But what if the person who killed Marquis wasn't after him? What if they were after Shay?"

"Shay?" Rakim raised back, surprised at the revelation. "If they wanted her, why didn't they kill her?"

"Maybe they didn't want to kill her. Maybe they had

other thoughts in mind, and maybe Marquis happened to turn up."

Rakim thought about that. "I don't know. I think we should follow up with those suspects."

They heard the phone ringing in the other room and ignored it. Shay would answer it.

"I do too. But it's just food for thought. We have to look at every possibility."

Rakim eyed him with admiration. "No wonder they say you're the man."

Braxton laughed. "I wouldn't go that far. It's been an interesting career."

"But you are putting it on the line."

The men looked at each other.

"Sometimes you have to take a chance when you know you're after what is right," Braxton told him.

"I'm talking about the relationship. What if in these few days you spend with Shay someone sees you that shouldn't? As discreet as you two may be, it can happen."

"I'm willing to take the chance."

"And lose everything you worked for?"

"She's everything to me now."

Rakim looked at him, really looked at him. "I can see she is. Welcome to the family."

The men came out of the kitchen and found the women with their heads huddled together. They were also giggling. Half of a strawberry cheesecake rested on the coffee table. Empty dessert plates sat nearby it.

"Let me tell you something, my brother," Rakim addressed Braxton. "If you want to make my sister happy, I mean really happy, just feed the child. That's all you have to do. That'll make her grin at you every time. Make her do anything you want."

"Oh, you, stop." Shay flung a plastic spoon at him.

He ducked. "It's true. You know you're greedy, girl. You ate everything up from me growing up."

"Liar. You ate up everything. Christina, you know what his plates look like. He piles them up enough for two people."

Christina was cracking up. "I'm staying out of this."

His dimples winking, Braxton strolled over to Shay. "Anything my baby wants, my baby gets, whether food or anything else." He slipped his arm around her shoulders.

Tauntingly, Shay looked at Rakim. "Now, see there."

He waved his hand at her. "Let me get out of here. Seriously, I have to get on this case." He pecked his sister on the forehead. "Now, you hold on. Hold on just like I said. Everything is going to be cool. You'll see."

As soon as they had gone, Shay gazed dismally at Braxton. "I guess you have to go do your job too?" She stepped up close in front of him. His eyes were sparkling, staring at her. They made her so warm.

"I'm going to do my job." He caressed her cheek. Sometimes he was compelled to touch it to see if she was as soft as she looked. "But I'm not leaving."

"You're not?" She was thrilled.

"I'm staying right here with you. Actually for a few days. I'm not comfortable with leaving you right away when that Vanessa character could be near and those calls nagging you and those mysterious footprints. No, I can't leave you right away. Rakim is getting a trace on those calls."

"The weirdo called again when you and Rakim were in the kitchen. They still didn't say anything. They just held the phone."

"See there. I have to stay. Plus, I felt like I was on my

honeymoon last night. I need some more honeymoon."
He picked her up. Up the stairs they went.

"Get Steele on the phone," Jamison ordered Patman.

Many miles from any home, in isolated woodlands, the two men were part of over twenty law enforcement officials scattered amongst the scene of a vicious murder scene. Blood was everywhere. The blood of an attractive thirty-something woman, who had been stabbed many times. They knew a psychopath was on the loose.

"He's not answering, sir," Patman said, holding the cellular phone to his ear. "The machine is picking up."

Jamison scratched at that fatty tip of his nose. "Try in a few more minutes."

"I'll do that." Patman tucked the telephone in his pocket. He also looked worriedly at his partner. "Sir, are you okay?" The medical examiner brushed by him, bending down to the victim. Patman moved slightly aside.

"Yes, I'm okay." Jamison just couldn't stop gawking at the woman. Other than the savageness of her death, there was something he found eerie. "Do you see it?" He turned to Patman.

"See what, sir?"

Both men shuffled around the site. The medical examiner hovering over the woman from one side was blocking their view. When their line of vision was unobstructed again, they observed her motionless, wounded form.

"Pretty woman," Patman commented. He rubbed across his mouth. "Very pretty. What a shame."

Jamison's tired eyes scattered over her. "That's not what I'm talking about."

"Then what, sir?"

"I'm talking about the resemblance."

"Resemblance?"

Even with her features bloodstained, Jamison could see it. "Yes. She looks like that Hilton woman. That Shay Hilton. So much it just makes you think."

Patman peered at the lifeless form that two physicians now attended to. With her caramel-hued skin, short-styled hair and large, baby-doll eyes staring straight up at the sky, she did resemble Shay Hilton. "I guess you're right, sir."

"There's no guessing in it." Studying the lifeless body, Jamison rubbed the half-inch growth along his chin. "It makes you wonder."

"Wonder what?"

"Nothing." He was wondering if there was some connection between this death and that Marquis Jackson murder. Though it couldn't be, he told himself. He didn't want it to be.

"Try Steele again."

Patman did as requested. He soon ended that call and dialed another number. Shuffling about, seeking a smoother connection, he spoke of the case and soon hung up. He trekked over to Jamison.

"Is he on his way?"

"No, sir. I didn't get Steele."

"Why the hell not?"

"He took two personal days. They said he is unavailable and referred me to his assisting counsel. That's who I spoke to."

Jamison raised a shaggy brow. "What the hell is Steele up to? I know he's not sick."

Far from being unwell, Braxton lounged next to Shay on her silken bed covers. Once they reached the upstairs, Braxton didn't want Shay to think all he wanted her for was lovemaking. Although that was in the forefront of his mind, he wanted her to know that they could communicate like they had in his home. So communicate they did, about anything and everything, and often their dialogue had nothing to do with the murder. Sitting atop the covers, they were simply snuggling and chattering. Even that felt delicious to them. Several times the mystery caller interrupted, choosing to be silent when Shay answered the phone. Despite it, even he couldn't steal their bliss.

"My agent called me today," Braxton shared with her.

With his arm around her shoulder, they were sitting against the headboard. Both faced forward where several fragrant candles adorned the dresser.

"Your agent called?" Shay was puzzled.

"He's the guy that sells my artwork."

Shay looked excited. "That's great. Was it about more sales?"

"Yes, actually. He told me about some society lady wanting to do a big gallery showing for me." He was gazing into the soothing candles.

"That sounds really nice."

"It is. But I usually let them do it without my being there, of course. You know how I like to keep my identity secret."

"And you know how I feel about that." She glanced up at him. With a serene expression, he was still staring at the candles. She joined him in getting lost in them too. They casted such a hypnotic, relaxing effect. "I think you should be bold with your talent."

"And you're absolutely right," he agreed with her.

"I'm glad you think so." So he was really listening to her and heeding her words. She loved a man who listened to her. It was another plus for him.

"In fact, I'm considering doing the show and making an appearance. My agent said that they could attract even more patrons that way. But best of all, part of the proceeds will go to the charity of my choice. Maybe one of these days, I'll even do my art full-time. Thanks to my woman believing so strongly in me. Get out this rat race law."

"Oh, Braxton, that's wonderful." She reached up and kissed his cheek.

As she tried to sink back into her former position, he wouldn't let her go. "You think that little bit of sugar is enough to hold me?"

Shay was gazing up into those eyes. "How much sugar can you handle?"

"I can handle everything you throw at me."

"Think so?" She lightly pressed her mouth on his.

"Know so." Swerving so he could face her, he slid his eyes up and down her body. At last gazing into her brown shimmering depths, he stared at her long and hard. Abruptly, his hand tugged at her sweat jacket. Carefully, he eased her out of it. The full view of her tight black jogging outfit opened his eyes. "Ooh, you're looking sexy today."

"You like it?" Shay stood on the floor, modeling it for him. Dramatically, she turned her butt. When she was in love she felt like being silly.

Springing up on the side of the bed, Braxton looked at her, his eyes clinging to the roundness she was shaking in front of him. "Don't tease me like that." He pulled her toward him by the hips. "You're playing with the wrong fellow."

She stood between his legs looking down at him. "Oh, yeah, what you going to do?"

"Give you something to really make you shake." His voice dropped. So did his head below her stomach. He began kneading his face into her.

Shay closed her eyes because it felt so good. The more he did it, the more she wanted them both out of their clothes.

Braxton heard her unspoken cry. Within a breath, he was on his feet, peeling Shay's jumpsuit off her. Soon after, she felt her panties and bra being peeled and kissed off as well. Although it wasn't soon enough for Braxton, she finally stood naked before him. The hungry stare roaming over her, making her feel sexier than ever, urged her on in undressing him as well.

"You're so beautiful, baby," he whispered. Now as nude as she was, his bottom was perched on the edge of the bed. She was again standing above him. "You're so beautiful, Shay." Frowning from the intensity of his desire, his fingers reached up to her face, caressed down to her breasts and wound up playing with her furry sweet patch.

"Ooh, Braxton," Shay moaned, rearing her head back. He was making her so wet.

"Yes, baby, I'm here. Here to make you happy." With such sensual adroitness, his fingers caressed and caressed, finally separating her sensitive folds.

"Braxton!" The moist, thrusting force of his tongue surprised her with such pleasure that she screamed. Erotically, lazily, swiftly, feather light and at times hard, he tantalized her secret garden. With each taste and tease of her, her screeches became louder. He became turned on turning her on. Reaching upward for her breasts, he squeezed her nipples with the same gentleness that he began to kiss her creamy love.

As if she had no control, Shay's limbs began quivering. His own love throbbing, he knew he had to please each of them more. Laying Shay on her stomach, he leaned down to her pretty toes. Slowly, savoring each inch, he began to kiss and suck them. Working his way up, the same sweet affection was lavished on the backs of her ankles, calves, thighs and soon her glistening buttocks.

To him the beautiful round cheeks looked as tasty as caramel candy.

Over and over he dragged his lips across them, feeling his erection becoming so steel-like it was reaching an erupting point. However, it was Shay's whimpers of rapture that made him desire to grant her the ultimate satisfaction. Careful not to put the brunt of his weight on her, he glided on her back. Kissing the sides of her face, he used his nimblest touch to part the backs of her legs.

"Oh, yes!" he moaned, pushing himself inside her. "You feel so good. Oh! Oh!"

Shay was in delirious hysteria from the incredible joy of his being inside her. So much so, she couldn't talk as his hips slapped forward against her backside. She could only move, seeking more of the sweet friction that only his steel-like hardness could grant her.

Just when she thought she couldn't bear anymore of the intolerable pleasure, Braxton turned her around. Smothering her breasts with his mouth and face, he slid his erection against her stomach, taunting her. She gazed down at it, caressing it. It looked like a snake about to jump at her.

"Please, baby. Put it in. I need you. I love you."

"Shay, I love you too." He raised up to look at her sensual beauty. The seductiveness of her eyes, the juiciness of her lips made him even harder. He was a breath away from exploding.

He poked her gently with the tip of his steel love before granting her the fullness of it. Biting her lips because of the maddening sensation of an approaching orgasm, she gyrated her hips with every drop of love that flamed in her blood for him.

Braxton couldn't take it anymore—the way she moved, the passion blazing between them, her sexiness, the love he felt for her, the love she felt for him and the intensity rushed to the core of him. Pounding her like a racing machine, he gave her all that was within him to give, as she did him. In one whirlwind of emotion, they both shook with an unutterable ecstasy before their exhausted bodies made them collapse in each other's arms.

Eleven

The lovemaking lingered on through the morning and afternoon. Much-needed sleep capped the unforgettable time for both of them. Yet when Shay woke up with the night descending on the sun, she was hungry. The meal she craved was Braxton. For her every inch of his wickedly sexy body would do.

She leaned over him, treating herself to kisses along his chest.

Feeling her warm mouth on him, he started to wake up feeling aroused. "What time is it?" Waking more, he stretched out his long, muscular arms.

More and more amorously christening his stomach, Shay was having too much fun to answer.

Dimples peeked from his cheeks when he looked down at her. "You just can't get enough of me, can you?"

"Un-un." She continued helping herself.

"I whipped you, didn't I?" He was playing with her. "And if you keep it up I'm going to whip you again."

"I'm the one who whipped you." She raised up, laying her head on his chest. "And I bet you won't soon forget it."

"Whooh, I sure won't." He brought his arms around her shoulder. "You made me feel so good, baby."

"You made me feel good, too."

He rose, leaning over her, staring down in her face. "You make me feel like I've never felt before. And I mean that with our lovemaking and everything else. We were born to love each other, and no one else."

"You mean that?" She gazed up at his eyes sparkling down at her.

"I never meant anything more." He stroked her cheek.

"What about that woman? How did you feel about her?"

"What woman?"

"The one you were committed to. The one who you painted so much. What happened between you two?"

Braxton looked aside.

Shay's gently turning his head back toward her made him look at her. "Please, tell me who she is, or was."

Knowing it was time to let it all go, the pain he'd held so long, Braxton laid down on his back. Facing the ceiling, he began, "Her name is Andrea. I met her in college. I fell in love with her like I'd never known at the time. She felt the same for me. She was even the one who inspired me to become a lawyer. Because she was so enthusiastic about the law. My parents loved her influence on me. They loved the way she pushed me to study and achieve good grades for law school.

They heard the phone ringing but chose to let the answering machine pick it up.

"We planned to get married. We planned to become rich lawyers and buy a mansion. We had never seen black people with mansions and we were determined to make sure we had one. During our senior year, we moved in together. We started making arrangements to get married after graduation. We were so in love I couldn't help painting it all, painting her. I filled our place up with our images of ecstasy. It was cluttered I had so many paintings."

The phone began ringing again. Braxton talked over it.

"Then one night, she was taking a little too long coming back from the library. I went to look for her, but by the time I found her, she was being worked on by the paramedics. She had been raped and stabbed by an animal wearing a ski mask. She was dying right there. But still she managed to speak to me. She told me to be a rich lawyer. She told me to buy a mansion. She told me to never forget how much she loved me. They never found her killer."

The emotion coming from him made her cuddle his face against her chest. "I'm so sorry."

"I thought if I went into prosecuting it would somehow lessen my anger toward the killer. If I could just get all the bad guys, I could somehow get the animal who did that to Andrea.

"She was the only one I loved . . . until you." He brought his face before hers. "And she never ever encouraged me the way you do with my art. She saw it as a hobby."

"But I know it's not. It's a gift you have to share with the world. I really think you should make that appearance at that gallery, Braxton."

"Maybe I will. I'll tell my agent to get in contact with the lady. She's some rich banker's wife."

Instantly Victoria Sheridan came to Shay's mind. Rakim's mother-in-law was a great lover of Ecstasy's work. On the other hand, there were plenty of rich banker's wives in Englewood Cliffs. Still, she was curious. "What is the woman's name who wants to give you the show?"

"Victoria Sheridan."

Victoria strolled back and forth along the study's plush olive carpet, contemplating her next move in saving her daughter's sanity. Janet hadn't eaten, bathed, slept and barely spoke. Her concern somewhere in space, she'd found comfort in a recliner cornered in the den.

"Mother, go home," Janet demanded suddenly. "I really don't need you here."

Victoria clutched her bosom she was so relieved to hear Janet speak. "You need me more than you know." She lifted a pitcher of icy sparkling cider from a nearby table, pouring some in a cup. Carrying it over to Janet, she announced, "I'm taking you to Dr. Weathers in the morning."

"That moron shrink." Janet waved off the idea just like she shoved the glass her mother extended out of her face.

"He's not stupid." Victoria turned up the frosty drink, drinking it herself. Emptying it, she sat the cup back on the table. "He's brilliant in his field. You have to get yourself together, darling. He can help you do that. Don't you want to feel good again?"

"I can never feel good again. Rakim is gone. *She* took him. He had to make a choice of whose life to save, and he chose *hers* first."

Janet had recounted the fight to Victoria, complete with the chandelier incident. It made Victoria want to bury Rakim alive. It was all the more reason why she would keep her secret.

Victoria pulled up a chair, situating herself in front of her haggard child. "Darling, all your friends have been calling." She caressed Janet's hand into her own. "Why don't you call them back?"

"I don't want to talk to any of them! They've probably all been laughing at me."

"Laughing at you about what?"

"About Rakim and that . . ." She couldn't even think of a word horrible enough to describe Christina. "They're flaunting themselves everywhere. My friends were probably calling to tell me they had seen them."

"Nonsense." But Victoria knew Janet was presumably right. That was how the people were in the circles they lived in. "Let's forget him, darling. If you don't want to go see Dr. Weathers, let's do something fun. Let's go for tea at Windoms, or go shopping at the mall, or go to New York for a play. I heard there's a new wonderful musical playing about that saxophone player. I can't remember the name. It's a . . ."

"You go, Mother." She brought her legs in the chair, folding them beneath her. "I feel like staying here."

"And did I tell you my wonderful news?"

"What news?"

"About the artist of artists, Ecstasy." She brushed a wayward hair off of Janet's damp forehead. "His agent is seeing if he will do a gallery showing that I'm arranging, and he even might reveal his identity. I'm dying to know who he really is. I wonder if he is as passionate as his portraits make him out to be."

Passion. David beheld it in vivid resplendence, approaching Shay's doorstep that evening. Stumbling on a rock that catapulted him toward a window that was a distance from the front door, he couldn't resist peeking inside when the pane nearly met his glasses. Blindless and with a flimsy curtain, the view was clear. Braxton and Shay were on the living room floor. Laying on top of her, he was attempting to kiss her lips off. Fully clothed, their bodies were performing motions like they weren't. David banged on the door.

"Who is it?" he heard Shay ask. She sounded nervous.

"David."

"It's only David," she said, unlocking the door.

"Hello, there." Smiling, Shay held out her hand for him to come in.

Braxton was standing behind her. "Hey, man."

David stepped in the house, then in a huff flung himself toward Braxton. "What, have you lost your mind?"

Braxton didn't appreciate being spoken to that way. "Man, what is your problem? Whatever it is, don't bring it in here."

"Your foolishness is my problem!" David leered at him and Shay. "I could see right in the window. I saw you two. I saw you!"

His bizarreness made Shay and Braxton glance at each other.

Was this all about male jealousy? Shay wondered. The kind that frightened her before. Or was it those headaches? He'd told her they were stressing him out. "David, are you okay?"

"I'm clear as day. Much more sane than you two. I could see you two in the window. Now do you know how many others could do that?" His glare shot to Braxton. "You're willing to jeopardize her freedom because of your raging libido?"

Braxton stepped up to him. "Now you wait one damn minute. What I do with my woman when I'm alone with her is our business."

"Your woman!" David's glasses slid down his nose. He pushed them back up.

"Come on, guys." Again, Shay found herself in the middle of two irate males she cared about. It was a position she loathed. "David, I appreciate your concern. And you're right, Braxton and I were being careless. I'll put something up to the window."

"Put something up to the window, my foot!" David threw his hands up in the air. "You need to get rid of this loser! You're always choosing losers! Always when the best man for you is right in your face!"

Shay was flabbergasted. She knew David desired her, but for him to rant like this wasn't at all like him. It was as if he were someone else.

"David, it isn't like you to behave this way. What's wrong?"

"What's wrong with me? Hell, what is wrong with you? It's not like you to give it up so fast. So into your sacred celibacy, you've been saving it for three years and you have the imbecility to give it to a jerk!"

With his fist in a ball, Braxton leaped for him.

Once more, Shay blocked the two men. "David, why are you doing this? Why?"

David clutched at the pain that was getting worse in his head. "Don't you know why? Don't you know I love you so much I would kill for you!" Leaving the trail of his words, David rushed to the door. It slammed behind him.

Shay winced at the loudness of the slam. "My goodness."

With his mouth stretched open, Braxton gawked at her. "You're right, my goodness. Did you hear what that nut just said? He's a suspect if I've ever seen one."

Straightaway, that angry circle he hadn't seen in a while returned. Shay's eyes narrowed with it. "Don't call him that. Don't dare call David that!"

"What? A nut or a suspect?"

"He's my friend. He's been there for me. And I don't appreciate you referring to him that way."

"But, baby, look at how he just acted. Listen to what he just said." He couldn't believe this intelligent woman was being so unreasonable.

"He's obviously not well."

"I know. He has a condition called lovesickness."

"What?"

"You heard what I said, Shay. He's hot for you."

Shay knew David was. Yet Braxton was making it sound like it was so bad that David would actually lose it. "David had nothing to do with Marquis's murder. He walked me to my door and he went home. And I won't stand for you harassing him about it."

"Well, we are going to have to agree to disagree on this one, because he is definitely going on my suspect list."

"No, he isn't! This goes no further."

"Yes, it does, Shay. I'm going to clear you, and I'm seeking the truth. That truth very well may be that David killed Marquis in a rage of jealousy over you. They were about to fight at the party. Anybody can see how much the man loves you."

"Braxton, don't pursue this. I mean it. If you do. . . ."

"If I do, what?" Pausing, he studied how upset she was about all this. "Were you two . . . were you two ever at all lovers?" He disliked her being this passionate about another man. "Let's be honest with each other now."

"No, we weren't lovers. We were always friends. Just friends. Can't a man and a woman be friends without *hitting it?*"

The phone began ringing. Each ignored it.

"Of course they can."

"Well, how dare you ask me that? How dare you even insult my friend?" She made a squinting frown. "You know, maybe we don't know each other as well as we thought we did."

"Come on, don't say that."

"No, it's true. Maybe I've just been so caught up with the romantic side of our relationship, I've overlooked your character. Maybe I don't know you as well as I thought."

"Shay, don't do this."

"Don't do what? Don't care about my friends? Mr. Steele, my good friend David was there long before you came in the picture, and maybe he'll be there when you go from it."

With that she stomped off in another room of the house. Braxton restrained from going after her. He wasn't in the mood. He had only been looking after Shay's welfare. In helping her and prosecuting this case, he had to seek the truth. He'd long learned in the law game that sometimes the truth was totally unexpected.

Plopping down on the couch, he couldn't understand how she could be so irrational. Most of all, how could she let David make them argue like this? Was David more to Shay than she revealed? Was she just loyal to her friends like that? Or was he himself simply feeling foolishly . . . jealous?

Moments later, he pushed open the door to her home office, approaching her desk. Sifting through a ton of papers in her new work space, she pretended he wasn't there.

He stood above her. "Can we forget that arguing about David and just get back to where we were before he came in?"

"You mean to the sex?" She still hadn't looked up at him. She was now writing editorial notes.

"No, I don't mean just that. I mean the closeness we have and that we were building on."

"I believe we were fooling ourselves." She was still writing.

"I know you don't mean that." He glimpsed down at the paper that seemed more important than him. He snatched the pen out of her hand.

A glare shot up at him. "Do you mind?"

He bent down. "I know you love me, like I love you,

and you know it's silly to let this little squabble get in the way of what we have."

Weakened looking into his eyes, Shay knew she could never, ever stop loving him. Still, his behavior about David had been ridiculous. To even utter that David was a murderer was ludicrous. To think that she was defending him because they were lovers was more ludicrous. Braxton was jealous. To use David as a pawn in that was very unattractive to her. She snatched her pen back, concentrating on her editorial.

"What is it going to take to stop you from being mad at me?"

She looked up at him. "Take back what you said about David."

No way he was doing that. David was a suspect. Shay was not going to jail for him. There had to be another way to butter her up. He looked down at all the papers. "This must be all the material for the next issue of the magazine?"

"Some of it is." She was still jotting down notes.

He noticed a pile of what looked like letters. Picking them up, on closer inspection they were communications to the editor. Reading them, he noticed that most merely expressed how much they enjoyed *Love & Relationships*. Braxton truly enjoyed them. He wished he could receive letters like these.

Only one person wrote that he disliked the publication. He claimed that one of the advice columnist's suggestions didn't help him in getting a woman. Braxton chuckled at that. Then he came to a grouping. A bunch of twenty or so letters, all dated within the last few months, claimed how the reader was the man for Shay. Strange things were written in the letters. He even told Shay how he had a collage of photos of her. The eeriest thing about them all was how he ended his love letters: "I love you, Shay, and we're going to be together. No matter what!"

"Why didn't you tell me about these?" Braxton was shaking the letters.

"Why didn't I tell you about what?" Continuing to be stern, Shay reached up for them. She browsed through them. "They're just letters."

"Letters from an obvious nutcase."

"So he likes me a little bit."

"Did you *really* read them?"

"So he's not wrapped too tight and likes me more than a little bit."

"He could be the one who has been calling and hanging around."

"I thought no one is supposed to know where I live."

"They're not. Rakim is even going to tell that Vanessa woman that if she told anyone your location, she could be arrested for interfering with a court proceeding."

"So who would have told where I live and my number?"

"I don't know. But I would definitely like a psychologist to see these letters."

"I can show them to David."

Braxton had had enough. David, David, David. He was sick of that name. He was sick of Shay's devotion to him. There had to have been something between them that she wasn't telling him about. What if it was still there?

"I'm going outside to get some air."

Braxton brushed against the door hurrying by it. Heading down the stairs, he knew he wasn't about to leave her alone with a possible psycho running loose. He was just going to stand in front of the house and clear his head. This murder mystery was getting more complicated by the second. Had someone been after Marquis? Was it Eric

Lebleau, Vanessa Collier or even David? Or with the reve-
lations of those letters, was someone after . . . Shay?
Worst of all, was the woman he'd been searching for his
whole life a little too concerned about another man?

Braxton opened the front door. A shocking sight made
him rush to the middle of the walkway.

"Call an ambulance quick!" Shay heard Braxton shouting from downstairs. "Hurry. Quick!"

Her heart racing, Shay dashed down the stairs, tripping
over a few. Out of the open door where the shouting came
from she went. Her hands flew up over her mouth seeing
David sprawled motionlessly on the path. "Oh, my God!
Did you do this to him?"

"Call an ambulance, Shay!"

Janet was no longer in need of medical attention. That
was what Victoria thought.

She was overjoyed when Janet agreed to clean herself
up and even visit Mariette French's Beauty Salon. Her
daughter wanted to look good. She hoped for another,
more suitable, worthy man.

Mariette not only had the most luxurious salon in
Englewood Cliffs, but she was also Victoria's friend. On
many occasions she had made her look ravishing for social
events. Janet had become one of her faithful customers
too. This evening Janet was going to have her hair treated,
a facial, a manicure, a pedicure and various body wraps.
Driven there by her chauffeur, Victoria stood at the door
waving her princess good-bye. Going back in the house,
she exhaled. Her child was on the road to recovery. She
was on the road of recovery from a man who Victoria
knew would soon know the meaning of hell on earth.
She'd made sure of it.

Not long after, Janet strolled into Mariette's salon. She

was immediately uplifted by the visual comforts. There was soft lighting, sprinkled over peach colored walls, chaises, sofas and carpeting. Mariette's even smelled as if it had been powdered with peach dust. Mostly though, this evening Janet was relieved that the parlor was nearly empty. That's one of the reasons she had chosen to come at the dinner hour on a Thursday night. All her friends were at the Daughters of Privilege meeting. She was supposed to be there too. So she knew hardly anyone would be at Mariette's during this time. Her and her rich friends were the main patronage. Janet couldn't face them. Surely, they had seen Rakim and Christina or heard about them. They were flaunting their love.

Marriette's never let the wealthy clientele wait and Janet was first pampered with a pedicure. With her eyes fluttered close, her toes were feeling like they were being made love to when she heard, "Janet, I'm so sorry."

Janet's eyes opened as wide as her mouth, seeing three of her friends standing above her. They began what sounded like an assault.

"Janet, we missed the meeting because we wanted to see you."

"We went by your house, but your mother said you were here."

"How have you been holding up?"

"Is he trying to take your trust fund?"

"How much has he asked for?"

"He doesn't know how good he had it."

"He could never fit in your world."

"I saw them one day in a restaurant. The press was following them. I assume because he's defending his sister."

"Do you really think she killed her ex?"

"Aren't you glad you're no longer in that family?"

"He's insane for leaving you for her."

"She's not that pretty."

"And her body. She needs some breast reduction."

"And hip reduction."

"A woman like that had to get him with sex."

"We weren't raised to be whores in the bedroom like she was."

"And he has nerve filing papers against you."

"On what grounds did he request the divorce?"

"He's the adulterer."

"He abandoned you."

Unable to respond to the hysteria of their words, Janet soon felt like she was dizzy. Shoving them out of her way, she ran through the salon and out of the door. She didn't stop running until her lack of breath told her no more.

She sank to the ground by a closed storefront. Crying, she'd never imagined something this awful could happen to her. This wasn't supposed to be an episode in her life. Someone else's, not hers. The love of her life no longer loving her was something she never dreamed in her worst nightmare.

Her entire life everything had been wonderful. Perfect. Like a princess always treated royally with a queen and king for parents was how she always felt. Why now did everything have to change? Why did she have to feel anguish unlike any other? Why this? Why did the man she love do this to her? She couldn't answer. But with her eyes drying as she pondered the injustice of it all, she did think of something she could do to remedy this situation. It would numb this tormenting pain. Uncaring that the chauffeur was scheduled to pick her up at Mariette's in two hours, she didn't call him to cancel. She simply hailed a taxi.

"Where to, lady?" The gaunt faced driver glimpsed back as she stepped inside.

"I want to go to a shop . . . that sells guns."

Twelve

With her head hung, Shay walked out of Englewood General Hospital into the deserted parking area. A shadowy male figure emerging toward her from an unlit section of the lot froze her tracks. Fright held her breath. As he came closer into view, she expelled her wind. It was Braxton. Because it was better if he made himself scarce when the ambulance arrived at her home, she'd left him behind.

"How is David?" He could see that she'd been crying.

"In surgery. He has a tumor." She couldn't possibly tell him what the tumor had made him do. Certainly he would have used it against David.

"Do they think they can operate without any damage?"

"This kind of surgery is very delicate. It's going to take a while before the doctors know anything. Just pray for him . . . if you can . . . I know I will."

"Shay, I know all about the tumor."

"What do you mean?" *How could he know?*

Sticking his hands in his pockets, Braxton hated bringing up what he was about to at a time like this. Yet it may have been crucial to her freedom. "I was in the hospital earlier. I inquired about David."

"They wouldn't give you any information. You're a stranger to him."

"I identified myself as the district attorney. Much of the staff knows who I am already. I . . . I told them David may be a murder suspect. That's how I got the information about his condition."

Shay couldn't believe what she was hearing. "No, you couldn't have done that. You couldn't have been that cruel. That man is in there fighting for his life, and because of some foolish jealousy you have of him, you're trying to put him in jail."

"Shay, you heard what he said. Plus we both know how angry he was at Marquis. They were about to come to blows. If he cares about you as much as you say that he does, he may have come in your house and finished what was started. We have to find out where he was at the time of the murder."

She was still amazed. "Is your career that important to you? To try to pin the murder on anyone? Especially someone who you think is important to me. A *man* who's important to me."

"It's about getting to the truth. It's about keeping your pretty butt out of prison."

"He didn't do it!"

"The doctor told me about the site of the tumor."

"He didn't."

"They said the site is in a part of the brain that makes one violent. Sometimes there are even blackouts, and the person may not remember what he did for a certain amount of time. He may have thought he was sleeping when in actuality, he may have been out doing something."

"For the last time, David did not murder Marquis."

"It's a possibility."

She couldn't take this anymore. The man she believed was a godsend was actually trying to put an innocent man in jail—one of the best friends she'd ever had. David had been there for her when she cried those nights and days about Marquis's betrayal. "I don't want you to come back to my place."

"Don't do this, Shay."

"I don't need you to stay another day with me." *And I won't impose on my brother and Christina either.* "I'll put extra locks on the doors."

"Why won't you listen to reason?" He gently gripped her arm.

"Because I don't hear any. Good-bye, Braxton." She jerked his hand off of her, heading toward her car.

Within seconds, Braxton stood in the parking lot alone. The way she said good-bye echoed all around him. She couldn't have meant *that* good-bye.

After a restless night, Braxton headed into the police station the next morning. Although he had kept in touch with his assisting counsel on various matters, particularly the Marquis Jackson murder, he wanted to reexamine the forensics report. As well, he wanted to see if any unexpected findings had turned up at the station.

Rakim had kept him abreast of his investigation. He'd been successful in clearing Marquis's agent as a suspect since the man had been attending a family reunion. The infamous members of his family who threatened Marquis had also been present. Unfortunately, he'd been unable to catch up with the seemingly busy Eric Lebleau. On the other hand, he had requestioned Vanessa Collier. Her alibi remained the same—she was in her hotel room. As much as Braxton appreciated Rakim's efforts, he planned an aggressive visit to those suspects during his day.

He had to find out who killed Marquis. There was no way he would let Shay rot in jail for something she didn't

do. That would kill him. He was far from ready to die.
Her love had awakened him. Awakened him so that last
night he barely slept thinking about her. He started to call
her. However, he knew she needed time to cool off. With
all his heart, he wished this David tragedy hadn't come
about. Certainly, he wanted the man to survive and thrive.
But with this news that his medical condition may have
made him violent—violent without him even remembering it—how could he ignore the likelihood of David being
a suspect?

Why had this caused such a rift between them? He was
only trying to help her. Never had he fallen in love so
deeply. Not even with Andrea. The emotion he felt for her
was so strong it felt like he breathed her. How could he
be without her if that good-bye was really good-bye?

"What are you doing, Steele?" Jamison was gawking
at Braxton.

Patman and he had come into the lounge to get their
usual black coffee. They found Braxton standing by the
machine, mindlessly filling his mug to the top with sugar
instead of his regular coffee with lots of cream.

Braxton sat the cup down on the counter. "I just have
things on my mind."

"I can see that," Jamison remarked. Braxton looked
tired to him. Not at all like the *GQ* type that made all the
secretaries and female cops swoon whenever he passed
their way. "You don't look good, Steele."

"You never look good, Jamison."

Patman cracked up. He sobered, seeing how annoyed
Jamison was at the outburst. He focused on Steele. "All
that sugar would have had you flying around here like a
kite." He snickered again. Neither Jamison nor Braxton
found anything funny.

"Well, you say you have something on your mind,"

Jamison told Braxton. "You'll have more when I show you something."

"What?"

Jamison led the way to the morgue. After undergoing the official process to view a body, Jamison snatched down the covers of a corpse in front of them.

Braxton was stunned. "Wow."

Jamison nodded. "I figured you would say something like that."

They were standing before the body of the young woman who was discovered stabbed to death.

"She looks just like Shay. Shay Hilton. The resemblance is amazing."

"That's what I said. They look too much alike. Poor kid, she wasn't even from around here. We found out she's a real estate agent. Married with two kids. The whole bit. She was just passing through town on business. But she ran into a monster."

Braxton frowned, thinking aloud. "This is so strange." With the victim looking so much like Shay, he wondered if the murder was in any way connected with the murder of Marquis Jackson. He really wondered.

"We're not going to talk about murder, or suspects or anything like that," Rakim promised Christina as they settled for an early lunch in the glamorous Muse Restaurant. Located in a tiny remote town a few miles from Englewood Cliffs, they were hoping to stay clear of reporters. They'd not only been hounding Rakim about the case but were also asking questions about his pending divorce from socialite Janet Hilton. Equally, they'd become intrigued with Christina. "We're only going to talk about me and you at this table right now." He hit his hand against the lace tablecloth, confirming his point.

Christina blew a smooch at him. "That's fine with me. Because this case has me worn out. We just need a little time-out, then we can go full steam batting for my girl."

"I'm with you, baby."

Smiling, her feline eyes scanned around the dusky oriental-styled ambience. "This is a nice place."

He did an observation too. "It certainly is."

"Nobody to bother you." She glanced at the tables. Patrons were engrossed in their meals and with each other.

"Nobody to follow you and hunt you down."

They looked at each other and laughed.

Flirtatiously, Christina played with her earring. "I guess we've become celebrities whether we wanted to or not."

"It'll be over soon, baby. It'll all be over. Then things will be normal. Shay will be out of this mess, and life will be life again."

"I hope so."

He leaned toward her, raising her hand. "And all we'll have to worry about is how many different ways we can please each other." He winked and brushed a kiss on her knuckles.

"You know that sounds good to me. You know I could make love to you all night long."

Rakim blushed. "Don't start. You're getting me excited. I want to take you home right now." He glimpsed a waiter finally approaching them.

Christina licked her tongue across her lips. "Maybe we can take the afternoon off. I'll make it worth your while."

"I know you will. Boy, do I know you will."

They were laughing when the waiter arrived.

Reaching in his pocket for a pad and a pen, the man grinned, revealing scattered teeth. "What will you two have?"

Before Christina could answer, the waiter pulled out a

camera. Lightbulbs started flashing in Christina's and Rakim's faces as the guy stated, "If you give me any information about your affair or the case, I'll be very fair. If you just open up a little."

The commotion attracted the attention of the real staff and security. When the reporter was dragged out, the portly host hurried to their table. "We apologize for this. We had no idea that man was the press. We respect every patron's right to privacy."

"It's all right, my brother. I believe you." Determined not to let the incident ruffle him, Rakim tucked his red napkin in his lap. "How can I let *him* ruin my day when I have such a beautiful lady sitting in front of me? I'm not."

The scowl the reporter put on Christina's face smoothed into a smile. "I'm not going to let him ruin my day either. Not when I have you."

David knew he had someone who cared about him too. When he woke in the recovery room, he was grateful for his family's presence. He had heard them praying for him, reminiscing with him, laughing with him, even when it was an arduous task for him to crack his eyes and respond. They had ridden with him through the tempestuous winds of the storm and now stood with him in the vivid colors of the rainbow.

Being near death was one of the most monumental experiences of his life. He thanked God that his parents and brothers had been there for him. That being as it may, he knew he had someone else he could count on. His loved ones told him she'd called endlessly inquiring about his condition. They further stressed that she wanted to stay with him all night. However, in light of her legal circumstances, the physicians didn't want to attract unwanted attention to the hospital. Still, David needed to just see her. With his life spared so much was clear to him now. "Please . . . please . . . I want to see Shay."

Thirteen

"I'm so glad you're alive, David. I'm so glad the doctors think you'll make a full recovery." She stroked his forehead as he managed a weak smile.

"I'm . . . glad to be . . . alive too."

"Soon you'll be walking right out of here. Getting back into that psychology practice of yours."

"Not . . . not so soon."

"You will be in full swing soon. I know you will. Think positive."

"I . . . am. I'm going to . . . travel."

Shay's brows raised with surprise. "Where are you traveling to?"

"All over. With my . . . with my friend."

"Your friend?"

David flushed. "A nurse."

"You're traveling with one of these nurses in this hospital?"

He grinned. "As soon as I'm . . . able."

"Really?"

"I knew her . . . I knew her a long . . . time ago."

"How long?"

"In school. We went to . . . elementary school together."

"And you met up here at the hospital?"

"She's my . . . she's my nurse."

"Isn't life something. They say if two people are meant to be together, somehow they will."

"And you're meant to be . . . with him."

"Who?"

"Steele."

Shay lowered her head. She was sure missing him. "I don't know about that, David."

"I know. I see . . . your eyes. They never . . . looked at me . . . that way."

"Don't say that."

He patted her hand. "It's okay. It's not your . . . fault. I know you . . . love me . . . one way. Love him . . . another way. We love . . . not by our choice. Not with our . . . minds. With . . . our . . . hearts."

"My mama used to say the same thing."

Eric Lebleau was certain he wasn't in love with the married woman he spent the night with during the time of the murder. Regardless, he was trying to evade telling Braxton where he was when he popped up at his office. It could have been the ruin of his career if it was revealed whose wife that woman was.

In the middle of Lebleau's office, Braxton was pacing. "Now, Mr. Lebleau . . ."

"Eric."

"Eric, then," Braxton corrected. "Eric, it has taken me a devil of a time catching up with you, and now that I'm here in your office, you're not going to tell me your whereabouts during the time of the murder."

"I can't."

"For the hundredth time, tell me why not." Staring at him, Braxton froze.

"I just can't."

"Do you know I could take you down to the station?"

Eric panicked. "For what? My prints aren't on that murder weapon. God knows, I don't believe Shay did it. But I didn't either." He reached across his desk for his bible. "I'm a man of God."

"So you say."

"It's true."

"A man of God has no qualms with the truth. You do."

"I'm being honest with you. I didn't have anything to do with it. I made peace with Marquis when I called him to my bedside when I believed I was going to die."

"So what's the problem with telling me where you were?"

"It's complicated."

"I can understand complications."

Debating if he should tell, Eric rubbed his hair back to his long ponytail. "I don't know. I can get myself and someone else in trouble."

"You'll feel damn more troubled in a jail cell."

"Look, you can't do that to me."

"Try me. You live in Shay Hilton's building. You had access to her apartment. You had access to the deceased. Now for the last time, where the hell were you?"

Eric stood up. Shaking his head, he peered out the window as he spoke. "I was with my minister's wife. She was here. We were making love."

Braxton was amused by his hypocrisy. "You sure are doing God's work."

Eric swerved around. "I made a mistake, all right."

"This is going to be verified with her."

"Just don't do it when the minister isn't around."

"I won't."

He didn't like the way Braxton was looking at him. "I became weak. Tempted. It happens to men. I bet it happened to you before." Though as he looked at Braxton, he began to wonder something. "I've never seen a prose-cutor work so hard when it would benefit the defense."

"I'm just looking for the truth."

"Right," Eric said, but when Braxton left, he was still wondering something. Had Shay gotten under the D.A.'s skin? Then again, he couldn't fault the guy. He'd been there too.

Roaming aimlessly through her house, Shay couldn't stop thinking of Braxton. She had already been missing him before meeting with David. But in talking with her thankful-to-be-alive friend, she'd realized what a precious love was slipping away. How many times in one's lifetime did a person experience the depth of emotion that she and Braxton shared? Rarely. Divorce statistics, marriage coun-selors, those talk shows with the spouses about to kill each other and so many realities in the world proved that true love should never be taken for granted. It should never be thrown away.

How many people out there in the world would have given anything to experience what she'd felt with Braxton? With what she was feeling for him now? It was happiness beyond description. It could only be felt.

She wanted to call him. Several times she started to. However, his failing to call her made her wonder. Maybe he believed her good-bye was good-bye. Worse, he didn't believe what they had was worth fighting for.

With her brain feeling like it would explode from all the thoughts, Shay decided she was going to lay down. The phone ringing brightened her mood. She swiped it hoping it was Braxton.

"Hello?"

Silence.

"Hello."

Silence again.

"Hello, would you get a life!"

Trying to get Shay out of his mind and concentrate on his job, Braxton walked up to Suite 4904 at the Berkshire Hotel. After knocking, a woman with too much makeup and too little clothes answered the door. Braxton thought she might have looked a little pretty if she hadn't made herself look so cheap and clownish.

She smiled as if someone had just told her a joke. "What can I do for you with your fine self?"

"I'm District Attorney Braxton Steele. Are you Vanessa Collier?"

"And I'm happy as a lock that I am if you're asking."

"May I speak with you please?"

"Surely."

Braxton took a seat on the suite's sofa while Vanessa went over to a miniature bar. "Can I get you something?"

"I don't drink on duty."

"Aw, you can't have a little drink with me? You don't follow protocol all the time, do you? Don't you ever loosen up?"

Braxton smiled dryly. "In our private lives we're allowed to do what we please. But now I'm on duty, and I'd like to ask you some questions about Marquis Jackson."

She poured herself a drink. "What about that dog?"

That he was, Braxton thought. "I'd like to know about your relationship with him." He watched her sashay across in front of him, sitting beside him on the sofa. "I'd also like to know where you were on the night of the murder."

"I already told that woman's lawyer where I was." She stirred the ice in her drink before sipping it. "I was here."

"Did anyone see you here?"

"He asked me that too." She took another drink, this time finishing the wine. Setting the glass on the table, she smiled over at him. "I told him the truth. I was here. No one saw me. End of story." She crossed her legs. "You know, you are so fine."

Braxton blushed. "My mom thinks so."

"No, really." She dragged her bottom across the cushions toward him. "You really are one good-looking man."

"Thank you."

"You're definitely my type. You married?"

"No."

"Good. I don't bother with them anymore. I got in a whole lot of trouble one time with one."

"Marquis was almost a married man."

"Almost. He didn't marry that woman. He didn't marry me either. But I'm glad about that."

"You are?"

"Hell, yeah. That dog. What didn't he do to me? He cheated. He lied. He was out of work sometimes. He was irresponsible. And in these last months together, he screwed like a mummy in traction."

Braxton buttoned his lips to stifle the laugh. "So why are you in Jersey? You obviously followed him from California."

"Because he took all the money out of our joint account. Took it and ran here to be with that woman."

"You mean Shay?"

"Who else? He was always talking about her. Complaining about her. Berating her. Telling me all her bad qualities. And, you know, I used to laugh. But then one night, that man called out that woman's name. He called it out when he was on top of *me!*" She pointed to herself.

"I guess that hurt pretty bad."

"It did more than hurt. It woke me up. You see all that denigrating of her he was doing was a front. He was still in love with that woman."

"So you came here to get him for all that, the money, the disloyalty?"

"I was so mad at him, I was following him around, waiting to make my move."

"Your move?"

"Yeah, I was going to make him suffer for all the misery he caused me."

"How?"

"Beat him. Get off my frustration at him."

Pretending he was ignorant about the cops being called to their home on several occasions for domestic violence, Braxton just looked at her. "So things were pretty tense between you two, in fact, sometimes violent?"

"You could say that. We had some real brawls. He has even called the cops on me."

"And why was that?"

"Because I released my frustration—the frustration that he gave me with all of his crap. I put something on him he would never forget. More than once, too. The last time all of his friends were laughing at him for letting a woman kick his ass. He wasn't even able to go to an audition because he looked so bad and was in such bad shape. He went to the hospital instead. But he brought it out in me. I would try my best to kill him."

Braxton cleared his throat. "So when you say that, are you *really* saying that you wanted him to die from the beating?"

"Why not?"

"You really wanted this man dead?"

"And buried. Thanks to that woman my wish has been granted. And I'm hanging around for the trial and after.

I have to see if I have any inheritance coming since I was his live-in partner for three years."

Braxton stood, extending his hand. "It has been interesting, Ms. Collier."

"Call me Vanessa."

Braxton headed toward the door. Her tugging his arm swung him around. Except he wasn't expecting her to grab him, forcing her lips into his. When he moved back grimacing, she was smiling. "I'd really like to get to know you better, Braxton."

With the back of his hand, he wiped the bright red lipstick off of his lips. "We'll be in touch."

When the handsome district attorney left her suite wiping off her lip prints, Vanessa wasn't the slightest bit offended. She was accustomed to being aggressive with men. That's how she usually snared the ones she wanted. She'd done the same with Marquis. She pursued him relentlessly, and when his relationship was in trouble, she took advantage of the situation. Unfortunately, their love affair didn't last. A few weeks after she hit California with Marquis, it was evident they were in grave trouble. Beyond the gloss of their physical affection, it always seemed to her that his mind was somewhere else. Somewhere so far she couldn't reach it, see it or understand it. Now she knew where. With the woman who'd taken his life.

Later mingling around the lobby bar with various men and women, Vanessa couldn't get that D.A. out of her mind. She even asked around about him and was pleased to find out he was well known and well liked. In fact, one woman described the outside of the huge mansion he owned. She even knew where it was.

Seconds later, Vanessa was powdering her face in her rental car's rearview mirror. Parked nearby Braxton's property, she didn't drive onto the land because she wanted to surprise him. Finally unlocking her door to make her move, she was staggered when another car passed her, making its way into the estate. It parked outside his door, and her eyes widened with shock when she saw who stepped out of it. It was Shay, the woman accused of murdering Marquis, a woman who shouldn't have been knocking on the district attorney's door. The shock of shocks, however, came when that door opened. Shay Hilton and Braxton Steele embraced.

"Now ain't this something. I think the police department would be very interested in this."

Fourteen

"I need to speak to the man in charge. Now!" With her hands on her hips, Vanessa stood over Patman's desk, her chest heaving with anxiousness. "I know something that is really going to shake things up with this Marquis Jackson case."

Skimming his eyes over her tawdry outfit, Patman threw his head toward a chair. "Take a seat."

She glanced over her shoulder at the metal chair he motioned to. It was a good distance away from his desk. After sliding it over, she seated herself in front of him. "I have to speak to the big guy in charge. He won't believe what I saw."

"Well the superior officers are out of the station right now. My partner, who has seniority over me, is out also. But maybe I can help you."

Vanessa assessed the weasel-like man. His appearance wasn't that of someone important. With his undeveloped physique and ordinary facial features, he definitely was no Braxton Steele. The way he slumped into the chair was also incomparable to the majestic posture Braxton had projected in his sitting, manner and movement. On the other hand, she knew Braxton Steele wasn't what he appeared to be. The so-called man of the law was all over that hussy when he'd been offered the chance to be all over her. That made Vanessa kicking mad. Another man she'd lost to Shay. This one was too fine. They weren't getting away with it.

"I saw the district attorney and Shay Hilton, the murder suspect, in front of his house hugging and kissing."

In shock, Patman's head lurched forward. "Could you say that again?"

Sourly, Vanessa twisted her red mouth. "Are you deaf or something? I said I saw Shay Hilton and Braxton Steele hugging and kissing in front of his house. *Hugging and kissing. The DA and the murder suspect.* Do you get it? Are you simple?"

Vanessa continued chattering about what she'd witnessed. Patman appeared like he was listening. In actuality her words became a blur. Eventually, he managed to make her leave the station without speaking to anyone else. He assured her he would handle everything. Matters like this had to be handled delicately. Otherwise, she could wind up being sued by Shay and Braxton.

Inside the mansion, the fireplace blazed as the glowing pair relaxed before it. He was so happy that she wasn't angry anymore. "I felt so empty with that tension between us."

"I felt exactly the same way, Braxton. The world even started looking differently, just somber everywhere I looked in that short amount of time."

"But it seemed like a long time."

"Didn't it though."

"I was having all kinds of thoughts, like you didn't want me anymore." He glided his finger along her cheek. "I was so down about it. Just tried to do my job and keep busy so I wouldn't think about you. It wouldn't work. I just kept thinking about you. I couldn't stop."

"The same with me." She stared in his eyes, the firelight reflected in them. "And I knew I took a chance coming here. But I just felt this strong need to be with you."

"I was working so hard today too. I said to myself, Maybe if I find that killer, I'll go tell her and she'll be wanting me again."

"I want you if you never find the killer."

He looked off, shaking his head. "I didn't have any luck with my investigation today either." He gazed back in her soft expression. "When I visited Eric Lebleau, I found out he was with his minister's wife getting busy during the murder."

"What?" Shay half laughed, half frowned. "So, he's still a louse."

"That's what I said. And I later verified his story with the woman and he was telling the truth."

"So he's off the suspect list."

"He's off."

"And Rakim told me that the agent has an alibi too."

"Sure does."

"So that leaves Vanessa."

"Whooh, Vanessa." Grinning, Braxton shook his head. "Vanessa, Vanessa, Vanessa."

Shay could see that something funny had happened. Whatever it was, it was funny to her even before he told it. "What did she do?"

"Now she's a piece of work. A real character." He shared his encounter with Vanessa, summing it up with, "And she gave me a smack on my lips when I left."

Shay thought that was funny. "You got to her. The woman couldn't help herself."

"Well I won't be visiting her anytime soon. If she needs to be questioned again Rakim can do it."

"With you getting to her like that, you may be able to get more out of her."

He speculated. "I don't know, baby. I get the feeling she didn't do it either."

"You do?"

"Yes. Actually, I kept thinking about those letters."

"What were you thinking?"

"I just kept thinking about them. In fact, I couldn't get them out of my mind. Then I think of those footprints. And those damn phone calls! I've been in constant touch with Rakim and the caller won't stay on long enough to get a trace."

"And whoever it is calls even more."

"We'll get them. And I'm going to lock them up and throw away the key."

"Do you really think the calls are linked to the murder?"

"It's just a feeling I get. I may be wrong, but it doesn't hurt to pursue it."

"Then that would mean they were after me, not Marquis."

"We have to consider that."

"Then why didn't they kill me? Why did they frame me?"

"They didn't kill you because their intention wasn't killing. It was romantic, like those weird letters. Now as far as the framing I haven't figured that out yet."

"So that means David is off your suspect list?"

"Pretty much. Although his condition could have led

him to do that, now I don't think that he did. It's just a feeling I get."

"I'm so glad you're not against him anymore." But looking weary, she crossed her arms, rubbing them. "On the other hand, this is really getting scary."

"Don't be afraid. I won't let anything happen to you. I'm going to take care of everything." Suddenly his gaze slid over her body. "Especially your needs. You look so good."

"So do you. Could we not talk about the case?"

"I'm with you, baby."

Tilting his head, he slipped his tongue in her mouth. When he let her go, Shay stood. "I want you to make love to me, Braxton."

"I want that too. More than anything." They began ascending the stairs.

Before they reached his bedroom, they passed his studio. Glancing in, Shay was drawn inside by a portrait she'd never seen. It was new.

"Oh, my God! It's us!" She stared at the striking image of them, relaxing before the fireplace on the day of the snowstorm. The detailing was such it was more radiant than a picture. Somehow it made them look more alive. "Braxton, you are so talented. I can see why your paintings have made you rich."

"You've made me rich." He wrapped her in his arms. "Money is nothing without some happiness in your life. I have that now." He hugged her.

She reared back, looking up at him with a mischievous glint in her eye. "Can you paint me?"

"Now?"

"Yes. We're feeling ecstasy. I know I am."

"Sure, baby. I'd love to paint you. But you know what happened the last time I tried to. You turned me on too much. I became too excited. Told myself I have to do that bad boy from memory. Then I won't kiss all over my lovely subject. My real live model does strange things to my body."

She was tickled. "I'm supposed to do strange things to your body, and you're supposed to do them to mine."

"Is that right?"

"That's right."

"So, young lady, do you want to model in one of my shirts again, or what you have on?" He glimpsed the blue rayon dress she was wearing. Since it showed off all her figure, he loved her in it. "You have such a beautiful body anything looks good on you."

"Even nothing." Shay reached to the back of her dress, unzipped it and slipped it off. Underneath the dress she was naked. "I came ready."

"I am ready." A banging started in Braxton's chest. A steel hardness seized his lower body. Staring at her, he pulled his tank top over his head and threw it wherever it wanted to go. "I'm so ready."

"Do you think you can paint me?" She shuffled toward the sofa and lay across it on her side.

Braxton began fluffing a pillow up against her back, but his hands maneuvered over to her breasts. His palm gently massaging the shape of them made her head sway back. Her eyes closed. "I missed this, Braxton."

"I missed it, too." His voice was muffled as his mouth began an erotic tug of her nipples. In the same moment, he rubbed across her ribs, stomach and the tender flesh below it.

"Do you like that, baby?" He was teasingly kissing her breasts and sensually mingling his fingers within her moist folds.

"Yes."

"Is it good enough for you?"

"Oh, yes." She was going mad from his kisses and his touch.

" 'Cause I'll do whatever it takes to make it even better." He felt her reaching for his sweat pants. Raising his hips, he helped her take them off. He was left only in shorts and a T-shirt.

Shay reached in his briefs, grabbing his love, while he still continued to thrill her with his touch. She was losing her mind.

Braxton enjoyed the lust in her slightly parted eyes. "You see how much you turn me on?"

"I love turning you on." She tugged his shorts down his leg and off of him. She felt his lengthy love mashing against her leg. "Please, I need to feel you." She stroked his broad back once he eased on top of her. "Please, give me your love."

He became more excited from the urgency in her tone and the feel of his body finally pressed against hers. Throwing his head back, closing his eyes, he guided himself within her tight drenched walls. The unbearably sweet feeling of being in her, of her silken skin against his, of her beautiful breasts on his chest and the erotic way she began to sway her hips, all made him push harder, harder, harder. He stopped when Shay screamed.

"Braxton, I've never felt like this." Loving the feel of him, she was motionless, enthralled by the sensation of their becoming one.

"Me either, baby." Passionately, he began kissing her face, neck, breasts, while moving himself back and forth within the splendor that seemed created only for him. "You just don't know what you do to me." Becoming enraptured by the fervent rhythm she began to fluctuate her hips, he distorted his face because of the unimaginable joy. Deeper he thrust, gliding his love to the sensual dance of ecstasy she tantalized him with.

Insatiably, he sought more of her addictive love, his tongue seeking the honey beyond her lips, his fingers squeezing her buttocks, his erection erotically grinding into her so that the intolerable ecstasy made her scream.

"It's so good, baby! Braxton, you make it so good!"

His heart touched by her words, he slow-danced his tongue out of her mouth and along her neck, all the while slowing and quickening his body motions, striving to hold on to the strain of love that was consuming them.

"I love you, baby," he whispered, rolling his tongue around her nipples. "I love you so much." He lightly pinched them between his teeth, before trying to suckle her entire breast in his mouth. "You taste so good."

"You do that so good." Mingling her fingers, through his head, she arched her chest forward for him to delight her more. She couldn't get enough of anything he did.

But suddenly she felt him ease off of her. Kissing her, he guided her body until she was on top. His love-drugged eyes gazing up at her, he played with her breasts, while she played with his chest and soon his love.

His eyes shut tight as she squeezed it, caressed it and kissed it softly. "Oh, baby."

Aching to thrill him more her lips loved him until he began to shudder. "I need to feel you again. I need you before I. . . ."

Shay needed to feel the fullness of him again too. Watching his agonized expression of pleasure, carefully she placed him inside her. Rocking her hips, she felt him matching her passionate stride.

"Oh! Oh!" he cried, as his body filled with fire that shook him.

"Braxton!" she screamed. Oceans of overwhelming

sensations were rushing down from her, making her shudder with him.

But no longer able to suppress the ultimate sensation of ecstasy, their bodies shook together in an earthquake of emotion. The love had been so good, so spine tingling, they couldn't have possibly seen the shadow by the window.

The remainder of the day, all night and much of the next day they made love. They were enjoying each other so much, Braxton hated to answer the phone when it began ringing incessantly. Since he'd told his agent that he'd make an appearance at the gallery opening featuring his work, he'd been expecting a call from him.

After they spoke, he regretted it.

"Why do you look so down?" Shay asked. "What did he say?"

"Victoria Sheridan wants to meet with me."

Shay's brows raised at her brother's mother-in-law's name.

"Unfortunately, this afternoon." He glimpsed his watch. "In about an hour."

"Ah, shucks." Shay looked like a disappointed little girl. "But we'll make the time up later. You sneak by my place as soon as you finish with her."

He smacked her mouth with a noisy kiss before swinging his legs over the side of the bed.

Some time later, Braxton drove off of his estate. Needing a little more time to get herself looking together, Shay walked out of his house and drove off of his property a short while later.

Eyes watched Shay. They were the eyes of the man in the car who began following her.

Arriving home, Shay was still feeling the magic of the spell Braxton had cast on her. The lovemaking, the passion between them, the loving humor, the talking, the under-standing of each other, the tenderness, and his protective-ness of her and constant efforts to clear her, made her feel like she was living a dream. It was one thing to dream of the perfect man, but to have him turn out more wonderful than any fantasy, was a blessing she would always be thank-ful for.

No other man could make her feel like Braxton did. His loving ways toward her and his kindness made it her pleasure to give the same to him. Love was power-ful, she knew from the fierce pounding still in her heart. It was no wonder that from the beginning of time eve-ryone was scrambling and fighting to taste just a bit of it in their lifetime. What was more precious than love? Nothing, the pounding in her heart assured her—the pounding that had Braxton's name reverberating with every rhythm.

Of all the wealth Shay had, it was incomparable to the joy Braxton gave her. The feeling he gave her made her happier than anything she had ever experienced. She'd felt so empty before, so alone even though she had those who loved her. Now she was so grateful that what her soul had ached for had finally appeared in her life—her soul mate, Braxton. Mounting the stairs to her bedroom, Shay couldn't stop smiling. She couldn't stop reliving how in-credibly he made love to her. She was aching to be in his arms again. A knock at the door made her heart jump with hope that the ache would be soothed. She rushed to the door, hoping it was Braxton. "Who is it?"

"Officer Patman."

Disappointed it wasn't Braxton, she still opened the door with a smile. She liked him much better than Jami-son. He wasn't so ready to put her in jail like his partner was.

"How you doing, Ms. Hilton?" His thin lips spread in a grin, he removed his hat.

"I'm wonderful."

He could see that from the glow on her face. "I was just checking around the area."

"Checking?"

"Yes. Seems there's someone on the loose. A woman was killed. Stabbed repeatedly."

"Oh, no. I've been so busy with my problems I haven't had time to find out what's going on in the world."

"Can I come in?"

She really wanted to get cozy and relax alone. Most of all, she wanted to get ready for Braxton. She wanted a repeat of their making up. Yet what could she say to this guy? He wasn't so bad. He would probably only hang around a minute. "Sure, you can come in."

Patman closed the door behind them. Immediately, Shay watched him surveying the place.

"Anything wrong?" she asked.

"Just checking to see how secure your place is. The locks, windows and such."

"Well, you're much more decent than your partner."

Patman chuckled. "Jamison is kind of hard sometimes." He was strolling about, still surveying.

"Kind of. He's awful."

"Don't worry. Things will be all right for you."

She was surprised he said that. "I'm glad you believe so."

"It will. You'll see. So what are you doing today?" He took a seat on the couch

Shay didn't feel like answering. She didn't want him on her couch. She wanted him to leave. She could sense the guy was lonely. Even so, she wasn't in the mood for entertaining him. "I'm very busy this afternoon actually." She hoped he received the hint.

He didn't. He made himself more comfortable, laying his arm over the back of the couch and swiveling toward her. "I bet it must be fun to run that magazine."

"It is. I love my work."

"I've read it, you know."

"You have?" She was surprised.

"It's a real nice magazine. Real interesting."

"Thank you."

There was an awkward silence amid him smiling up at her. "So you still didn't say what you were going to do today."

She was trying not to get annoyed. "Lots of things. I'm sure you're busy too."

"Do you have a boyfriend you're spending the day with?"

Shay knew it could have been a normal question. Normal for a single lonely man. Coming from this man, though, it made her feel odd. "Officer Patman, I don't mean to be rude, but I really have so much to do."

He didn't look happy about the brush off. "I understand." He stood, sauntering to the door.

Opening it for him, Shay offered, "Take care."

Stepping along the walkway, he threw over his shoulder. "You too."

Wanting to scream her gladness that he left, Shay hurried over to the CD rack that was crammed with old and new music. She was so happy about Braxton and her straightening things out, she was anxious to hear some romantic ballads. After locating Maxwell's latest CD, she was about to put it in the player when the phone rang.

Her heart banging, she picked up the phone. "Hello?"

"Shay?"

She exhaled her relief hearing Rakim's voice. "Hey, big bro, what you doing?"

"Working hard on your case. I'm close by, too."

"Anything new?"

"Actually, I wanted to see those letters. Braxton called and told me about them."

"Sure. They're here."

"Well, Christina and I'll be over. We'll bring an early dinner too."

"Sounds good to me."

"What do you want Chinese, Italian, Thai food?"

"Hmm." She thought. "How about some *fried* chicken?"

"Cool. Christina loves fried chicken, too."

"How about getting it from that place on Valley Road?" She was groping her fingers through her hair, feeling how dry it was. She needed some conditioning.

"Oh, yes. That chicken is off the hook."

"Kind of reminds me of Mama's chicken." Her lips curled at the fond memory.

"You know, I was thinking the same thing."

"Okay, I'm going to hang up now. I want you to hurry up and come on over here with that chicken. And bring enough for Braxton. He'll be coming over too."

"Will do. See you soon."

As soon as Shay hung up, she realized she forgot to tell him whom Braxton had an appointment with. Wouldn't he be surprised hearing that it was his soon-to-be-ex-mother-in-law? She would tell him when he came over.

Just wanting to indulge in a moment of leisure, Shay strolled upstairs to her room, and fell backward on her bed. Moments swept by as she lay there, unable to stop thinking of Braxton. But when her fitted dress became uncomfortable, she wanted to put on an outfit more comfortable for lounging around the house. Seeking something softer, looser or baggier, she went over to her closet. As she looked for something that was homelike but sexy enough to please Braxton's eye, she reached for a muted green stretch pants with a matching top. Neither piece was tight. Each simply fitted well.

Laying them on her bed, she stood above it, taking off the dress. Removing it, she tossed it aside, then began to dress. But as she was finished, from the side of her eye, she swore she saw a blur of a figure. Her head snapped to the direction. There was no one there. Could that have been Rakim, she wondered, hurrying into the hallway. Christina and he did have a key.

"Rakim?" From side to side she looked, seeing no one and nothing unusual. "Rakim?" she called again, inspecting the downstairs. Again, there was no one. As well, the doors and windows were all securely locked.

Returning to the hallway upstairs, she knew she had nothing to worry about. Taking a detour into the guest room, checking around for a second, she knew she was probably feeling a little chicken because Patman had told her about that murder. That's all it was. Shay believed there was no need to worry since Rakim, Christina and Braxton would be there soon. She headed back down the hall toward her room. She knew she wouldn't be alone long. Entering the room that assumption became an eye-popping reality. Her heart jumped at the sight of the man standing in the midst of her bedroom.

"What are you doing in here!"

Fifteen

"You heard me!" Shay was livid that her privacy had been invaded. "What are you sneaking around my house for? For more evidence? I thought you were different. I thought that Jamison was the tyrant. Not you."

Patman's lips formed a crooked grin. "I am different, sweetheart."

"I'm not your sweetheart." Shay swore with disgust. "Now you get out of my house." She pointed toward the door she was standing near. "You have no court order to search here!"

"I don't need one."

"What do you mean you don't need one?"

"I'm not here on official business."

"What?" She was mystified. "What are you talking about?"

"I'm not here on official business. This is personal."

Frowning, she knew what this was sounding like but didn't want to accept it. "Patman, just leave my house. You must have been drinking, or you're on drugs or something because I know good and well you didn't come up in my bedroom to try and seduce me. I know you can't mean that."

Patman's grin formed into a hard line. "Why can't I mean that? Do you think you're too good for me?"

"You have lost your mind."

"I haven't lost anything!" His foot made a step forward. "Do you think you're only good enough for that arrogant prosecutor? I saw you last night, this morning and today! *I saw you!*"

Braxton had been waiting in the study of Victoria Sheridan's daughter's home for so long, he couldn't help thinking of what he loved more than art, more than anything. What he loved so passionately was Shay.

His body still hadn't recovered from the paradise she had delivered him to. He kept envisioning her face and remembering the feel of her body. He kept inhaling and smelling not this home's numerous plants, but the strawberry fragrance he had tasted from her moist body. Just thinking about it, he had to close his eyes and relive it all over again. He couldn't wait to love her again.

Yet it was more than her body that mesmerized him so. It was what he'd discovered in her—the beauty and sexiness within that couldn't help manifesting outwardly. She was kind and loving in a way he'd never even dreamed about. And the way she understood him, his dreams, his heart, guaranteed him she was his soul mate. No other woman could give him what she did. Everything he'd been looking for in a lover, he'd found it in her. But there was even more. He thanked God for her. He *would* thank Him for her. And he would clear her name. There was no way he could live without this woman. For the rest of his life he wanted to do everything in his power to make her happy. He wanted to make every day special. Each day he would love her, give her, listen to her, protect her, encourage her, uplift her, make her laugh, and overall be her man in good times and bad. Love was something else, he thought as he sat there. It made the world look different, prettier, brighter. He wasn't even impatient that Victoria Sheridan was making him wait.

"Mr. Steele?"

Braxton saw a short stout elderly woman making quick steps to him from a glistening tiled corridor.

She extended one hand. "My apologies, Mr. Steele." With the other hand she held a newspaper.

Braxton returned the handshake. "It's very nice to meet you, Ms. Sheridan." They sat across from each other at a tea table.

She raised the newspaper, shaking it. "This is the reason I took so long with you."

"The paper? Something interesting in today's news?"

"Something terrible." She unfolded it, sliding a photo of Rakim and Christina dining at a restaurant. A full page article was devoted to them. "This is my daughter's husband, soon to be ex, philandering with this woman, humiliating my daughter. I've had to hide it from her, and I've been making so many calls to them. I'm going to take legal action against this." Pausing, she patted her bosom. "I was so glad to find out your identity—to find out who the artist Ecstasy really was. I was shocked that it was our town prosecutor. You're an amazing man, Mr. Steele."

Braxton smiled. "I'm glad you enjoy my work."

"I enjoy both of your careers. I'm so glad you're going to prosecute that Shay Hilton."

"And why is that?"

"She's my son-in-law's sister."

"And?"

"And he's treated my daughter like dirt."

"She had nothing to do with that."

"The apple falls from the same tree. She's going to pay for what she did. Rakim is going to look like a fool defending her. And while she's rotting in jail he's going to rot too."

"How is that?"

"Having his sister in prison. I always told Janet he loved Shay more than anything on this earth. But now his precious Shay is going far away. I hope they never see each other again."

Braxton watched the veins bulging in her neck. "That's pretty harsh."

"Not harsh enough. And I have faith you'll convict her. I'll be right there at the trial." She patted his hand. "You have a solid case. All the evidence pointing to her, and that person calling, hearing them arguing before it happened."

Contemplating what she'd said, wondering why it made him feel so strange, his thoughts were interrupted by her daughter's sudden appearance into the study.

"This is Ecstasy, darling," Victoria told Janet. "He's actually Braxton Steele. Remember I was telling you about the exhibit I'm planning."

Janet acted as if she didn't even see Braxton or her mother. Neither was acknowledged verbally or visually as she proceeded in the room. She had overheard the maid talking to the chauffeur about the article in the paper. Knowing it was delivered to them each day, she was determined to find it. She saw it on the tea table between her mother and their guest.

Victoria grabbed it. "You don't need to see this."

Janet snatched the paper out of her hand and fled from the room.

Victoria was trembling. "Oh, this is really going to set her off." She stood, turning in various directions.

Braxton came around to her. "Ms. Sheridan, are you okay? Is there anything I can do?"

"No. There's nothing you can do. My daughter is having a breakdown and. . . . Oh, I'll have to finish our meeting another time. I have to take care of Janet. I'm afraid of what she might do."

Inside her room, Janet tossed the paper harshly against the floor when she finished reading it. *This is it! This is it! I've had enough!* Grabbing her cell phone, she quickly dialed the private investigator. She'd had him tailing Christina and Rakim.

"Hello?" a nasal male voice spoke.

"It's Janet. Where are they?"

"They're headed toward his sister's place."

"Good." Her eyes scattered frantically as she mentally planned.

"Do you want more pictures?"

"No, I'll handle it."

She hung up while he was still talking. She rushed to her drawer. She pulled out her gun.

Braxton was trying to console Victoria Sheridan when she saw her daughter rushing by the study window, hurrying to her car.

"Janet, you're in no condition to drive!" she yelled, hurrying out the door behind her. Braxton followed her. "Janet, where are you going?"

Janet jumped in her car. Victoria tried to get in too. Janet took off.

In a breath, Victoria was in the chauffeur's car, directing the driver to follow her daughter. Not far behind them, Braxton headed down the highway not so much intrigued by these dramatics as he was the conversation he'd had with Victoria.

The grudge she had against Shay was such that it was bizarre. Yet as he thought more about what was said in those few moments, something else was more bizarre. How did Victoria know that on the night of the murder someone had called the police, telling them about an argument between the victim and a woman? That information was withheld from the public. How did she know that, unless. . . .

Trembling by the portal of her bedroom, Shay was wondering how she could get away from this lunatic before he went off.

"How could you be with him?" he asked her.

Shay's heart began banging in her chest. "You mean because he's the prosecutor against me?"

"No, I don't mean that! I could care less about that!" His foot moved forward. "I mean because you knew there was someone out there with deep feelings for you. I've written you so many letters."

Shay swallowed. "So that was you?" She made a baby step back. "I didn't know it was you."

"Because I was afraid you wouldn't like me. But that one time. . . ."

She made another step back. "What one time?"

"That time I thought I saw you stranded in the car, I decided to let you know how I felt. But it was just someone who looked like you. So I pretended it was you. But she was mean to me, and fighting me off and looking at me like I was the bottom of her shoe and calling me names, names like my aunt used to call me, those horrible names."

He was so terrifying Shay felt like her entire body was one giant racing heartbeat.

"You didn't kill that girl, did you? That's not the girl who was stabbed was it?"

"She did a bad thing in treating me that way. I had my hunting knife and I showed her she could never do that to me again. You could never do that to me. But it wasn't you, was it? I wanted to be with you so bad. But I was so, so afraid of letting you know it was me. I would just call to hear your voice. Just to hear it."

"That was you?"

"Yes, it was me. But now a call won't do." He began unbuckling his belt.

Shay stepped back. Moving further, she soon raced out of the door. Patman caught her by the hair in the living room. Fighting him off, she punched, bit and kicked, all the while tumbling over furnishings, breaking each one in their path. Enraged by her resistance, he slapped her all over the room. Finally, smashing a vase in his face she managed to get away.

"You shouldn't have done that!" His fingers wiped the blood that leaped from his gashed cheek. But feeling its pain and stinging didn't stop him from running out of the door and across the highway. That's where he saw her disappear into the woods.

Sixteen

Teasing and playing with each other, Rakim and Christina stopped when they saw the open door at Shay's house. Hurrying up the pathway to see if anything happened, it was as if a nightmare had descended when they saw the state of the house. Nearly every movable object was broken.

"What happened here?" Christina frowned at what she was beholding. She dropped the food she'd been holding in the nearest chair. She could barely breathe she was so scared for Shay.

Stepping further into the room, Rakim grabbed his head. "Oh, no, something has happened to my sister." His eyes wildly searching, he spotted some blood on the floor. "She's bleeding." He ran throughout the house, searching for her.

"I'll get the police." Christina swiped up the telephone.

Jamison wasn't in the station to get the call from Shay Hilton's home. The fact that Patman had left work early two days ago, hadn't returned and hadn't called had the hairs standing on the back of his neck. Something wasn't right. On his break, he drove over to his partner's apartment. Knocking hard, he grew more worried when no one answered. He started yelling through the door. Yelling so loud that the landlord next door heard him.

A tall middle-aged woman walked out of her apartment. "May I help you, officer?"

"You seen Patman?"

"No, maybe Mr. Patman isn't home."

"I've worked with the guy for the last three months. He's never been out sick, and if he was he's responsible enough to call in for a sick day. We haven't heard from him. Do you know who can open up this door?"

"I can." She searched through her pocket, pulling out a bunch of keys.

"He's one sloppy one all right," Jamison remarked a few moments later. Clothes were strewn on the sofa. Dirty dishes piled in the sink. Flies buzzed around them. The landlord was trailing Jamison as he looked throughout Patman's living room and kitchen. Heading into the bedroom, he stopped stone-still at the entrance.

Beholding what she did, the landlord's feet froze too. "Jesus, what is this?"

"Something sick," Jamison answered, stepping closer to it. Narrowing his eyes, he finally reached the candles and the urn and her face. It was some kind of shrine—a shrine to Shay Hilton. Photos of various sizes were everywhere. They appeared like they'd been cut out of a magazine and blown up. Jamison assumed they were from her publication. He turned to the landlord. "You see people. You work with them every day, but you never know them."

Something told him to look elsewhere in the room, inside drawers, under the bed, within the closet. Inside a shoebox is where he saw bloody knives.

He called into the station, requesting that forensics and other officers get over to Patman's house. He gave the address. They gave him one too. According to a frantic call to the station something big was happening at Shay Hilton's temporary home.

"I'm going to find you," Patman warned Shay. Dusk was descending on the sky and out in the woods, the trees shading the land made it even darker. Patman hated that it made it easier for her to hide.

Stooped within some bushes that covered her, Shay was afraid to breathe. Patman's thick shoes had passed her face several times in his hunt for her. Never had she been so afraid. Except for when he suddenly stood above her. Bending down, he parted the bushes. She was in full view.

"There you are. Why are you hiding from me? Don't you know how much I care about you? Don't you have any idea? I just couldn't stand you last night with that maniac, breathing all over you and doing everything under the sun. I threw up watching you. I have to wash you. I want you to take off all your clothes and go over there." His head pointed to a pond. "I'm going to wash his filth off you, and then show you what it's like to really make love."

He reached for Shay. As he did, her foot raised and smashed his face. He fell holding his broken nose and watched her running away. She was really going to get it when he caught her, he thought. She wasn't even aware she was running deeper into the woods. That was perfect for him.

Rakim and Christina were pacing frantically throughout the room when they heard a car drive up. Believing it was the police answering their call, they hurried over to the front door. Opening it, the hateful eyes of Janet greeted them. Afterward they saw her brandish the gun.

They both moved backward.

At a point, Rakim stopped. "Put that thing down, Janet."

"Yes, put it down, darling." Victoria emerged, running behind her daughter.

"Get away, Mother." Steadily, she was looking at Rakim and Christina. "Please leave and let me get them out of my sight forever. They can't do what they've done to me and get away with it."

"Darling, don't do this. You'll ruin everything." Victoria was crying. She even attempted to reach for the gun.

Janet whacked her on the arm with it. "Stay back."

Rubbing her arm, Victoria moved aside. "If you wound them, they'll win. You'll go to jail."

"No, Mother. They have to pay." She saw Christina hiding behind Rakim. "Show yourself, slut, and take your death like a woman."

Christina was so scared of that gun she didn't even know if any part of her body could move.

"Did you hear what I said?"

"Leave her alone, Janet." Rakim began easing toward her. "Just put the gun down."

"Yes, put it down, Janet." Braxton entering the room didn't turn her around.

She continued to aim. "You two really deserve to die."

Victoria began to cry. "Don't do it! Don't ruin everything."

"How did you know that there was a call to the police station on the night of the murder, Victoria?" Braxton was right behind her.

She wouldn't acknowledge him. "Darling, put the gun away."

"What was your connection to him?" Braxton pressed.

"Look, my child is my only concern." Her tears worsened. "You should try to help her. Get that gun out of her hands. Not badger me."

"The gun isn't going, Mother. I'm killing these two. Right now." Janet's finger bent the trigger.

Rakim made a leap toward Janet.

Shots rang, reaching the outside, rushing Jamison inside. Several other officers dashed in the house after him. Some attended to Rakim and Christina who lay wounded. After checking on them, and calling for paramedics, Braxton stood beside Jamison reading Janet her rights.

Braxton stepped over to Victoria, who had sank to her knees. She became hysterical when Janet was handcuffed and escorted outside.

"It's all ruined now!" she cried. "My baby's life is ruined. I did everything for her. Everything."

Braxton bent down to her to meet her bloodshot eyes. "Like framing Shay?"

Victoria cried as she spoke. "What does anything matter now? What does anything mean anymore? Nothing without my child. With what has happened to her."

"I know you had something to do with the murder."

Dazedly, she nodded. "Oh, yes, I did. I went to her apartment that night." She began rocking. "I was looking for Rakim. He'd made my daughter so upset with that carrying on with that woman. He'd left her so saddened. I was going to give him a piece of my mind. Security let me up without any problem. They knew me. I had friends in that high rise.

"When I reached Shay's apartment the door was slightly open. I peeked inside. And that's when I saw a man beating another man with a candlestick. I only saw the back of him. I was so frightened I moved back out of the way, hiding on a stairwell. I was afraid he'd come after me.

"Then I heard nothing. I thought he was gone. So I

came out of the stairwell. But I saw him running down the hall, the back of him. I peeked back at the suite door, and the man he had been beating was laying on the floor. Blood was everywhere. Everything was broken. And Shay, she walked to the door and looked and saw all this. And she fainted. She fainted right there.

"But I wasn't going to help her. I thought of my daughter. Of how Rakim had made her suffer. I would make him suffer too. I would take the most precious thing in the world to him and destroy it. That was Shay. So, wearing my gloves, I took the candlestick, wiped off the thick coating of blood with my hanky. And I wiped off all the killer's prints. Then I smeared some of Marquis's blood back on it. And lastly, I wrapped Shay's hand around it. She would be convicted of a murder she didn't do. And Rakim would never have any peace knowing that."

Braxton was too angry with her to speak. He wanted to strangle her.

Jamison lifted her by the arm before motioning to another cop to come for her.

"Do you remember anything about that man that could help us find him?"

"Yes. He was an officer. A skinny, young officer."

Jamison hit his fist against his pocket. "Damn it! It's Patman."

A scream from outdoors made Braxton and Jamison bolt toward the sound, which came from the woods.

Other officers followed. All slowed and hid when they located Shay and Patman. With her back against him, he had her locked with one arm. With the other hand, he waved his gun.

"Do you know how much I love you? I knew I loved you when I read what you wrote in the magazine. Then I saw you. You were so beautiful. But I was so afraid you wouldn't like me. Women don't usually fall at their feet for me. But I'm not bad. Not like my aunt said I was.

"I protected you. I was at that ceremony. I was on duty that night and I dragged out that actor. I was so angry with him. Then I went up to see you. And I was so angry when I saw that Steele there. And I followed that guy to your place. I could get in that building anytime I want without signing anything. Officers get respect. And I got to him before he got to you. I think he was going to rape you. But not me. I'm going to love you. Right now."

He released Shay and reached to rip her top. Braxton charging at him diverted his attention, allowing Shay to run. She froze when behind her she heard a shot. With the tumult of the shooting behind her back, Shay slowly curved around, praying Braxton hadn't been the one who was wounded. Her prayer was answered when she saw him coming toward her. Not far away, it was Patman, who lay squirming, bloodied, and surrounded on the ground. That is until he became motionless.

Once in each other's arms, Braxton and Shay's tight embrace expressed what their overwhelmed emotions wouldn't allow their mouths to speak intelligently. Watching them from afar, Jamison suspected something had developed between those two. Their tender display undoubtedly confirmed it.

He walked over to them. "I guess you two are thanking your lucky stars to be alive."

Smiling, Braxton uncoupled from Shay, but clutched her hand. "You know that."

"I owe you an apology," Jamison went on.

"For always messing with me?" Braxton teased.

"I'm not talking to you."

Shay's eyes widened. "You mean to me, officer?"

Jamison lips curled into a smile that looked like it hurt.

"Yes, I was wrong, Ms. Hilton. I was wrong about you and I apologize. I hope you'll forgive me one day."

Jamison strolled off, stopping when he heard Shay call, "Jamison?"

He spun around. Braxton and Shay looked amused.

"Don't call me, Ms. Hilton. Call me Shay."

Grinning, Jamison did a thumbs up sign.

Hours later, Shay relaxed before the fireplace in Braxton's home, waiting for him to bring down a special gift. She couldn't believe it all was over. The nightmare that had overtaken her life was no more. It was as if something that had covered her and smothered her was at last taken away. Now she could breathe.

She thanked God that her brother and Christina would recover. Rakim's arm would heal and so would Christina's shoulder. Equally as wonderful, David was doing so well he would be released soon. And she learned that the nurse he was talking about traveling with hadn't just told him that to help him get well. When Shay visited him earlier, she showed Shay the travel brochure for their trip. They were intent on rekindling a romance that had long ago been denied them both. Shay could see from the glow in David's eyes that he really cared about the nurse. Not long ago, he'd looked at Shay that way.

But mostly she thanked God for the man who saved her life, critically wounding a mad man who meant to destroy her. Watching him coming down the stairs, she knew Braxton was a gift from God. And not because of the covered painting he was carrying to her.

"What's that?" She watched him joining her before the fireplace.

"A gift for my beautiful woman." Staring in her eyes, he handed it to her.

Anxiously, Shay uncovered it. A portrait of Braxton and her making love took her breath away. "This is so beautiful, baby." She hugged and kissed him, before gazing at it again. "Which one of the wonderful moments is this one? One of our hot moments from last night?"

"No." He put the portrait aside. "It's an image of ecstasy to come. You and I making love—making love as husband and wife. That's if you can stand being married to an artist. I'm giving up the law. I just want to do what makes me happiest. I want to be with who makes me happy. And that's you. Forever with you. I thank God that you came into my life, Shay. And I'm going to show you that every day if you marry me."

"How can I not marry you when God sent you to me. I thank Him for you. He sent you just for me. You're such a blessing in my life."

Dear Reader

It's been a true blessing to me that you picked up this book and allowed me to share this story with you. I hoped that Shay and Braxton would become real to you and after taking this journey with them you would feel as happy, hopeful, and touched by the magic of love as they did.

Thank you all for the e-mails, letters and cards. Each one is a gift, and I appreciate every word. The response to A TASTE OF LOVE has been incredible, and the touching letters that I still receive about MOST OF ALL has made me think of writing sequels to them both. I hope I can continue writing stories that you enjoy. PASSIONATE SURRENDER is the tentative title of my next release.

Please feel free to write me about IMAGES OF EC-STASY or my other novels at:

PO Box 020648, Brooklyn, New York 11202-0648
Or
E-mail me at LoureBus@aol.com
Visit my Web site at http://www.LoureBussey.com

I hope you are blessed in everything you do and everything you dream of.

Until next time,
Louré Bussey

ABOUT THE AUTHOR

Louré Bussey, a graduate of Borough Of Manhattan Community College, has published 56 short stories and is the author of five other novels: NIGHTFALL, MOST OF ALL, TWIST OF FATE, LOVE SO and A TASTE OF LOVE. She is also a singer/songwriter with a soon-to-be released CD entitled "Louré" (songs performed and written by the author, which are based on her best-selling novels).

BOOK YOUR PLACE ON OUR WEBSITE AND MAKE THE ARABESQUE ROMANCE CONNECTION!

We've created a customized website just for our very special Arabesque readers, where you can get the inside scoop on everything that's going on with Arabesque romance novels.

When you come online, you'll have the exciting opportunity to:

- View covers of upcoming books

- Learn about our future publishing schedule (listed by publication month and author)

- Find out when your favorite authors will be visiting a city near you

- Search for and order backlist books

- Check out author bios and background information

- Send e-mail to your favorite authors

- Join us in weekly chats with authors, readers and other guests

- Get writing guidelines

- AND MUCH MORE!

Visit our website at
http://www.arabesquebooks.com

Coming in August from
Arabesque Books . . .

THE BUSINESS OF LOVE by Angela Winters
1-58314-150-2   **$5.99US/$7.99CAN**

The heir to a hotel chain, Maya Woodson is determined to make her plan to go public a success—even if she is at odds with handsome Trajan Matthews, the investment expert who's overseeing the deal. But when a crime endangers the chain's future—and their careers—Maya and Trajan must discover what they cherish most . . . if they are to find a love-filled future.

FIRST LOVE by Cheryl Faye
1-58314-117-0   **$5.99US/$7.99CAN**

When shy Lena Caldwell and Quincy Taylor strike up a friendship, it isn't long before a sweetly sensual fire is sparked. But as their attraction grows, Quincy's past mistakes inject doubt into their newfound romance and the two must confront their insecurities to find a love worth fighting for.

SOULFUL SERENADE by Linda Hudson-Smith
1-58314-140-5   **$5.99US/$7.99CAN**

Hillary Houston has it all—personality, looks, talent, and now, sexy engineer Brandon Blair. But when Hillary is offered the chance to become a recording superstar, Brandon's threatened with the possibility of losing the woman of his dreams . . . unless he can find a way to keep her forever.

ADMISSION OF LOVE by Niobia Bryant
1-58314-164-2   **$5.99US/$7.99CAN**

When supermodel Chloe Bryant settles down in her mother's rural South Carolina town, she is at instant odds with handsome, reserved Devon Jamison. But amid hidden hurt and unexpected romantic rivals, Devon and Chloe begin to discover what they both really desire—to gain the dream they want most and have always waited for . . .

Please Use the Coupon on the Next Page to Order

Have A Sizzling Summer
With Arabesque Books